Nancy Mitford

LOVE IN A COLD CLIMATE

Introduction by Flora Fraser

Vintage Books
A Division of Random House, Inc.
New York

TO LORD BERNERS

Library of Congress Cataloging-in-Publication Data

Mitford, Nancy, 1904–1973.
Love in a cold climate / by Nancy Mitford ; introduction
by Flora Fraser. —1st Vintage Books ed.
p. cm.
Originally published: London : H. Hamilton, 1949.
1. Upper class—Fiction.   2. England—Fiction.
I. Title.
PR6025.I88L68 2010
823'.914—dc22
2010021927

Vintage ISBN: 978-0-307-74082-3

www.vintagebooks.com

Printed in the United States of America
10 9 8 7 6 5 4 3 2

INTRODUCTION

WHEN NANCY MITFORD sent a typescript of *Love in a Cold Climate* in October 1948 to her friend Evelyn Waugh for his comments, he wrote back: "The manuscript was a delight to read, full of wit & fun & fantasy. Whole passages . . . might be used verbatim in a book." But he wanted her to do a complete rewrite before she published: "the book must be saved. So start again."[i] Nancy declined, but she might so easily have agreed. Waugh had been a close friend since she made her London debut in the 1920s and a regular correspondent since she followed a lover to Paris after the war. He was also one of Britain's premier novelists and one to whom she often turned for literary advice. Indeed he suggested the title of her earlier novel, *The Pursuit of Love* (1945), as well as the title of *Love in a Cold Climate,* which refers to the seeming inability, for much of the book and to her mother, Lady Montdore's fury, of beautiful Lady Polly to fall in love or attract any marriage proposals.

[i] ed. Charlotte Mosley, *The Letters of Nancy Mitford and Evelyn Waugh* (London: Sceptre, 1997), pp. 109–110: Evelyn Waugh to Nancy Mitford, October 24, 1948.

Nancy felt bolstered in her refusal to oblige Waugh by the runaway success she had enjoyed with *The Pursuit of Love*. Admittedly the romantic adventures of the Hon. Linda Radlett portrayed there had been extremely autobiographical, and so perhaps easier for her to narrate than *Cold Climate*'s plot involving Lady Polly, the Montdore millions, and Cedric, the Nova Scotia–born heir. But Fanny, or the Hon. Frances Logan, Linda's cousin and Polly's friend, was a narrator who had "worked" in *Pursuit* and "works" too in *Cold Climate*. Readers of *Pursuit* had loved too the characters of Uncle Matthew and Aunt Sadie, whom Nancy had based on her parents, Lord and Lady Redesdale. Uncle Matthew and Aunt Sadie play important parts in *Cold Climate*. Mitford had a readership now, and she had found a landscape that could paint and rework.

She had, by her own account, worked hard, very hard, writing and reworking *Cold Climate* before she sent it to Waugh. Even today the sections covering Fanny's and Polly's contrasting youths, adolescences and romances read with a frightening wit and fluency. Take Fanny's awed description of Lady Montdore the morning after a weekend house party ended at Hampton. The hostess was "drinking strong tea in bed among masses of lace pillows, her coarse grey hair frizzed out and wearing what appeared to be a man's striped flannel pyjama top under a feathered wrap."

With Polly's disastrous marriage and the astonishing transformation of her mother, Lady Montdore, following the arrival at Hampton of young Cedric, a darker vein obtrudes. The climax to the book, apparently a happy if sophisticated ending, is like a devastating train crash whose images linger long in the mind. The wonder is that Waugh wanted to tinker with Mitford's extraordinarily successful and intricate arrangement. Mitford later wrote that she considered *Cold Climate* her best novel.[ii] At any rate now she ignored

---

Waugh's advice and published *Love in a Cold Climate* in July 1949 to considerable acclaim.

There were those who found the openly homosexual character Cedric hard to stomach, and *Ladies' Home Journal* refused to serialize the book. But Nancy was pleased with the "human dragonfly" portrait that she had drawn of Cedric, using as her exquisite model the Hon. Stephen Tennant, friend of Cecil Beaton and later supposedly one of the models for Sebastian in Waugh's *Brideshead Revisited*. Anyway she was used to controversy, and, having worked in the London bookshop G. Heywood Hill, knew that it helped sell books. Moreover, she was no stranger to outrage. Nancy's mother Lady Redesdale remonstrated at one point in the 1920s, "Whenever I see the words 'Peer's daughter' in a headline. . . . I know it's going to be something about one of you children."[iii]

With the exploits of Nancy's younger sisters—she was the eldest of the six Mitford daughters and older too than their only brother, Tom—we are not concerned here. But there is no doubt that Nancy shocked her parents with her choice of friends, once she had made her debut in London, in the 1920s and 30s. With a variety of writers and aesthetes such as Evelyn Waugh and Harold Acton and other smart or bright young people in attendance, the capital's gossip columns avidly in pursuit, Nancy shingled her hair, wore trousers, smoked cigarettes—and wrote the occasional column herself. There was not much money about, much gaiety, many parties, and much offense given to almost everyone of a more traditional outlook.

In particular, the openness about homosexual liaisons within this loose amalgam of revelers and the "camp" appearance of the men in question repulsed many. But at the same time, and as the interwar novels that Nancy's friends wrote—Waugh's *Vile Bodies* and *Handful of Dust*, Henry Green's *Party Going* and Anthony Powell's *Afternoon Men*—bear witness, these Bright Young Things

---

[iii] Jessica Mitford, *Hons and Rebels* (London: Phoenix, 1999), p. 9

who found their elders and the certainties of prewar England hilarious had not found anything to put in place of those certainties. *Love in a Cold Climate*, though written in Paris and in 1948, both holds its own against the books mentioned above and is witness to that same despair. However, there is one difference: the character of Fanny.

In Fanny Wincham née Logan and in *Cold Climate*, Nancy Mitford developed—as she did not in *Pursuit* where Cousin Linda is the focus—an "I person" whom we accompany through several stages of growth. Fanny is first seen as a nervous adolescent but becomes a willing bride, a confident wife, and loving mother. And her character, the husband she chooses and loves (an Oxford don), and her married home (a North Oxford terraced house) are utterly unlike those of anyone in Nancy's original "set." Her domestic concerns are quite unlike those either of the mistress of a grand country house and London residence, or of a Bright Young Thing going to parties and drinking cocktails. There is even, heaven forbid, hardly a servant to create "the servant problem." "I was obliged to get up very early and cook Alfred's breakfast, but I did not mind. He was my own husband, and the cooking took place in my own kitchen; it all seemed like heaven to me," writes Fanny in *Cold Climate*.

The reader may think himself or herself fully engaged with the beautiful blankness of Polly, the lecherous attentions of Boy Dougdale, or the tantrums of Lady Montdore. In fact, Mitford has us keeping half an eye on Fanny and her fretting that Alfred might read a book or commit some other heinous crime while staying with Uncle Matthew. We are seeing in Fanny the woman that Nancy Mitford might have been, had she married the right man instead of moody, feckless Peter Rodd, had she had the children that agonizingly never appeared, had she enjoyed prolonged domestic contentment rather than intermittent doses of happiness with Gaullist politician and womanizer Gaston Palewski. In Fanny Wincham—the choice of name echoes that of Fanny Price, the cousin at Mansfield Park—Mitford created, for all the snobbery that pervades her world, a woman who is truly modern and middleclass in the best sense of the word. Fanny's values are never those of her Radlett cousins at Alconleigh, nor is her head turned by the impossibly magnificent life at Hampton with the Montdores. For Mitford makes it clear that life is fairly conventional and down-to-earth at home with Aunt Emily and Uncle Davey, who have been to Fanny as mother and father ever since her own mother, "the Bolter," left her father.

Nancy Mitford used to say later in life that she had never loved her mother, and Lady Redesdale, especially to her elder children when they were young, appears to have been a vague and remote figure. In Mitford's depiction of Fanny's relatively "normal" home life before marriage, her marriage to the intelligent, austere Alfred, and her love of her home and family we may see the poignant wish of Nancy Mitford for what might have been. But these were not wishes that she voiced outside of the pages of her book.

For her family as well as for her friends, Nancy Mitford kept up a front. For the public she was the stylish lady writer, photographed in Parisian chic, holidaying in Venice or in the South of France with princes and millionaires. Her correspondence, her conversation were legendary for their verbal fireworks. But after she had died in great pain in Versailles in 1973, tended by the sisters who had loved her but had suffered too from her sarcasm and spikey wit, one of them wrote to another, "I know she had success as a writer but what is that compared to things like proper husbands and lovers and children—think of the loneliness of all these years, so *sad*."[iv] Despite all her artistry, in short, there had been no one for whom Nancy came first.

With Fanny, however, and with *Cold Climate* Mitford triumphed. She created someone who always came first with her Alfred, and he

[iv] ed. Charlotte Mosley, *The Mitfords: Letters between Six Sisters* (London: Harper Perennial, 2008), p. 596: Deborah, Duchess of Devonshire to Jessica Mitford Treuhaft, 8 July 1973

with her. The curiosity is that when Mitford went on to write a book exclusively about Fanny, *Don't Tell Alfred* (1960), Fanny no longer came first with her husband. In that novel, Alfred has been appointed British Ambassador to Paris and official duties occupy him. *Don't Tell Alfred* is a hilarious portrait of high society life in Paris and of internal embassy politics, with Fanny's escapades as ambassadress central to the plot but the ambassador himself a largely absent figure and, when present, more irritated than loving. That, however, is another story. Meanwhile glorious *Love in a Cold Climate* awaits.

Flora Fraser is the author of *Princesses: The Six Daughters of George III; Beloved Emma: The Life of Emma, Lady Hamilton; Pauline Bonaparte: Venus of Empire;* and *The Unruly Queen: The Life of Queen Caroline.*

LOVE IN A COLD CLIMATE

PART ONE

Chapter 1

I AM OBLIGED TO begin this story with a brief account of the Hampton family, because it is necessary to emphasise the fact once and for all that the Hamptons were very grand as well as very rich. A short session with Burke or with Debrett would be quite enough to make this clear, but these large volumes are not always available, while the books on the subject by Lord Montdore's brother-in-law, Boy Dougdale, are all out of print. His great talent for snobbishness and small talent for literature have produced three detailed studies of his wife's forebears, but they can only be read now by asking a bookseller to get them at second hand. (The bookseller will put an advertisement in his trade paper, *The Clique*: "H. Dougdale, any by." He will be snowed under with copies at about a shilling each and will then proudly inform his customer that he has "managed to find what you want," implying hours of careful search on barrows, dirt cheap, at 30/- the three.) *Georgiana Lady Montdore and Her Circle*, *The Magnificent Montdores* and *Old Chronicles of Hampton*, I have them beside me as I write, and see that the opening paragraph of the first is:

"Two ladies, one dark, one fair, both young and lovely, were driving briskly towards the little village of Kensington on a fine May morning. They were Georgiana, Countess of Montdore and her great friend Walburga, Duchess of Paddington, and they made a delightfully animated picture as they discussed the burning question of the hour—should one or should one not subscribe to a parting present for poor dear Princess Lieven?"

This book is dedicated, by gracious permission, to Her Royal Highness, the Grand Duchess Peter of Russia, and has eight full-page illustrations.

IT MUST BE said that when this trilogy first came out it had quite a vogue with the lending-library public.

"The family of Hampton is ancient in the West of England, indeed Fuller, in his *Worthies* mentions it as being of stupendous antiquity."

Burke makes it out just a shade more ancient than does Debrett, but both plunge back into the mists of mediaeval times from which they drag forth ancestors with P. G. Wodehouse names, Ugs and Berts and Threds, and Walter Scott fates. "His Lordship was attainted—beheaded—convicted—proscribed—exiled—dragged from prison by a furious mob—slain at the Battle of Crécy—went down in the White Ship—perished during the third crusade—killed in a duel." There were very few natural deaths to record in the early misty days. Both Burke and Debrett linger with obvious enjoyment over so genuine an object as this family, unspoilt by the ambiguities of female line and deed poll. Nor could any of those horrid books, which came out in the nineteenth century, devoted to research and aiming to denigrate the nobility, make the object seem less genuine. Tall, golden-haired barons, born in wedlock and all looking very much alike, succeeded each other at Hampton, on lands which had never been bought or sold, generation after generation until, in 1770, the Lord Hampton of the day brought back, from a visit to Versailles, a French bride, a Mademoiselle de Montdore. Their son had brown eyes, a dark skin and presumably, for it is powdered in all the pictures of him, black hair. This blackness did not persist in the family. He married a golden-haired heiress from Derbyshire, and the Hamptons reverted to their blue-and-gold looks, for which they are famous to this day. The son of the Frenchwoman was rather clever and very worldly; he dabbled in politics and wrote a book of aphorisms, but his chief claim to fame was his great and lifelong friendship with the Regent, which procured him, among other favours, an earldom. His mother's family having all perished during the Terror in France, he took her name as his title. Enormously rich, he spent enormously; he had a taste for French objects of art and acquired, during the years which followed the Revolution, a splendid collection of such things, including many pieces from the royal establishments, and others which had been looted out of the Hotel de Montdore in the rue de Varenne. To make a suitable setting for this collection, he then proceeded to pull down at Hampton the large plain house that Adam had built for his grandfather and to drag over to England stone by stone (as modern American millionaires are supposed to do) a Gothic French chateau. This he assembled round a splendid tower of his own designing, covered the walls of the rooms with French panelling and silks and set it in a formal landscape which he also designed and planted himself. It was all very grand and very mad, and in the between wars period of which I write, very much out of fashion. "I suppose it is beautiful," people used to say, "but frankly I don't admire it."

This Lord Montdore also built Montdore House in Park Lane and a castle on a crag in Aberdeenshire. He was really much the most interesting and original character the family produced, but no member of it deviated from a tradition of authority. A solid, worthy, powerful Hampton can be found on every page of English history, his influence enormous in the West of England and his counsels not unheeded in London.

The tradition was carried on by the father of my friend, Polly Hampton. If an Englishman could be descended from the gods it would be he, so much the very type of English nobleman that those who believed in aristocratic government would always begin by pointing to him as a justification of their argument. It was generally felt, indeed, that if there were more people like him the country would not be in its present mess, even Socialists conceding his excellence, which they could afford to do since there was only one of him and he was getting on. A scholar, a Christian, a gentleman, finest shot in the British Isles, best-looking Viceroy we ever sent to India, a popular landlord, a pillar of the Conservative Party, a wonderful old man, in short, who nothing common ever did or mean. My cousin Linda and I, two irreverent little girls whose opinion makes no odds, used to think that he was a wonderful old fraud, and it seemed to us that in that house it was Lady Montdore who really counted. Now Lady Montdore was forever doing common things and mean, and she was intensely unpopular, quite as much disliked as her husband was loved, so that anything he might do that was considered not quite worthy of him, or which did not quite fit in with his reputation, was immediately laid at her door. "Of course she made him do it." On the other hand, I have often wondered whether without her to bully him and push him forward and plot and intrigue for him and "make him do it," whether, in fact, without the help of those very attributes which caused her to be so much disliked, her thick skin and ambition and boundless driving energy, he would ever have done anything at all noteworthy in the world.

This is not a popular theory. I am told that by the time I really knew him, after they got back from India, he was already tired out and had given up the struggle, and that when he was in his prime he had not only controlled the destinies of men but also the vulgarities of his wife. I wonder. There was an ineffectiveness about Lord Montdore which had nothing to do with age; he was certainly beautiful to look at, but it was an empty beauty, like that of a woman who has no sex appeal; he looked wonderful and old, but it seemed to me that, in spite of the fact that he still went regularly to the House of Lords, attended the Privy Council, sat on many committees, and often appeared in the Birthday Honours, he might just as well have been made of cardboard.

Lady Montdore, however, was flesh and blood all right. She was born a Miss Perrotte, the handsome daughter of a country squire of small means and no particular note, so that her marriage to Lord Montdore was a far better one than she could reasonably have been expected to make. As time went on, when her worldly greed and snobbishness, her terrible relentless rudeness had become proverbial and formed the subject of many a legendary tale, people were inclined to suppose that her origins must have been low or transatlantic, but, in fact, she was perfectly well born and had been decently brought up, what used to be called "a lady," so that there were no mitigating circumstances, and she ought to have known better.

No doubt her rampant vulgarity must have become more evident and less controlled with the years. In any case, her husband never seemed aware of it and the marriage was a success. Lady Montdore soon embarked him upon a public career, the fruits of which he was able to enjoy without much hard work, since she made it her business to see that he was surrounded by a host of efficient underlings, and though he pretended to despise the social life which gave meaning to her existence, he put up with it very gracefully, exercising a natural talent for agreeable conversation and accepting as his due the fact that people thought him wonderful.

"Isn't Lord Montdore wonderful? Sonia, of course, is past a joke, but he is so brilliant, such a dear, I do love him."

The people who benefited by their hospitality were fond of pretending that it was solely on his account that they ever went to the house at all, but this was great nonsense because the lively quality, the fun of Lady Montdore's parties had nothing whatever to do with him, and, hateful as she may have been in many ways, she excelled as a hostess.

In short, they were happy together and singularly well suited. But for years they suffered one serious vexation in their married life: they had no children. Lord Montdore minded this because he naturally wanted an heir, as well as for more sentimental reasons. Lady Montdore minded passionately. Not only did she also want an heir, but she disliked any form of failure, could not bear to be thwarted and was eager for an object on which she could concentrate such energy as was not absorbed by society and her husband's career. They had been married nearly twenty years, and quite given up all idea of having a child when Lady Montdore began to feel less well than usual. She took no notice, went on with her usual occupations and it was only two months before it was born that she realized she was going to have a baby. She was clever enough to avoid the ridicule which often attaches to such a situation by pretending to have kept the secret on purpose, so that instead of roaring with laughter, everybody said, "Isn't Sonia absolutely phenomenal?"

I know all this because my uncle Davey Warbeck has told me. Having himself for many years suffered (or enjoyed) most of the distempers in the medical dictionary, he is very well up in nursing-home gossip.

The fact that the child, when it was born, turned out to be a daughter, never seems to have troubled the Montdores at all. It is possible that, as Lady Montdore was under forty when she was born, they did not at first envisage her as an only child and by the time they realized that they would never have another, they loved her so much that the idea of her being in any way different, a different person, a boy, had become unthinkable. Naturally they would have liked to have had a boy, but only if it could have been as well as, and not instead of, Polly. She was their treasure, the very hub of their universe.

Polly Hampton had beauty, and this beauty was her outstanding characteristic. She was one of those people you cannot think of except in regard to their looks which, in her case, were unvarying, independent of clothes, of age, of circumstances and even of health. When ill or tired, she merely looked fragile, but never yellow, withered or diminished; she was born beautiful and never, at any time when I knew her, went off or became less beautiful, but on the contrary her looks always steadily improved. The beauty of Polly and the importance of her family are essential elements of this story. But, whereas the Hamptons can be studied in various books of reference, it is not much use turning to old *Tatlers* and seeing Polly as Lenare, as Dorothy Wilding saw her. The bones, of course, are there; hideous hats, old-fashioned poses cannot conceal them; the bones and the shape of her face are always perfection. But beauty is more, after all, than bones, for, while bones belong to death and endure after decay, beauty is a living thing; it is, in fact, skin deep, blue shadows on a white skin, hair falling like golden feathers on a white smooth forehead, embodied in the movement, in the smile and, above all, in the regard of a beautiful woman. Polly's regard was a blue flash, the bluest and most sudden thing I ever saw, so curiously unrelated to the act of seeing that it was almost impossible to believe that those opaque blue stones observed, assimilated, or did anything except confer a benefit upon the object of their direction.

No wonder her parents loved her. Even Lady Montdore, who would have been a terrible mother to an ugly girl, or to an eccentric, wayward boy, had no difficulty in being perfect to a child who must, it seemed, do her great credit in the world and crown her ambitions; literally, perhaps, crown. Polly was certainly destined for an exceptional marriage—was Lady Montdore not envisaging something very grand indeed when she gave her the name Leopoldina? Had this not a royal, a vaguely Coburg flavour which might one day be most suitable? Was she dreaming of an altar, an Archbishop, a voice saying, "I, Albert Christian George Andrew Patrick David take thee Leopoldina"? It was not an impossible dream. On the other hand, nothing could be more wholesome and unpretentious than "Polly."

MY COUSIN LINDA Radlett and I used to be borrowed from a very early age to play with Polly, for, as so often happens with the parents of only children, the Montdores were always much preoccupied with her possible loneliness. I know that my own adopted mother, Aunt Emily, had the same feeling about me and would do anything rather than keep me alone with her during the holidays. Hampton Park is not far from Linda's home, Alconleigh, and she and Polly, being more or less of an age, seemed destined to become each other's greatest friends. For some reason, however, they never really took to each other much, while Lady Montdore disliked Linda, and as soon as she was able to converse at all pronounced her conversation "unsuitable." I can see Linda now, at luncheon in the big dining room at Hampton (that dining room in which I have, at various times in my life been so terrified, that its very smell, a bouquet left by a hundred years of rich food, rich wine, rich cigars and rich women, is still to me as the smell of blood is to an animal), I can hear her loud singsong Radlett voice, "Did you ever have worms, Polly? I did. You can't imagine how fidgetty they are. Then, oh, the heaven of it, Doctor Simpson came and wormed me. Well, you know how Doc Simp has always been the love of my life—so you do see . . ."

This was too much for Lady Montdore and Linda was never asked to stay again. But I went for a week or so almost every holiday, packed off there on my way to or from Alconleigh, as children are, without ever being asked if I enjoyed it or wanted to go. My father was related to Lord Montdore through his mother. I was a well-behaved child, and I think Lady Montdore quite liked me; anyhow, she must have considered me "suitable," a word which figured prominently in her vocabulary, because at one moment there was a question of my going to live there during the term, to do lessons with Polly. When I was thirteen, however, they went off to govern India, after which Hampton and its owners became a dim, though always alarming, memory to me.

Chapter 2

BY THE TIME the Montdores and Polly returned from India, I was grown-up and had already had a season in London. Linda's mother, my Aunt Sadie (Lady Alconleigh), had taken Linda and me out together, that is to say, we went to a series of debutante dances where the people we met were all as young and as shy as we were ourselves, and the whole thing smelt strongly of bread and butter; it was quite unlike the real world, and almost as little of a preparation for it as children's parties are. When the summer ended Linda became engaged to be married, and I went back to my home in Kent, to another aunt and uncle, Aunt Emily and Uncle Davey, who had relieved my own divorced parents of the boredom and the burden of bringing up a child.

I was finding it dull at home, as young girls do, when, for the first time, they have neither lessons nor parties to occupy their minds, and then one day into this dullness fell an invitation to stay at Hampton in October. Aunt Emily came out to find me—I was sitting in the garden—with Lady Montdore's letter in her hand.

"Lady Montdore says it will be rather a grown-up affair, but she particularly wants you as company for Polly. She says there will be two young men for you girls, of course. Oh, what a pity it happens to be Davey's day for getting drunk. I long to tell him, he'll be so much interested."

There was nothing for it, however, but to wait. Davey had quite passed out and his stertorous breathing could be heard all over the house. Davey's lapses into insobriety had no vice about them; they were purely therapeutic. The fact is he was following a new regime for perfect health, much in vogue at that time, he assured us, on the Continent.

"The aim is to warm up your glands with a series of jolts. The worst thing in the world for the body is to settle down and lead a quiet little life of regular habits; if you do that it soon resigns itself to old age and death. Shock your glands, force them to react, startle them back into youth, keep them on tiptoe so that they never know what to expect next, and they have to keep young and healthy to deal with all the surprises."

Accordingly, he ate in turns like Gandhi and like Henry VIII, went for ten-mile walks or lay in bed all day, shivered in a cold bath or sweated in a hot one. Nothing in moderation. "It is also very important to get drunk every now and then." Davey, however, was too much of a one for regular habits to be irregular otherwise than regularly, so he always got drunk at the full moon. Having once been under the influence of Rudolph Steiner, he was still very conscious of the waxing and waning of the moon and had, I believe, a vague idea that the waxing and waning of the capacity of his stomach coincided with its periods.

Uncle Davey was my one contact with the world, not the world of bread-and-butter misses, but the great wicked world itself. Both my aunts had renounced it at an early age so that, for them, its existence had no reality, while their sister, my mother, had long since disappeared from view into its maw. Davey, however, had a modified liking for it, and often made little bachelor excursions into it from which he would return with a bag of interesting anecdotes. I could hardly wait to have a chat with him about this new development in my life.

"Are you sure he's too drunk, Aunt Emily?"

"Quite sure, dear. We must leave it until to-morrow."

Meanwhile she wrote (she always answered letters by return of post) and accepted. But the next day when Davey re-appeared looking perfectly green and with an appalling headache ("Oh, but that's splendid, don't you see, such a challenge to the metabolism, I've just spoken to Dr. England and he is most satisfied with my reaction"), he was rather doubtful whether she had been right to do so.

"My darling Emily, the child will die of terror, that's all," he said. He was examining Lady Montdore's letter. I knew quite well that what he said was true. I had known it in my heart ever since Aunt Emily had read me the letter, but nevertheless I was determined to go; the idea had a glittering fascination for me.

"I'm not a child any longer, Davey," I said.

"Grown-up people have died of terror at Hampton before now," he replied. "Two young men for Fanny and Polly, indeed! Two old lovers of two of the old ladies there, if I know anything about it. What a look, Emily! If you intend to launch this poor child in high society you must send her away armed with knowledge of the facts of life, you know. But I really don't understand what your policy is. First of all, you take care that she should only meet the most utterly innocuous people, keep her nose firmly to Pont Street—quite a point of view, don't think I'm against it for a moment—but then all of a sudden you push her off the rocks into Hampton and expect that she will be able to swim."

"Your metaphors Davey—it's all those spirits," Aunt Emily said, crossly for her.

"Never mind the spirits and let me tell poor Fanny the form. First of all, dear, I must explain that it's no good counting on these alleged young men to amuse you, because they won't have any time to spare for little girls, that's quite certain. On the other hand, who is sure to be there is the Lecherous Lecturer, and, as you are probably still just within his age group, there's no saying what fun and games you may not have with him."

"Oh, Davey," I said, "you are dreadful."

The Lecherous Lecturer was Boy Dougdale. The Radlett children had given him this name after he had once lectured at Aunt Sadie's Women's Institute. The lecture, it seemed, (I was not there at the time) had been very dull, but the things the lecturer did afterwards to Linda and Jassy were not dull at all.

"You know what secluded lives we lead," Jassy had told me when next I was at Alconleigh. "Naturally it's not very difficult to arouse our interest. For example, do you remember that dear old man who came and lectured on the Toll Gates of England and Wales? It was rather tedious, but we liked it—he's coming again, Green Lanes this time. . . . Well, the Lecherous Lecturer's lecture was duchesses and, of course, one always prefers people to gates. But the fascinating thing was after the lecture he gave us a foretaste of sex. Think what a thrill! He took Linda up onto the roof and did all sorts of blissful things to her; at least she could easily see how they would be blissful with anybody except the Lecturer. And I got some great sexy pinches as he passed the nursery landing when he was on his way down to dine. Do admit, Fanny."

Of course my Aunt Sadie had no inkling of all this, she would have been perfectly horrified. Both she and Uncle Matthew always had very much disliked Mr. Dougdale, and, when speaking of the lecture, she said it was exactly what she would have expected, snobbish, dreary and out of place with a village audience, but she had such difficulty filling up the Women's Institute programme month after month in such a remote district that when he had himself written and suggested coming she had thought, "Oh, well . . . !" No doubt she supposed that her children called him the Lecherous Lecturer for alliterative rather than factual reasons, and, indeed, with the Radletts you never could tell. Why, for instance, would Victoria bellow like a bull and half kill Jassy whenever Jassy said, in a certain tone of voice, pointing her finger with a certain look, "Fancy?" I think they hardly knew why, themselves.

When I got home I told Davey about the Lecturer, and he had

roared with laughter but said I was not to breathe a word to Aunt Emily or there would be an appalling row and the one who would really suffer would be Lady Patricia Dougdale, Boy's wife.

"She has enough to put up with as it is," he said, "and besides, what would be the good? Those Radletts are clearly heading for one bad end after another, except that for them nothing ever will be the end. Poor dear Sadie just doesn't realize what she has hatched out, luckily for her."

All this happened a year or two before the time of which I am writing and the name of Lecturer for Boy Dougdale had passed into the family language so that none of us children ever called him anything else, and even the grown-ups had come to accept it, though Aunt Sadie, as a matter of form, made an occasional vague protest. It seemed to suit him perfectly.

"Don't listen to Davey," Aunt Emily said. "He's in a very naughty mood. Another time we'll wait for the waning moon to tell him these things. He's only really sensible when he's fasting, I've noticed. Now we shall have to think about your clothes, Fanny. Sonia's parties are always so dreadfully smart. I suppose they'll be sure to change for tea? Perhaps if we dyed your Ascot dress a nice dark shade of red that would do? It's a good thing we've got nearly a month."

Nearly a month was indeed a comforting thought. Although I was bent on going to this house party, the very idea of it made me shake in my shoes with fright, not so much as the result of Davey's teasing as because ancient memories of Hampton now began to revive in force, memories of my childhood visits there and of how little, really, I had enjoyed them. Downstairs had been so utterly terrifying. It might be supposed that nothing could frighten somebody accustomed, as I was, to a downstairs inhabited by my uncle Matthew Alconleigh. But that rumbustious ogre, that eater of little girls was by no means confined to one part of his house. He raged and roared about the whole of it, and indeed the safest place to be in, as far as he was concerned, was downstairs in Aunt Sadie's drawing room, since she alone had any control over him. The terror at

Hampton was of a different quality, icy and dispassionate, and it reigned downstairs. You were forced down into it after tea, frilled up, washed and curled, when quite little, or in a tidy frock when older, into the Long Gallery where there would seem to be dozens of grown-ups, all, usually, playing bridge. The worst of bridge is that out of every four people playing it, one is always at liberty to roam about and say kind words to little girls.

Still, on the whole, there was not much attention to spare from the cards and we could sit on the long white fur of the polar bear in front of the fireplace, looking at a picture book propped against its head, or just chatting to each other until welcome bedtime. It quite often happened, however, that Lord Montdore, or Boy Dougdale, if he was there, would give up playing in order to amuse us. Lord Montdore would read aloud from Hans Andersen or Lewis Carroll and there was something about the way he read that made me squirm with secret embarrassment; Polly used to lie with her head on the bear's head, not listening, I believe, to a single word. It was far worse when Boy Dougdale organized hide and seek or sardines, two games of which he was extremely fond, and which he played in what Linda and I considered a stchoopid way. The word stupid, pronounced like that, had a meaning of its own in our language when we (the Radletts and I) were little; it was not until after the Lecturer's lecture that we realized its full implication and that Boy Dougdale had not been stupid so much as lecherous.

When bridge was in progress, we would at least be spared the attention of Lady Montdore, who, even when dummy, had eyes for nothing but the cards; but if by chance there should not be a four staying in the house she would make us play racing demon, a game which has always given me an inferiority feeling because I do pant along so slowly.

"Hurry up, Fanny—we're all waiting for that seven, you know, don't be so moony, dear."

She always won at demon by hundreds, never missing a trick. She never missed a detail of one's appearance, either—the shabby old pair of indoor shoes, the stockings that did not quite match each other, the tidy frock too short and too tight, grown out of, in fact—it was all chalked up on the score.

That was downstairs. Upstairs was all right, perfectly safe, anyhow, from intrusion, the nursery being occupied by nurses, the schoolroom by governesses and neither being subject to visits from the Montdores who, when they wished to see Polly, sent for her to go to them. But it was rather dull, not nearly as much fun as staying at Alconleigh. No Hons' cupboard (the Hons was the Radlett secret society and the Hons' cupboard its headquarters), no talking bawdy, no sallies into the woods to hide the steel traps or to unstop an earth, no nests of baby bats being fed with fountain-pen fillers in secret from the grown-ups, who had absurd ideas about bats, that they were covered with vermin, or got into your hair. Polly was a withdrawn, formal little girl, who went through her day with the sense of ritual, the poise, the absolute submission to etiquette of a Spanish Infanta. You had to love her, she was so beautiful and so friendly, but it was impossible to feel very intimate with her.

She was the exact opposite of the Radletts, who always "told" everything. Polly "told" nothing, and if there were anything to tell it was all bottled up inside her. When Lord Montdore once read us the story of the Snow Queen (I could hardly listen, he put in so much expression) I remember thinking that it must be about Polly and that she surely had a glass splinter in her heart. For what did she love? That was the great puzzle to me. My cousins and I poured out love, we lavished it to right and to left, on each other, on the grown-ups, on a variety of animals and, above all, on the characters (often historical or even fictional) with whom we were *in* love. There was no reticence, and we all knew everything there was to know about each other's feelings for every other creature, whether real or imaginary. Then there were the shrieks. Shrieks of laughter and happiness and high spirits which always resounded through Alconleigh, except on the rare occasions when there were floods. It was shrieks or floods in that house, usually shrieks. But Polly did not pour or lavish or shriek, and I never saw her in tears. She was always the same, always charming, sweet and docile, polite, interested in what one said, rather amused by one's jokes, but all without exuberance, without superlatives, and certainly without any confidences.

Nearly a month then to this visit about which my feelings were so uncertain. All of a sudden, not only not nearly a month but now, to-day, now this minute, and I found myself being whirled through the suburbs of Oxford in a large black Daimler. One mercy, I was alone, and there was a long drive, some twenty miles, in front of me. I knew the road well from my hunting days in that neighbourhood. Perhaps it would go on nearly for ever. Lady Montdore's writing paper was headed Hampton Place, Oxford, station Twyfold. But Twyfold, with the change and hour's wait at Oxford which it involved, was only inflicted upon such people as were never likely to be in a position to get their own back on Lady Montdore, anybody for whom she had the slightest regard being met at Oxford. "Always be civil to the girls, you never know who they may marry," is an aphorism which has saved many an English spinster from being treated like an Indian widow.

So I fidgetted in my corner, looking out at the deep intense blue dusk of autumn, profoundly wishing that I could be safe back at home or going to Alconleigh or, indeed, anywhere rather than to Hampton. Well-known landmarks kept looming up; it got darker and darker but I could just see the Merlinford road, branching off with a big sign post, and then in a moment, or so it seemed, we were turning in at lodge gates. Horrors! I had arrived.

Chapter 3

Ascrunch of gravel, the car gently stopped and exactly as it did so the front door opened, casting a panel of light at my feet. Once inside, the butler took charge of me, removed my nutria coat (a coming-out present from Davey), led me through the hall, under the great steep Gothic double staircase up which rushed a hundred steps, halfway to heaven, meeting at a marble group which represented the sorrows of Niobe, through the octagonal ante-chamber, through the green drawing room and the red drawing room into the Long Gallery where, without asking it, he pronounced my name, very loud and clear, and then abandoned me.

The Long Gallery was, as I always remember it being, full of people. There were perhaps twenty or thirty on this occasion, a few very old ones, contemporaries of Lady Montdore, sitting stiffly round a tea table by the fire, while further down the room, glasses instead of cups in their hands, the rest of the party stood watching games of backgammon. Younger than Lady Montdore, they still seemed elderly to me, being about the age of my own mother. They were chattering like starlings in a tree, did not stop their chatter when I came in, when Lady Montdore introduced me to them, merely broke off what they were saying, stared at me for a moment and went straight on again. However, when she pronounced my name, one of them said,

"Not the Bolter's daughter?"

I was quite accustomed to hearing my mother referred to as the Bolter, indeed nobody, not even her own sisters, ever called her anything else, so, when Lady Montdore paused with a disapproving look at the speaker, I piped up, "Yes."

It then seemed as though all the starlings rose in the air and settled on a different tree, and that tree was me.

"The Bolter's girl?"

"Don't be funny—how could the Bolter have a grown-up daughter?"

"Veronica, do come here a minute, do you know who this is? She's the Bolter's daughter, that's all."

"Come and have your tea, Fanny," said Lady Montdore. She led me to the tea table and the starlings went on with their chatter about my mother in eggy-peggy, a language I happened to know quite well.

"Eggis sheggee reggeally, peggoor sweggeet! I couldn't be more interested, naturally, when you come to think of it, considering that the very first person the Bolter ever bolted with, was my husband— wasn't it, Chad? Tiny me got you next, didn't I, my angel, but not until she had bolted away from you again."

"I don't believe it. The Bolter can't be more than thirty-six. I know she can't, we used to go to Miss Vacani together, and you used to come, too, Roly—couldn't remember it better—poker and tongs on the floor for the sword dance and Roly in his tiny kilt. What do you say, darling—can she be more than thirty-six?"

"That's right. Do the sum, birdbrain. She married at eighteen, eighteen and eighteen are thirty-six. Correct—no?"

"Well, steady on though, how about the nine months?"

"Not nine, darling, nothing like nine, don't you remember how bogus it all was and how shamingly huge her bouquet had to be, poor sweet? It was the whole point."

"Careful, Veronica. Really, Veronica always goes too far. Come on, let's finish the game. . . ."

I had half an ear on this rivetting conversation, and half on what Lady Montdore was saying. Having given me a characteristic and well-remembered look, up and down, a look which told me what I knew too well, that my tweed skirt bulged behind and why had I no gloves? (why, indeed, left them in the motor no doubt and how would I ever have the courage to ask for them?), said in a most friendly way that I had changed more in five years than Polly had, but that Polly was now much taller than I. How was Aunt Emily? And Davey?

"You'll have your tea?" she said.

That was where her charm lay. She would suddenly be nice just when it seemed that she was about to go for you tooth and nail; it was the charm of a purring puma. She now sent one of the men off to look for Polly.

"Playing billiards with Boy, I think," and poured me out a cup of tea.

"And here," she said, to the company in general, "is Montdore."

She always called her husband Montdore to those she regarded as her equals, but to borderline cases such as the estate agent or Dr. Simpson he was Lord Montdore, if not His Lordship. I never heard her refer to him as "my husband." It was all part of the attitude to life that made her so generally un-beloved, a determination to show people what she considered to be their proper place and keep them in it.

The chatter did not continue while Lord Montdore, radiating wonderful oldness, came into the room. It stopped dead, and those who were not already standing up, respectfully did so. He shook hands all round, a suitable word for each in turn.

"And this is my friend Fanny? Quite grown-up now, and do you remember that last time I saw you, we were weeping together over the 'Little Match Girl'?"

Perfectly untrue, I thought. Nothing about human beings ever had the power to move me as a child. *Black Beauty* now . . . !

He turned to the fire, holding his thin white hands which shook a little to the blaze, while Lady Montdore poured out his tea. There was a long silence in the room. Presently he took a scone, buttered it, put it in his saucer, and turning to another old man said, "I've been wanting to ask you."

They sat down together, talking in low voices, and by degrees the starling chatter broke loose again.

I was beginning to see that there was no occasion to feel alarmed in this company, because, as far as my fellow guests were concerned, I was clearly endowed with protective colouring, their momentary initial interest in me having subsided, I might just as well not have been there at all, and could keep happily to myself and observe their antics. The various house parties for people of my own age that I had been to during the past year had really been much more unnerving, because there I knew that I was expected to play a part, to sing for my supper by being, if possible, amusing. But here, a child once more among all these old people, it was my place to be seen and not heard. Looking round the room, I wondered vaguely which were the young men Lady Montdore had mentioned as being specially invited for Polly and me. They could not yet have arrived, as certainly none of these were the least bit young, all well over thirty, I should have said, and probably all married, though it was impossible to guess which of the couples were husbands and wives, because they all spoke to each other as if they all were, in voices and with endearments which, in the case of my aunts, could only have meant that it was their own husbands they were addressing.

"Have the Sauveterres not arrived yet, Sonia?" said Lord Montdore coming up for another cup of tea.

There was a movement among the women. They turned their heads like dogs who think they hear somebody unwrapping a piece of chocolate.

"Sauveterres? Do you mean Fabrice? Don't tell me Fabrice is married? I couldn't be more amazed."

"No, no, of course not. He's bringing his mother to stay. She's an old flame of Montdore's—I've never seen her, and Montdore hasn't for quite forty years. Of course, we've always known Fabrice, and he came to us in India; he's such fun, a delightful creature. He was very much taken up with the little Ranee of Rawalpur; in fact, they do say her last baby . . ."

"Sonia . . . !" said Lord Montdore, quite sharply for him. She took absolutely no notice.

"Dreadful old man the Rajah, I only hope it was. Poor creatures, it's one baby after another; you can't help feeling sorry for them, like little birds, you know. I used to go and visit the ones who were kept in purdah and of course they simply worshipped me, it was really touching."

Lady Patricia Dougdale was announced. I had seen the Dougdales from time to time while the Montdores were abroad because they were neighbours at Alconleigh and although my Uncle Matthew by no means encouraged neighbours it was beyond even his powers to suppress them altogether and prevent them from turning up at the meets, the local point to points, on Oxford platform for the 9.10 and Paddington for the 4.45, or at the Merlinford market. Besides, the Dougdales had brought house parties to Alconleigh for Aunt Sadie's dances when Louisa and Linda came out and had given Louisa, for a wedding present, an antique pin cushion, curiously heavy because full of lead. The romantic Louisa, making sure it was curiously heavy because full of gold, "Somebody's savings, don't you see?" had ripped it open with her nail scissors, only to find the lead, with the result that none of her wedding presents could be shown, for fear of hurting Lady Patricia's feelings.

Lady Patricia was a perfect example of beauty that is but skin deep. She had once had the same face as Polly, but the fair hair had now gone white and the white skin yellow, so that she looked like a classical statue that has been out in the weather, with a layer of snow on its head, the features smudged and smeared by damp. Aunt Sadie said that she and Boy had been considered the handsomest couple in London, but of course that must have been years ago; they were old now, fifty or something, and life would soon be over for them. Lady Patricia's life had been full of sadness and suffering, sadness in her marriage and suffering in her liver. (Of course I am now quoting Davey.) She had been passionately in love with Boy, who was younger than she, for some years before he had married her, which he was supposed to have done because he could not resist the relationship with his esteemed Hampton family. The great sorrow of his life was childlessness, since he had set his heart on a quiverful of little half-Hamptons, and people said that the disappointment had almost unhinged him for a while, but that his niece, Polly, was now beginning to take the place of a daughter, he was so extremely devoted to her.

"Where is Boy?" Lady Patricia said when she had greeted, in the usual English way of greeting, the people who were near the fire, sending a wave of her gloves or half a smile to the ones who were further off. She wore a felt hat, sensible tweeds, silk stockings and beautifully polished calf shoes.

"I do wish they'd come," said Lady Montdore. "I want him to help me with the table. He's playing billiards with Polly. I've sent word once, by Rory—oh, here they are."

Polly kissed her aunt and kissed me. She looked round the room to see if anybody else had arrived to whom she had not yet said, "How do you do?" (she and her parents, as a result, no doubt, of the various official positions Lord Montdore had held, were rather formal in their manners) and then turned back again to me.

"Fanny," she said, "have you been here long? Nobody told me."

She stood there, rather taller now than me, embodied once more instead of a mere nebulous memory of my childhood, and all the complicated feelings that we have for the beings who matter in our lives, came rushing back to me. My feelings for the Lecturer came rushing back, too, uncomplicated.

"Ha!" he was saying, "here, at last, is my lady wife." He gave me the creeps, with his crinkly black hair going grey now and his perky, jaunty figure. He was shorter than his wife and tried to make up for this by having very thick soles to his shoes. He always looked horribly pleased with himself; the corners of his mouth turned up when his face was in repose, and if he was at all put out they turned up even more in a maddening smile.

Polly's blue look was now upon me. I suppose she also was rediscovering a person only half-remembered, quite the same person really, a curly little black girl, Aunt Sadie used to say, like a little pony which at any moment might toss its shaggy mane and gallop off. Half an hour ago, I would gladly have galloped but now I felt happily inclined to stay where I was.

As we went upstairs together, Polly put her arm round my waist saying, with obvious sincerity, "It's too lovely to see you again. The things I've got to ask you! When I was in India I used to think and think about you. Do you remember how we both had black velvet dresses with red sashes for coming down after tea and how Linda had worms? It does seem another life, so long ago. What is Linda's fiancé like?"

"Very good-looking," I said. "Very hearty. They don't care for him much at Alconleigh, any of them."

"Oh, how sad. Still, if Linda does . . . Fancy, though, Louisa married and Linda engaged already! Of course before India we were all babies really, and now we are of marriageable age, it makes a difference, doesn't it?" She sighed deeply.

"I suppose you came out in India?" I said. Polly, I knew, was a little older than I was.

"Well, yes, I did, I've been out two years, actually. It was all very dull, this coming out seems a great, great bore. Do you enjoy it, Fanny?"

I had never thought about whether I enjoyed it or not and found it difficult to answer her question. Girls have to come out, I knew. It is a stage in their existence, just as the public school is for boys, which must be passed before life, real life, could begin. Dances are supposed to be delightful. They cost a lot of money and it is most good of the grown-ups to give them, most good, too, of Aunt Sadie to have taken me to so many. But at these dances, although I quite enjoyed going to them, I always had the uncomfortable feeling that I missed something; it was like going to a play in a foreign language. Each time I used to hope that I should see the point, but I never did, though the people round me were all so evidently seeing it. Linda, for instance, had seen it clearly but then she had been successfully pursuing love.

"What I do enjoy," I said, truthfully, "is the dressing up."

"Oh, so do I! Do you think about dresses and hats all the time, even in church? I do, too. Heavenly tweed, Fanny, I noticed it at once."

"Only it's bagging," I said.

"They always bag, except on very smart little thin women, like Veronica. Are you pleased to be back in this room? It's the one you used to have, do you remember?"

Of course I remembered. It always had my name in full "The Honble Frances Logan" written in a careful copperplate on a card on the door, even when I was so small that I came with my nanny, and this had greatly impressed and pleased me as a child.

"Is this what you're going to wear to-night?" Polly went up to the huge red four-poster where my dress was laid out.

"How lovely—green velvet and silver. I call that a dream, so soft and delicious, too." She rubbed a fold of the skirt against her cheek. "Mine's silver lamé. It smells like a bird cage when it gets hot, but I do love it. Aren't you thankful evening skirts are long again? But I want to hear more about what coming out is like in England."

"Dances," I said, "girls' luncheon parties, tennis, if you can, dinner parties to go to, plays, Ascot, being presented. Oh, I don't know, I expect you can just about imagine."

"And all going on like the people downstairs?"

"Chattering all the time? Well, but the downstairs people are old, Polly, coming out is with people of one's own age, you see."

"They don't think they're old a bit," she said, laughing.

"Well," I said, "all the same, they are."

"I don't see them as so old myself, but I expect that's because they seem young beside Mummy and Daddy. Just think of it, Fanny, your mother wasn't born when Mummy married, and Mrs. Warbeck was only just old enough to be her bridesmaid. Mummy was saying so before you came. No, but what I really want to know about coming out here is, what about love? Are they all always having love affairs the whole time? Is it their one and only topic of conversation?"

I was obliged to admit that this was the case.

"Oh, bother. I felt sure, really, you would say that. It was so in India, of course, but I thought perhaps in a cold climate . . . ! Anyway, don't tell Mummy if she asks you. Pretend that English debutantes don't bother about love. She is in a perfect fit because I never fall in love with people; she teases me about it all the time. But it isn't any good, because if you don't you don't. I should have thought, at my age, it's natural not to."

I looked at her in surprise, it seemed to me highly unnatural, though I could well understand not wanting to talk about such things to the grown-ups, and specially not to Lady Montdore if she happened to be one's mother. But a new idea struck me.

"In India," I said, "could you have fallen in love?" Polly laughed.

"Fanny darling, what do you mean? Of course I could have. Why not? I just didn't happen to, you see."

"White people?"

"White or black," she said, teasingly.

"Fall in love with blacks?" What would Uncle Matthew say?

"People do, like anything. You don't understand about Rajahs, I see, but some of them are awfully attractive. I had a friend there who nearly died of love for one. And I'll tell you something, Fanny. I honestly believe Mamma would rather I fell in love with an Indian than not at all. Of course there would have been a fearful row, and I should have been sent straight home, but even so she would have thought it quite a good thing. What she minds so much is the not at all. I bet you anything she's only asked this Frenchman to stay because she thinks no woman can resist him. They could think of nothing else in Delhi. I wasn't there at the time, I was in the hills with Boy and Auntie Patsy. We did a heavenly, heavenly trip. I must tell you about it, but not now."

"But would your mother like you to marry a Frenchman?" I said. At this time love and marriage were inextricably knotted in my mind.

"Oh, not marry, good gracious, no. She'd just like me to have a little weakness for him, to show that I'm capable of it. She wants to see if I'm like other women. Well, she'll see. There's the dressing bell—I'll call for you when I'm ready. I don't live up here any more, I've got a new room over the porch. Heaps of time, Fanny, quite an hour."

Chapter 4

My BEDROOM WAS in the tower, where Polly's nurseries had been when she was small. Whereas all the other rooms at Hampton were classical in feeling, the tower rooms were exaggeratedly Gothic, the Gothic of fairy-story illustrations. In this one the bed, the cupboards and the fireplace had pinnacles; the wallpaper was a design of scrolls and the windows were casements. An extensive work of modernisation had taken place all over the house while the family was in India, and looking round I saw that in one of the cupboards there was now a tiled bathroom.

In the old days I used to sally forth, sponge in hand, to the nursery bathroom which was down a terrifying, twisting staircase, and I could still remember how cold it used to be outside, in the passages, though there was always a blazing fire in my room. But now the central heating had been brought up to date and the temperature everywhere was that of a hot-house. The fire which flickered away beneath the spires and towers of the chimney-piece was merely there for show, and no longer to be lighted at 7 A.M., before one was awake, by a little maid scuffling about like a mouse. The age of luxury was ended and that of comfort had begun. Being conservative by nature, I was glad to see that the decoration of the room had not been changed at all, though the lighting was very much improved. There was a new quilt on the bed, the mahogany dressing table had acquired a muslin petticoat and a triple looking-glass, and the whole room and bathroom were close carpeted. Otherwise everything was exactly as I remembered it, including two large yellow pictures which could be seen from the bed, Caravaggio's "The Gamesters" and "A Courtesan" by Raphael.

I dressed for dinner, passionately wishing that Polly and I could have spent the evening together upstairs, supping off a tray, as we used to do, in the schoolroom. I was dreading this grown-up dinner ahead of me because I knew that once I found myself in the dining room, seated between two of the old gentlemen downstairs, it would no longer be possible to remain a silent spectator. I should be obliged to try and think of things to say. It had been drummed into me all my life, especially by Davey, that silence at meal times is antisocial.

"So long as you chatter, Fanny, it's of no consequence what you say. Better recite out of the A.B.C. than sit like a deaf mute. Think of your poor hostess—it simply isn't fair on her."

In the dining room, between the man called Rory and the man called Roly, I found things even worse than I had expected. The protective colouring, which had worked so well in the drawing room, was now going on and off like a deficient electric light. I was visible, one of my neighbours would begin a conversation with me and seem quite interested in what I was telling him when, without any warning at all, I would become invisible and Rory and Roly were both shouting across the table at the lady called Veronica, while I was left in mid-air with some sad little remark. It then became too obvious that they had not heard a single word I had been saying but had all along been entranced by the infinitely more fascinating conversation of this Veronica lady. All right then, invisible, which really I much preferred, able to eat happily away in silence. But no, not at all, unaccountably visible again.

"Is Lord Alconleigh your uncle then? Isn't he quite barmy? Doesn't he hunt people with bloodhounds by full moon?"

I was still enough of a child to accept the grown-ups of my own family without a question and to suppose that each in their own way was more or less perfect, and it gave me a shock to hear this stranger refer to my uncle as quite barmy.

"Oh, but we love it," I began. "You can't imagine what fun . . ." No good, even as I spoke I became invisible.

"No, no, Veronica, the whole point was he bought the microscope to look at his own . . ."

"Well, I dare you to say the word at dinner, that's all," said Veronica. "Even if you know how to pronounce it, which I doubt, it's too shame-making, not a dinner thing at all. . . ." And so they went on backwards and forwards.

"I couldn't think Veronica much funnier, could you?"

The two ends of the table were quieter. At one, Lady Montdore was talking to the Duc de Sauveterre, who was politely listening to what she said, but whose brilliant, good-humoured little black eyes were nevertheless slightly roving, and, at the other, Lord Montdore and the Lecturer were having a lovely time showing off their fault-less French by talking in it across the old Duchesse de Sauveterre to each other. I was near enough to listen to what they were saying, which I did during my periods of invisibility and, though it may not have been as witty as the conversation round Veronica, it had the merit of being, to me, more comprehensible. It was all on these lines:

Montdore: "*Alors, le Duc du Maine était le fils de qui?*"

Boy: "*Mais, dîtes donc, mon vieux, de Louis XIV.*"

Montdore: "*Bien entendu, mais sa mère?*"

Boy: "*La Montespan.*"

At this point, the Duchess, who had been munching away in silence and not apparently listening to them said, in a loud and very disapproving voice, "*Madame* de Montespan."

Boy: "*Oui—oui—oui, parfaitement, Madame la Duchesse.*" (In

an English aside to his brother-in-law, "The Marquise de Montespan was an aristocrat, you know. They never forget it.")

"Elle avait deux fils d'ailleurs, le Duc du Maine et le Comte de Toulouse, et Louis XIV les avait tous deux légitimés. Et sa fille a épousé le Régent. Tout cela est exacte, n'est-ce pas, Madame la Duchesse?"

But the old lady for whose benefit this linguistic performance was presumably being staged was totally uninterested in it. She was eating as hard as she could, only pausing in order to ask the footman for more bread. When directly appealed to, she said, "I suppose so."

"It's all in St. Simon," said the Lecturer. "I've been reading him again and so must you Montdore. Simply fascinating." Boy was versed in all the court memoirs that had ever been written, thus acquiring a reputation for great historical knowledge.

"You may not like Boy, but he does know a lot about history, there's nothing he can't tell you."

All depending on what you wanted to find out. The Empress Eugenie's flight from the Tuileries, yes, the Tolpuddle Martyr's martyrdom, no. Boy's historical knowledge was a sublimation of snobbery.

Lady Montdore now turned to her other neighbour, and everybody else followed suit. I got Rory instead of Roly, which was no change as both by now were entirely absorbed in what was going on on the other side of the table, and the Lecturer was left to struggle alone with the Duchess. I heard him say, *"Dans le temps j'étais très lié avec le Duc de Souppes, qu'est-ce qu'il est devenu, Madame la Duchesse?"*

"How, you are a friend to that poor Souppes?" she said. "He is such an annoying boy." Her accent was very strange, a mixture of French and Cockney.

"Il habite toujours ce ravissant hôtel dans la rue du Bac?"

"I suppose so."

"Et la vieille duchesse est toujours en vie?"

But his neighbour was now quite given over to eating and he never got another word out of her. At the end of each course she craned to see what was coming next; when plates were given round after the pudding she touched hers and I heard her say approvingly to herself, "*Encore une assiette chaude, très-très bien.*" She was loving her food.

I was loving mine, too, especially now that the protective colouring was in perfect order again, and indeed continued to work for the rest of the evening with hardly another breakdown. I thought what a pity it was that Davey could not be here for one of his overeating days. He always complained that Aunt Emily never really provided him with enough different dishes on these occasions to give his metabolism a proper shock.

"I don't believe you understand the least bit what I need," he would say, crossly for him. "I've got to be giddy, exhausted from overeating, if it's to do me any good. That feeling you have after a meal in a Paris restaurant is what we've got to aim at, when you're too full to do anything but lie on your bed like a cobra, for hours and hours, too full even to sleep. Now there must be a great many different courses to coax my appetite—second helpings don't count; I must have them anyway, a great many different courses of really rich food, Emily dear. Naturally, if you'd rather, I'll give up the cure, but it seems a pity, just when it's doing me so much good. If it's the house books you're thinking of, you must remember there are my starvation days. You never seem to take them into account at all."

But Aunt Emily said the starvation days made absolutely no difference to the house books and that he might call it starvation but anybody else would call it four square meals.

Some two dozen metabolisms round this table were getting a jolly good jolt, I thought, as the meal went on and on. Soup, fish, pheasant, beefsteak, asparagus, pudding, savoury, fruit. Hampton food, Aunt Sadie used to call it, and indeed it had a character of its own which can best be described by saying that it was like mountains of the very most delicious imaginable nursery food, plain and wholesome, made of the best materials, each thing tasting strongly of itself. But, like everything else at Hampton, it was exaggerated. Just as Lady Montdore was a little bit too much like a Countess, Lord Montdore too much like an elder statesman, the servants too perfect and too deferential, the beds too soft and the linen too fine, the motor cars too new and too shiny and everything too much in apple-pie order, so the very peaches there were too peach-like. I used to think, when I was a child, that all this excellence made Hampton seem unreal compared with the only other houses I knew, Alconleigh and Aunt Emily's little house. It was like a noble establishment in a book or a play, not like somebody's home, and in the same way the Montdores, and even Polly, never quite seemed to be real flesh-and-blood people.

By the time I was embarked on a too peach-like peach, I had lost all sense of fear, if not of decorum, and was lolling about as I would not have dared to at the beginning of dinner, boldly looking to right and to left. It was not the wine. I had only had one glass of claret and all my other glasses were full (the butler having paid no attention to my shakes of the head) and untouched. It was the food; I was reeling drunk on food. I saw just what Davey meant about a cobra, everything was stretched to its capacity and I really felt as if I had swallowed a goat. I knew that my face was scarlet, and looking round I saw that so were all the other faces, except Polly's.

Polly, between just such a pair as Rory and Roly, had not made the least effort to be agreeable to them, though they had taken a good deal more trouble with her than my neighbours had with me. Nor was she enjoying her food. She picked at it with a fork, leaving most of it on her plate, and seemed to be completely in the clouds, her blank stare shining, like the ray from a blue lamp, in the direction of Boy, but not as though she saw him really or was listening to his terribly adequate French. Lady Montdore gave her a dissatisfied look from time to time, but she noticed nothing. Her thoughts were evidently far away from her mother's dinner table, and after awhile her neighbours gave up the struggle of getting yes and no out of her, and, in chorus with mine, began to shout back chat at the lady called Veronica.

This Veronica was small and thin and sparkling. Her bright gold hair lay on her head like a cap, perfectly smooth, with a few flat curls above her forehead. She had a high bony nose, rather protruding pale-blue eyes and not much chin. She looked decadent, I thought, my drunkenness putting that clever grown-up word into my mind no doubt, but all the same it was no good denying that she was very, very pretty and that her clothes, her jewels, her make-up and her whole appearance were the perfection of smartness. She was evidently considered to be a great wit and as soon as the party began to warm up after a chilly start it revolved entirely round her. She bandied repartee with the various Rorys and Rolys, the other women of her age-group merely giggling away at the jokes but taking no active part in them, as though they realized it would be useless to try and steal any of her limelight, while the even older people at the two ends of the table kept up a steady flow of grave talk, occasionally throwing an indulgent glance at Veronica.

Now that I had become brave, I asked one of my neighbours to tell me her name, but he was so much surprised at my not knowing it that he quite forgot to answer my question.

"Veronica?" he said, stupefied. "But surely you know Veronica?"

It was as though I had never heard of Vesuvius. Afterwards I discovered that her name was Mrs. Chaddesley Corbett, and it seemed strange to me that Lady Montdore, whom I had so often been told was a snob, should have only a Mrs., not even an Hon. Mrs., to stay and treat her almost with deference. This shows how innocent, socially, I must have been in those days, since every schoolboy (every Etonian, that is) knew all about Mrs. Chaddesley Corbett. She was to the other smart women of her day as the star is to the chorus, and had invented a type of looks, as well as a way of talking, walking and behaving, which was slavishly copied by the fashionable set in England for at least ten years. No doubt the reason why I had never heard her name before was that she was such miles, in smartness, above the bread-and-butter world of my acquaintance.

It was terribly late when at last Lady Montdore got up to leave the table. My aunts never allowed such long sitting in the dining room because of the washing up and keeping the servants from going to bed, but that sort of thing simply was not considered at Hampton, nor did Lady Montdore turn to her husband, as Aunt Sadie always did, with an imploring look and a "Not too long, darling," as she went, leaving the men to their port, their brandy, their cigars and their traditional dirty stories which could hardly be any dirtier, it seemed to me, than Veronica's conversation had become during the last half hour or so.

Back in the Long Gallery some of the women went upstairs to "powder their noses." Lady Montdore was scornful.

"I go in the morning," she said, "and that is that. I don't have to be let out like a dog at intervals."

If Lady Montdore had really hoped that Sauveterre would exercise his charm on Polly, she was in for a disappointment. As soon as the men came out of the dining room, where they had remained for quite an hour ("This English habit," I heard him say, "is terrible"), he was surrounded by Veronica and her chorus and never given a chance to speak to anybody else. They all seemed to be old friends of his, called him Fabrice and had a thousand questions to ask about mutual acquaintances in Paris, fashionable foreign ladies with such unfashionable English names as Norah, Cora, Jennie, Daisy, May and Nellie.

"Are all Frenchwomen called after English housemaids?" Lady Montdore said, rather crossly, as she resigned herself to a chat with the old Duchess, the group round Sauveterre having clearly settled down for good. He seemed to be enjoying himself, consumed, one would say, by some secret joke, his twinkling eyes resting with amusement rather than desire, on each plucked and painted face in turn, while in turn, and with almost too obvious an insincerity they asked about their darling Nellies and Daisys. Meanwhile, the husbands of these various ladies, frankly relieved, as Englishmen always are, by a respite from feminine company, were gambling at the other end of the long room, playing, no doubt, for much higher stakes than they would have been allowed to by their wives and with a solid, heavy masculine concentration on the game itself, undisturbed by any of the distractions of sex. Lady Patricia went off to bed; Boy Dougdale began by inserting himself into the group round Sauveterre but finding that nobody there took the slightest notice of him, Sauveterre not even answering when he asked about the Duc de Souppes, beyond saying evasively, "I see poor Nina de Souppes sometimes," he gave up, a hurt, smiling look on his face, and came and sat with Polly and me and showed us how to play backgammon. He held our hands as he shook the dice, rubbed our knees with his, generally behaving I thought, in a stchoopid and lecherous way. Lord Montdore and the other very old man went off to play billiards; he was said to be the finest billiards player in the British Isles.

Meanwhile poor Lady Montdore was being subjected to a tremendous interrogation by the Duchess, who had relapsed, through a spirit of contradiction perhaps, into her native tongue. Lady Montdore's French was adequate, but by no means so horribly wonderful as that of her husband and brother-in-law, and she was soon in difficulties over questions of weights and measures; how many hectares in the park at Hampton, how many metres high was the tower, what it would cost, in francs, to take a house boat for Henley, how many kilometers they were from Sheffield? She was obliged to appeal the whole time to Boy, who never failed her, of course, but the Duchess was not really very much interested in the answers, she was too busy cooking up the next question. They poured out in a relentless torrent, giving Lady Montdore no opportunity whatever to escape to the bridge table as she was longing to do. What sort of electric-light machine was there at Hampton, what was the average weight of a Scotch stag, how long had Lord and

Lady Montdore been married (*"Tiens!"*) how was the bath water heated, how many hounds in a pack of fox hounds, where was the Royal Family now? Lady Montdore was undergoing the sensation, novel to her, of being a rabbit with a snake. At last she could bear it no more and broke up the party, taking the women off to bed very much earlier than was usual, at Hampton.

Chapter 5

As this was the first time I had ever stayed away in such a large grand grown-up house party, I was rather uncertain what would happen, in the morning, about breakfast, so before we said good night I asked Polly.

"Oh," she said vaguely, "nine-ish, you know," and I took that to mean, as it meant at home, between five and fifteen minutes past nine. In the morning I was woken up at eight by a housemaid, who brought me tea with slices of paper-thin bread and butter, asked me, "Are these your gloves, miss, they were found in the car?" and then, after running me a bath, whisked away every other garment within sight, to add them no doubt to the collection she had already made of yesterday's tweed suit, jersey, shoes, stockings and underclothes. I foresaw that soon I should be appearing downstairs in my gloves and nothing else.

By nine o'clock I was bathed and dressed and quite ready for some food. Curiously enough, the immense dinner of the night before, which ought to have lasted me a week, seemed to have made me hungrier than usual. I waited a few minutes after the stable clock struck nine, so as not to be the first, and then ventured downstairs, but was greatly disconcerted in the dining room to find the table still in its green baize, the door into the pantry wide open and the menservants, in striped waistcoats and shirt sleeves, engaged upon jobs which had nothing to do with an approaching meal, such as sorting out letters and folding up the morning papers. They looked at me, or so I imagined, with surprise and hostility. I found them even more frightening than my fellow guests and was about to go back to my bedroom as quickly as I could when a voice behind me said, "But it's terrible, looking at this empty table."

It was the Duc de Sauveterre. My protective colouring was off, it seemed, by morning light. In fact he spoke as if we were old friends. I was very much surprised, more so when he shook my hand, and most of all when he said, "I also long for my porridge, but we can't stay here. It's too sad. Shall we go for a walk while it comes?"

The next thing I knew I was walking beside him, very fast, running almost to keep up, in one of the great lime avenues of the park. He talked all the time, as fast as he walked.

"Season of mists," he said, "and mellow fruitfulness. Am I not brilliant to know that? But this morning you can hardly see the mellow fruitfulness for the mists."

And indeed there was a thin fog all round us, out of which loomed great yellow trees. The grass was soaking wet and my indoor shoes were already leaking.

"I do love," he went on, "getting up with the lark and going for a walk before breakfast."

"Do you always?" I said.

Some people did, I knew.

"Never, never, never. But this morning I told my man to put a call through to Paris, thinking it would take quite an hour, but it came through at once, so now I am at a loose end with time on my hands. Do I not know wonderful English?"

This ringing up of Paris seemed to me a most dashing extravagance. Aunt Sadie and Aunt Emily only made trunk calls in times of crisis, and even then they generally rang off in the middle of a sentence when the three-minute signal went. Davey, it is true, spoke to his doctor in London most days, but that was only from Kent, and in any case Davey's health could really be said to constitute a perpetual crisis. But Paris, abroad!

"Is somebody ill?" I ventured.

"Not exactly ill, but she bores herself, poor thing. I quite understand it. Paris must be terrible without me. I don't know how she can bear it. I do pity her, really."

"Who?" I said, curiosity overcoming my shyness, and indeed it would be difficult to feel shy for long with this extraordinary man.

"My fiancée," he said, carelessly.

Alas! Something had told me this would be the reply, my heart sank and I said, dimly, "Oh! How exciting! You are engaged?"

He gave me a sidelong whimsical look.

"Oh, yes," he said, "engaged!"

"And are you going to be married soon?"

But why, I wondered had he come away alone, without her? If I had such a fascinating fiancé I would follow him everywhere, I knew, like a faithful spaniel.

"I don't imagine it will be very soon," he said gaily. "You know what it is with the Vatican. Time is nothing to them—a thousand ages in their sight are as an evening gone. Do I not know a lot of English poetry?"

"If you call it poetry. It's a hymn, really. But what has your marriage got to do with the Vatican? Isn't that in Rome?"

"It is. There is such a thing as the Church of Rome, my dear young lady, which I belong to, and this Church must annul the marriage of my affianced—do you say affianced?"

"You could. It's rather affected."

"My inamorata, my Dulcinea (brilliant?) must annul her marriage before she is at liberty to marry me."

"Goodness! Is she married already?"

"Yes, yes, of course. There are very few unmarried ladies going about, you know. It's not a state that lasts very long with pretty women."

"My aunt Emily doesn't approve of people getting engaged when they are married. My mother is always doing it and it makes Aunt Emily very cross."

"You must tell your dear Aunt Emily that in many ways it is rather convenient. But all the same, she is quite right. I have been a fiancé too often and for too long and now it is time I was married."

"Do you want to be?"

"I am not so sure. Going out to dinner every night with the same person, this must be terrible."

"You might stay in?"

"To break the habit of a life time is rather terrible, too. The fact is, I am so accustomed now to the engaged state that it's hard to imagine anything different."

"But have you been engaged to other people before this one?"

"Many, many times," he admitted.

"So what happened to them all?"

"Various unmentionable fates."

"For instance, what happened to the last one before this?"

"Let me see. Ah, yes—the last one before this did something I couldn't approve of, so I stopped loving her."

"But can you stop loving people because they do things you don't approve of?"

"Yes, I can."

"What a lucky talent," I said. "I'm sure I couldn't."

We had come to the end of the avenue and before us lay a field of stubble. The sun's rays were now beginning to pour down and dissolve the blue mist, turning the trees, the stubble and a group of ricks into objects of gold. I thought how lucky I was to be enjoying such a beautiful moment with so exactly the right person and that this was something I should remember all my life. The Duke interrupted these sentimental reflections, saying:

"Behold how brightly breaks the morning

Though bleak our lot our hearts are warm. . . .

Am I not a perfect mine of quotations? Tell me, who is Veronica's lover now?"

I was once more obliged to confess that I had not known Veronica before, and I knew nothing of her life. He seemed less astounded by this news than Roly had been, but looked at me reflectively, saying, "You are very young. You have something of your mother. At first I thought not, but now I see there is something."

"And who do you think Mrs. Chaddesley Corbett's lover is?" I said. I was more interested in her than in my mother at the moment, and, besides, all this talk about lovers intoxicated me. One knew of course that they existed, because of the Duke of Monmouth, and so on, but so near, under the very same roof as oneself, that was indeed exciting.

"It doesn't make a pin of difference," he said, "who it is. She lives, as all those sort of women do, in one little tiny group or set, and sooner or later everybody in that set becomes the lover of everybody else, so that when they change their lovers it is more like a cabinet reshuffle than a new government. Always chosen out of the same old lot, you see."

"Is it like that in France?" I said.

"With society people? Just the same all over the world, though in France I should say there is less reshuffling on the whole than in England; the ministers stay longer in their posts."

"Why?"

"Why? Frenchwomen generally keep their lovers if they want to because they know that there is one infallible way of doing so."

"No!" I said. "Oh, do tell."

I was more fascinated by this conversation every minute.

"It's very simple. You must give way to them in every respect."

"Goodness!" I said, thinking hard.

"Now, you see, these English *femmes du monde*, these Veronicas and Sheilas and Brendas and your mother, too, though nobody could say she stays in one little set—if she had done that she would not be so déclassée—they follow quite a different plan. They are proud and distant, out when the telephone bell rings, not free to dine, unless you ask them a week before; in short, *elles cherchent à se faire valoir*, and it never, never succeeds. Even Englishmen, who are used to it, don't like it, after a bit. Of course no Frenchman would put up with it for a day. So they go on reshuffling."

"They're very nasty ladies, aren't they?" I said, having formed that opinion the night before.

"Not at all, poor things. They are *les femmes du monde, voilà tout*, I love them, so easy to get on with. Not nasty at all. And I love *la mère* Montdore. How amusing she is, with her snobbishness. I am very much for snobs, they are always so charming to me."

"And Lord Montdore—and Polly?"

"Lord Montdore is a terrible old hypocrite, very English, very nice, but Polly now . . . ! There is something I don't quite understand about Polly. Perhaps she does not have a properly organized sex life, yes, I expect it is that. She seems so dreamy. I must see what I can do for her—only there's not much time." He looked at his watch.

I said primly that very few well-brought-up English girls of nineteen have a properly organized sex life. Mine was not organized at all, I knew, but I did not seem to be so specially dreamy.

"But what a beauty, even in that terrible dress. When she has had a little love she may become one of the beauties of our age. It's not certain; it never is with Englishwomen. She may cram a felt hat on her head and become a Lady Patricia Dougdale. Everything depends on the lover. So this Boy Dougdale, what about him?"

"Stupid," I said, meaning, really, "stchoopid."

"But you are impossible, my dear. Nasty ladies, stupid men—you really must try and like people more or you'll never get on in this world."

"How d'you mean, get on?"

"Well, get all those things like husbands and fiancés, and get on with them. They are what really matter in a woman's life, you know."

"And children?" I said.

He roared with laughter. "Yes, yes, of course, children. Husbands first, then children, then fiancés, then more children. . . . Then you have to live near the Parc Monceau because of the nannies. It's a whole programme having children, I can tell you, especially if you happen to prefer the Left Bank, as I do."

I did not understand one word of all this.

"Are you going to be a Bolter," he said, "like your mother?"

"No, no," I said. "A tremendous sticker."

"Really? I'm not quite sure."

Soon, too soon for my liking, we found ourselves back at the house.

"Porridge," said the Duke, again looking at his watch.

The front door opened upon a scene of great confusion. Most of the house party, some in tweeds and some in dressing gowns, were assembled in the hall, as were various outdoor and indoor servants, while a village policeman, who, in the excitement of the moment had brought his bicycle in with him, was conferring with Lord Montdore. High above our heads, leaning over the balustrade in front of Niobe, Lady Montdore, in a mauve satin wrap, was shouting at her husband:

"Tell him we must have Scotland Yard down at once, Montdore. If he won't send for them I shall ring up the Home Secretary myself. Most fortunately I have the number of his private line. In fact, I think I'd better go and do it now."

"No, no, my dear, please not. An Inspector is on his way, I tell you."

"Yes, I daresay, but how do we know it's the very best Inspector? I think I'd better get on to my friend. I think he'd be hurt with me if I didn't, the dear thing. Always so anxious to do what he can."

I was rather surprised to hear Lady Montdore speak so affectionately of a member of the Labour Government, this not being the attitude of other grown-ups, in my experience, but when I came to know her better I realized that power was a positive virtue in her eyes and that she automatically liked those who were invested with it.

My companion, with that look of concentration which comes over French faces when a meal is in the offing, did not wait to hear any of this. He made a bee line for the dining room, but although I was also very hungry indeed after my walk, curiosity got the better of me and I stayed to find out what it all meant. It seemed that there had been a burglary during the night and that nearly everybody in the house, except Lord and Lady Montdore, had been roundly robbed of jewels, loose cash, furs and anything portable of the kind that happened to be lying about. What made it particularly annoying for the victims was that they had all been woken up by somebody prowling in their rooms, but had all immediately concluded that it must be Sauveterre, pursuing his well-known hobby, so that the husbands had merely turned over with a grunt, saying, "Sorry, old chap, it's only me, I should try next door," while the wives had lain quite still in a happy trance of desire, murmuring such words of encouragement as they knew in French. Or so, at least, they were saying about each other, and, when I passed the telephone box on my way upstairs to change my wet shoes, I could hear Mrs. Chaddesley Corbett's bird-like twitters piping her version of the story to the outside world. Perhaps the cabinet changes were becoming a little bit of a bore, after all, and these ladies did rather long, at heart, for a new policy.

The general feeling was now very much against Sauveterre, whose fault the whole thing clearly was. It became positively inflamed when he was known to have had a good night's rest, to have got up at eight to telephone to his mistress in Paris and then to have gone for a walk with that little girl. ("Not the Bolter's child for nothing," I heard somebody say bitterly.) The climax was reached when he was seen to be putting away a huge breakfast of porridge and cream, kedgeree, eggs, cold ham and slice upon slice of toast covered with Cooper's Oxford. Very un-French, not at all in keeping with his reputation, unsuitable behaviour too, in view of the well-known frailty of his fellow guests. Britannia felt herself slighted by this foreigner. Away with him! And away he went, immediately after breakfast, driving hell for leather to Newhaven to catch the boat for Dieppe.

"Castle life," explained his mother, who placidly remained on until Monday, "always annoys Fabrice and makes him so nervous, poor boy."

I never saw Sauveterre again and it was to be many years before I even heard his name, but in the end I found myself adopting his little boy, so small is the world, so strange is fate.

Chapter 6

THE REST OF that day was rather disorganized. The men finally went off shooting, very late, while the women stayed at home to be interviewed by various Inspectors on the subject of their lost possessions. Of course the burglary made a wonderful topic of conversation and indeed nobody spoke of anything else.

"I couldn't care less about the diamond brooch. After all, it's well insured and now I shall be able to have clips instead which will be far and away smarter. Veronica's clips always make me miserable, every time I see her, and, besides, that brooch used to remind me of my bogus old mother-in-law too much. But I couldn't think it more hateful of them to have taken my fur tippet. Burglars never seem to realize one might feel the cold. How would they like it if I took away their wife's shawl?"

"Oh, I know. I'm in a terrible do about my bracelet of lucky charms—no value to anybody else—it really is too too sick-making. Just when I had managed to get a bit of hangman's rope, Mrs. Thompson too, did I tell you? Roly will never win the National now, poor sweet."

"With me it's Mummy's little locket she had as a child. I can't think why my ass of a maid had to go and put it in. She never does as a rule."

These brassy ladies became quite human as they mourned their lost trinkets, and now that the men were out of the house they suddenly seemed very much nicer. I am speaking of the Veronica chorus, for Mrs. Chaddesley Corbett herself, in common with Lady Montdore and Lady Patricia, was always exactly the same, whatever the company.

At tea time the village policeman reappeared with his bicycle, having wiped the eye of all the grand detectives who had come from London in their shiny cars. He produced a perfect jumble-sale heap of objects which had been discarded by the burglars under a haystack and nearly all the little treasures were retrieved, with high cries of joy, by their owners. As the only things which now remained missing were jewels of considerable value, and as these were felt to be the business of the Insurance Companies, the party continued in a much more cheerful atmosphere. There was, however, a distinctly noticeable current of anti-French feeling. The Norahs and Nellies would have had a pretty poor reception if any of them had turned up just then, and Boy, if it was possible for him to have enough of a Duchess, must have been having enough of this one, since all but he fled from the machine-gun fire of questions, and he was obliged to spend the next two days practically alone with her.

I WAS HANGING about, as one does at house parties, waiting for the next meal; it was not yet quite time to dress for dinner on Sunday evening. One of the pleasures of staying at Hampton was that the huge Louis XV map table in the middle of the Long Gallery was always covered with every imaginable weekly newspaper neatly laid out in rows and rearranged two or three times a day by a footman whose sole occupation this appeared to be.

I seldom saw the *Tatler* and *Sketch*, as my aunts would have thought it a perfectly unwarranted extravagance to subscribe to such papers, and I was greedily gulping down back numbers when Lady Montdore called to me from a sofa where, ever since tea, she had been deep in talk with Mrs. Chaddesley Corbett. I had been throwing an occasional glance in their direction, wondering what it could all be about and wishing I could be a fly on the wall to hear them, thinking also that it would hardly be possible for two women to look more different. Mrs. Chaddesley Corbett, her bony little silken legs crossed and uncovered to above the knee, perched rather than sat on the edge of the sofa. She wore a plain beige kasha dress, which must certainly have been made in Paris, and certainly designed for the Anglo-Saxon market, and smoked cigarette after cigarette with a great play of long thin white fingers, flashing with rings and painted nails. She did not keep still for one moment, though she was talking with great earnestness and concentration.

Lady Montdore sat well back on the sofa, both her feet on the ground. She seemed planted there, immovable and solid, not actually fat, but solid through and through. Smartness, even if she had sought after it, would hardly be attainable by her in a world where it was personified by the other and had become almost as much a question of build, of quick and nervous movement as of actual clothes. Her hair was shingled, but it was grey and fluffy, by no means a smooth cap, her eyebrows grew at will, and when she remembered to use lipstick and powder they were any colour and slapped on anyhow, so that her face, compared with that of Mrs. Chaddesley Corbett was as a hayfield is to a lawn, her whole head looking twice as large as the polished little head beside her. All the same she was not disagreeable to look at. There was a healthiness and liveliness about her face which lent it a certain attraction. Of course she seemed to me, then, very old. She was, in fact, about fifty-eight.

"Come over here, Fanny."

I was almost too much surprised to be alarmed by this summons and hurried over, wondering what it could all be about.

"Sit there," she said, pointing to a needlework chair, "and talk to us. Are you in love?"

I felt myself becoming scarlet in the face. How could they have guessed my secret? Of course I had been in love for two days now, ever since my morning walk with the Duc de Sauveterre. Passionately, but, as indeed I realized, hopelessly in love. In fact the very thing that Lady Montdore had intended for Polly had befallen me.

"There you are, Sonia," said Mrs. Chaddesley Corbett triumphantly, tapping a cigarette with nervous violence against her jewelled case and lighting it with a gold lighter, her pale blue eyes never meanwhile leaving my face. "What did I tell you? Of course she is, poor sweet, just look at that blush, it must be something quite new and horribly bogus. I know, it's my dear old husband. Confess, now! I couldn't mind less, actually."

I did not like to say that I still, after a whole weekend, had no idea at all which of the many husbands present hers might be, but stammered out as quick as I could, "Oh, no, no, not anybody's husband, I promise." Only a fiancé, and such a detached one at that.

They both laughed.

"All right," said Mrs. Chaddesley Corbett, "we're not going to worm. What we really want to know, to settle a bet, is, have you always fancied somebody ever since you can remember? Answer truthfully, please."

I was obliged to admit that this was the case. From a tiny child, ever since I could remember, in fact, some delicious image had been enshrined in my heart, last thought at night, first thought in the morning. Fred Terry as Sir Percy Blakeney, Lord Byron, Rudolph Valentino, Henry V, Gerald du Maurier, blissful Mrs. Ashton at my school, Steerforth, Napoleon, the guard on the 4.45, image had succeeded image. Latterly it had been that of a pale, pompous young man in the Foreign Office who had once, during my season in London, asked me for a dance, had seemed to me the very flower of cosmopolitan civilization, and had remained the pivot of existence until wiped from my memory by Sauveterre. For that is what always happened to these images. Time and hateful absence blurred them, faded them but never quite obliterated them until some lovely new broom image came and swept them away.

"There you are, you see," Mrs. Chaddesley Corbett turned triumphantly to Lady Montdore. "From kiddie car to hearse, darling, I couldn't know it better. After all, what would there be to think about when one's alone, otherwise?"

What, indeed? This Veronica had hit the nail on the head. Lady Montdore did not look convinced. She, I felt sure, had never harboured romantic yearnings and had plenty to think about when she was alone, which, anyhow, was hardly ever.

"But who is there for her to be in love with, and, if she is, surely I should know it," she said.

I guessed that they were talking about Polly and this was confirmed by Mrs. Chaddesley Corbett saying, "No, darling, you wouldn't, you're her mother. When I remember poor Mummy and her ideas on the subject of my ginks . . ."

"Now, Fanny, tell us what you think. Is Polly in love?"

"Well, she says she's not, but . . ."

"But you don't think it's possible not to be fancying someone? Nor do I."

I wondered. Polly and I had had a long chat the night before, sprawling on my bed in our dressing gowns, and I had felt almost certain then that she was keeping something back which she would half have liked to tell me.

"I suppose it might depend on your nature?" I said, doubtfully.

"Anyhow," said Lady Montdore, "there's one thing only too certain. She takes no notice of the young men I provide for her and they take no notice of her. They worship me, of course, but what is the good of that?"

Mrs. Chaddesley Corbett caught my eye, and I thought she gave me half a wink. I liked her more every minute. Lady Montdore went on:

"Bored and boring. I can't say I'm looking forward to bringing her out in London very much if she goes on like this. She used to be such a sweet easy child, but her whole character seems to have changed, now she is grown-up. I can't understand it."

"Oh, she's bound to fall for some nice chap in London, darling," said Mrs. Chaddesley Corbett. "I wouldn't worry too much, if I were you. Whoever she's in love with now, if she is in love, which Fanny and I know she must be, is probably a kind of dream and she only needs to see some flesh and blood people for her to forget about it. It so often happens, with girls."

"Yes, my dear, that's all very well, but she was out for two years in India, you know. There were some very attractive men there, polo, and so on; not suitable, of course. I was only too thankful she didn't fall in love with any of them, but she could have, it would not have been unnatural at all. Why, poor Delia's girl fell in love with a Rajah, you know."

"I couldn't blame her less," said Mrs. Chaddesley Corbett. "Rajahs must be perfect heaven—all those diamonds."

"Oh, no, my dear—any Englishwoman has better stones than they do. I never saw anything to compare with mine when I was there. But this Rajah was rather attractive, I must say, though of course Polly didn't see it; she never does. Oh, dear, oh, dear! Now, if only we were a French family, they seem to arrange things so very much better. To begin with, Polly would inherit all this, instead of those stupid people in Nova Scotia—so unsuitable—can you imagine Colonials living here?—and, to go on with, we should find a husband for her ourselves, after which he and she would live partly at his place with his parents and partly here with us. Think how sensible that is. The old French tart was telling me the whole system last night."

Lady Montdore was famous for picking up words she did not quite understand and giving them a meaning of her own. She clearly took the word tart to mean old girl, trout, body. Mrs. Chaddesley Corbett was delighted. She gave a happy little squeak and rushed upstairs, saying that she must go and dress for dinner. When

I came up ten minutes later she was still telling the news through bathroom doors.

AFTER THIS, LADY Montdore set out to win my heart, and, of course, succeeded. It was not very difficult. I was young and frightened, she was old and grand and frightening, and it only required a very little charm, an occasional hint of mutual understanding, a smile, a movement of sympathy to make me think I really loved her. The fact is that she had charm, and since charm allied to riches and position is almost irresistible, it so happened that her many haters were usually people who had never met her, or people she had purposely snubbed or ignored. Those whom she made efforts to please, while forced to admit that she was indefensible, were very much inclined to say ". . . but all the same she has been very nice to me and I can't help liking her." She herself, of course, never doubted for one moment that she was worshipped, and by every section of society.

Before I left Hampton on Monday morning Polly took me up to her mother's bedroom to say good-bye. Some of the guests had left the night before, the others were leaving now, all rolling away in their huge rich motor cars, and the house was like a big school breaking up for the holidays. The bedroom doors we passed were open, revealing litters of tissue paper and unmade beds, servants struggling with suitcases and guests struggling into their coats. Everybody seemed to be in a struggling hurry all of a sudden.

Lady Montdore's room—I remembered it of old—was enormous, more like a ballroom than a bedroom, and was done up in the taste of her own young days when she was a bride. The walls were panelled in pink silk covered with white lace, the huge wicker-work bed on a dais had curtains of pink shot silk, there was a lot of white furniture with fat pink satin upholstery outlined in ribbon roses. Silver flower vases stood on all the tables, and photographs in silver frames, mostly of royal personages, with inscriptions cordial in inverse ratio to the actual importance of the personage, reigning monarchs having contented themselves with merely a

Christian name, an R, and perhaps a date, while ex-kings and queens, archduchesses and grand dukes had scattered Dearest and Darling Sonia and Loving all over their trains and uniform trousers.

In the middle of all this silver and satin and silk, Lady Montdore cut rather a comic figure drinking strong tea in bed among masses of lace pillows, her coarse grey hair frizzed out, and wearing what appeared to be a man's striped flannel pyjama top under a feathered wrap. The striped pyjamas were not the only incongruous touch in the room. On her lacy dressing table with its big, solid silver looking-glass and among her silver and enamel brushes, bottles and boxes with their diamond cypher, were a black Mason Pearson hair brush and a pot of Pond's cold cream, while dumped down in the middle of the royalties were a rusty nail file, a broken comb and a bit of cotton wool. While we were talking, Lady Montdore's maid came in and with much clicking of her tongue was about to remove all these objects when Lady Montdore told her to leave them, as she had not finished.

Her quilt was covered with newspapers and opened letters and she held the *Times* neatly folded back at the Court Circular, probably the only part of it she ever looked at, since news, she used to say, can always be gleaned, and far more accurately too, from those who make it. I think she felt it comfortable, rather like reading prayers, to begin the day with their Majesties having attended Divine Service at Sandringham and Mabell Countess of Airlie having succeeded the Lady Elizabeth Motion as Lady in Waiting to the Queen. It indicated that the globe was still revolving in accordance with the laws of nature.

"Good morning, Fanny dear," she said. "This will interest you, I suppose."

She handed me the *Times* and I saw that Linda's engagement to Anthony Kroesig was announced at last.

"Poor Alconleighs," she went on, in tones of deep satisfaction. "No wonder they don't like it! What a silly girl! Well, she always has been, in my opinion. No place. Rich, of course, but banker's money; it comes and it goes and however much of it there may be it's not like marrying all this."

"All this" was a favourite expression of Lady Montdore's. It did not mean all this beauty, this strange and fairy-like house set in the middle of four great avenues rushing up four artificial slopes, the ordered spaces of trees and grass and sky seen from its windows, or the aesthetic joy given by the treasures it contained, for she was not gifted with the sense of beauty and if she admired anything at all it was rather what might be described as stockbroker's picturesque. She had made herself a little garden round a Cotswold well-head, rustic, with heather and rambler roses, and to this she would often retire in order to sketch the sunset. "So beautiful it makes me want to cry." She had all the sentimentality of her generation, and this sentimentality, growing like a green moss over her spirit, helped to conceal its texture of stone, if not from others, at any rate from herself. She was convinced that she was a woman of profound sensibility.

"All this," on her lips, meant position allied to such solid assets as acres, coal mines, real estate, jewels, silver, pictures, incunables, and other possessions of the sort. Lord Montdore owned an almost incredible number of such things, fortunately.

"Not that I ever expected poor little Linda to make a suitable marriage," she went on. "Sadie is a wonderful woman, of course, and I'm devoted to her, but I'm afraid she hasn't the very smallest idea how to bring up girls."

Nevertheless, no sooner did Aunt Sadie's girls show their noses outside the schoolroom than they were snapped up and married, albeit unsuitably, and perhaps this fact was rankling a little with Lady Montdore whose mind appeared to be so much on the subject.

The relations between Hampton and Alconleigh were as follows: Lady Montdore had an irritated fondness for Aunt Sadie, whom she half admired for an integrity which she could not but recognize and half blamed for an unworldliness which she considered out of place in somebody of her position; she could not endure Uncle Matthew and thought him mad. Uncle Matthew, for his part, revered Lord Montdore who was perhaps the only person in the world whom he looked up to, and loathed Lady Montdore to such a degree that he used to say he longed to strangle her. Now that Lord Montdore was back from India, Uncle Matthew continually saw him at the House of Lords, and on the various county organizations which they both attended, and he would come home and quote his most banal remark as if it were the utterance of a prophet. "Montdore tells me . . . Montdore says . . ." And that was that— useless to question it; what Lord Montdore believed on any subject was final in the eyes of my uncle.

"Wonderful fella, Montdore. What I can't imagine is how we ever got on without him in this country all those years. Terribly wasted among the blackamoors when he's the kind of fella we need so badly, here."

He even broke his rule about never visiting other people's houses in favour of Hampton. "If Montdore asks us I think we ought to go."

"It's Sonia who asks us," Aunt Sadie would correct him, mischievously.

'The old she-wolf. I shall never know what can have come over Montdore to make him marry her. I suppose he didn't realize at the time how utterly poisonously bloody she is."

"Darling—darling . . . !"

"Utterly bloody. But if Montdore asks us I think we should go."

As for Aunt Sadie, she was always so vague, so much in the clouds, that it was never easy to know what she really thought of people, but I believe that though she rather enjoyed the company of Lady Montdore in small doses, she did not share my uncle's feelings about Lord Montdore, for when she spoke of him there was always a note of disparagement in her voice.

"Something silly about his look," she used to say, though never in front of Uncle Matthew, for it would have hurt his feelings dreadfully.

"So that's Louisa and poor Linda accounted for," Lady Montdore went on. "Now you must be the next one, Fanny."

"Oh, no," I said. "Nobody will ever marry me." And indeed I

could not imagine anybody wanting to. I seemed to myself so much less fascinating than the other girls I knew, and I despised my looks, hating my round pink cheeks and rough curly black hair which never could be made to frame my face in silken cords, however much I wetted and brushed it, but would insist on growing the wrong way, upwards, like heather.

"Nonsense. And don't you go marrying just anybody, for love," she said. "Remember that love cannot last; it never, never does; but if you marry all this it's for your life. One day, don't forget, you'll be middle-aged and think what that must be like for a woman who can't have, say, a pair of diamond earrings. A woman of my age needs diamonds near her face, to give a sparkle. Then at meal times, sitting with all the unimportant people for ever and ever. And no car. Not a very nice prospect, you know. Of course," she added as an afterthought, "I was lucky, I had love as well as all this. But it doesn't often happen and when the moment comes for you to choose, just remember what I say. I suppose Fanny ought to go now and catch her train—and when you've seen her off, will you find Boy, please, and send him up here to me, Polly? I want to think over the dinner party for next week with him. Goodbye then, Fanny—let's see a lot of you now we're back."

On the way downstairs we ran into Boy.

"Mummy wants to see you," Polly said, gravely posing her blue look upon him. He put his hand to her shoulder and massaged it with his thumb.

"Yes," he said, "about this dinner party, I suppose. Are you coming to it, old girl?"

"Oh, I expect so," she said. "I'm out now, you see."

"Can't say I'm looking forward to it very much. Your mother's ideas on *placement* get vaguer and vaguer. Really, the table last night, the *duchesse is* still in a temper about it! Sonia really shouldn't have people at all if she can't treat them properly."

A phrase I had often heard on the lips of my Aunt Emily, with reference to animals.

Chapter 7

Back at home I was naturally unable to talk of anything but my visit. Davey was much amused and said he had never known me so chatty.

"But my dear child," he said, "weren't you petrified? Sauveterre and the Chaddesley Corbetts . . . ! Even worse than I had expected."

"Well, yes, at first I thought I'd die. But nobody took any notice of me, really, except Mrs. Chaddesley Corbett and Lady Montdore. . . ."

"Oh! And what notice did they take, may I ask?"

"Well, Mrs. Chaddesley Corbett said Mummy bolted first of all with Mr. Chaddesley Corbett."

"So she did," said Davey. "That boring old Chad, I'd quite forgotten. You don't mean to say Veronica told you so? I wouldn't have thought it possible, even of her."

"No, she said it to somebody else—eggy-peggy."

"I see. Well, then what about Sonia?"

"Oh, she was sweet to me."

"She was, was she? This is indeed sinister news."

"What is sinister news?" said Aunt Emily, coming in with her dogs. "It's simply glorious out, I can't imagine why you two are stuffing in here on this heavenly day."

"We're gossiping about the party you so unwisely allowed Fanny to go to. And I was saying that if Sonia has really taken a fancy to our little one, which it seems she has, we must look out for trouble, that's all."

"What trouble?" I said.

"Sonia's terribly fond of juggling with people's lives. I never shall forget when she made me go to her doctor. . . . I can only say he very nearly killed me. It's not her fault if I'm here today. She's entirely unscrupulous. She gets a hold over people much too easily, with her charm and her prestige, and then forces her own values on them."

"Not on Fanny," Aunt Emily said, with confidence. "Look at that chin."

"You always say look at Fanny's chin, but I never can see any other signs of her being strong-minded. Any of the Radletts can make her do whatever they like."

"You'll see," said Aunt Emily. "Siegfried is quite all right again, by the way. He's had a lovely walkie."

"Oh, good," said Davey. "Olive oil's the thing."

They both looked affectionately at the Pekingese, Siegfried.

But I wanted to get some more interesting gossip out of Davey about the Hamptons. I said coaxingly, "Go on, Davey, do go on telling about Lady Montdore. What was she like when she was young?"

"Exactly the same as she is now."

I sighed. "No, but I mean what did she look like?"

"I tell you, just the same," said Davey. "I've known her ever since I was a little tiny boy and she hasn't changed one scrap."

"Oh, Davey . . ." I began. But I left it at that. It's no good, I thought, you always come up against this blank wall with old people, they always say about each other that they have never looked any different, and how can it be true? Anyway, if it is true they must have been a horrid generation, all withered or blowsy, and grey at the age of eighteen, knobbly hands, bags under the chin, eyes set in a little map of wrinkles, I thought crossly, adding up all these things on the faces of Davey and Aunt Emily as they sat there, smugly thinking that they had always looked exactly the same. Quite useless to discuss questions of age with old people, they have such peculiar ideas on the subject. "Not really old at all, only seventy," you hear them saying, or "Quite young, younger than me, not much more than forty." At eighteen this seems great nonsense, though now, at the more advanced age which I have reached, I am beginning to understand what it all meant, because Davey and Aunt Emily, in their turn, seem to me to look as they have looked ever since I knew them first, when I was a little child, between twenty and thirty years ago.

"Who else was there?" asked Davey, "the Dougdales?"

"Oh, yes. Isn't the Lecturer stchoopid?"

Davey laughed. "And lecherous?" he said.

"No, I must say not actually lecherous, not with me."

"Well, of course he couldn't be with Sonia there, he wouldn't dare. He's been her young man for years, you know."

"Don't tell me!" I said, fascinated. That was the heaven of Davey, he knew everything about everybody, quite unlike my aunts, who, though they had no special objection to our knowing gossip, now that we were grown-up, had always forgotten it themselves, being totally uninterested in the doings of people outside their own family. "Davey—how could she?"

"Well, Boy is very good-looking," said Davey. "I should say, rather, how could he? But, as a matter of fact, I think it's a love-affair of pure convenience, it suits them both perfectly. Boy knows the Gotha by heart, and all that kind of thing. He's like a wonderful extra butler, and Sonia, on her side, gives him an interest in life. I quite see it."

One comfort, I thought, such elderly folk couldn't do anything, but again I kept it to myself because I knew that nothing makes people crosser than being considered too old for love, and Davey and the Lecturer were exactly the same age; they had been at Eton together. Lady Montdore, of course, was even older.

"Let's hear about Polly," said Aunt Emily, "and then I really must insist on you going out of doors before tea. Is she a real beauty, just as we were always being told by Sonia that she would be?"

"Of course she is," said Davey, "doesn't Sonia always get her own way?"

"So beautiful, you can't imagine," I said. "And so nice, the nicest person I ever met."

"Fanny is such a hero-worshipper," said Aunt Emily, amused.

"I expect it's true though, anyway about the beauty," said Davey. "Because, quite apart from Sonia always getting what she wants, Hamptons do have such marvellous looks, and, after all, the old girl herself is very handsome. In fact, I see that she would improve the strain by giving a little solidity—Montdore looks too much like a collie dog."

"And who is this wonderful girl to marry?" said Aunt Emily. "That will be the next problem for Sonia. I can't see who will ever be good enough for her?"

"Merely a question of strawberry leaves," said Davey, "as I imagine she's probably too big for the Prince of Wales, he likes such tiny little women. You know, I can't help thinking that now Montdore is getting older he must feel it dreadfully that he can't leave Hampton to her. I had a long talk about it the other day with Boy in the London Library. Of course, Polly will be very rich—enormously rich, because he can leave her everything else—but they all love Hampton so much, I think it's very sad for them."

"Can he leave Polly the pictures at Montdore House? Surely they must be entailed on the heir?" said Aunt Emily.

"There are wonderful pictures at Hampton," I butted in. "A Raphael and a Caravaggio in my bedroom alone." They both laughed at me, hurting my feelings, rather.

"Oh, my darling child, country-house bedroom pictures! But the ones in London are a world-famous collection, and I believe they can all go to Polly. The young man from Nova Scotia simply gets Hampton and everything in it, but that is an Aladdin's Cave, you know, the furniture, the silver, the library—treasures beyond value. Boy was saying they really ought to get him over and show him something of civilization before he becomes too transatlantic."

"I forget how old he is," said Aunt Emily.

"I know," I said. "He's six years older than I, about twenty-four now. And he's called Cedric, like Lord Fauntleroy. Linda and I used to look him up when we were little to see if he would do for us."

"You would. How typical," said Aunt Emily. "But I should have thought he might really do for Polly—settle everything."

"It would be too much unlike life," said Davey. "Oh, bother, talking to Fanny has made me forget my three o'clock pill."

"Take it now," said Aunt Emily, "and then go out, please, both of you."

FROM THIS TIME on I saw a great deal of Polly. I went to Alconleigh, as I did every year, for some hunting, and from there I often went over to spend a night or two at Hampton. There were no more big house parties but a continual flow of people and, in fact, the Montdores and Polly never seemed to have a meal by themselves. Boy Dougdale came over nearly every day from his own house at Silkin which was only about ten miles away. He quite often went home to dress for dinner and came back again to spend the evening, since Lady Patricia, it seemed, was not at all well, and liked to go to bed early. Boy never seemed to me quite like a real human being, and I think the reason for this was that he was always acting some part. Boy, the Don Juan, alternated with Boy, the Squire of Silkin and Boy, the Cultivated Cosmopolitan. In none of these parts was he quite convincing. Don Juan only made headway with very unsophisticated women, except in the case of Lady Montdore, and she, whatever their relationship may have been in the past, was treating him by now more as a private secretary than as a lover. The squire played cricket with the village youths and lectured the village women, but never seemed like a real squire for all his efforts, and the cultivated cosmopolitan gave himself away every time he put brush to canvas or pen to paper.

When he was with Lady Montdore they occupied much of their time painting, water-colour sketches out of doors in the summer and large set pieces in oils, using a north bedroom as a studio in the winter. They covered acres of canvas and were such great admirers of their own and each other's work that the opinion of the outside world meant but little to them. Their pictures were always framed and hung about their two houses, the best ones in rooms and the others in passages.

By the evening Lady Montdore was ready for some relaxation. "I like to work hard all day," she would say, "and then have agreeable company and perhaps a game of cards in the evening."

There were always guests for dinner, an Oxford don or two, with whom Lord Montdore could show off about Livy, Plotinus and the Claudian family, Lord Merlin, who was a great favourite of Lady Montdore and who published her sayings far and wide, and the more important county neighbours strictly in turns. They seldom sat down fewer than ten people. It was very different from Alconleigh.

I enjoyed these visits to Hampton. Lady Montdore terrified me less and charmed me more, Lord Montdore remained perfectly agreeable and colourless, Boy continued to give me the creeps and Polly became my best-friend-next-to-Linda.

Presently Aunt Sadie suggested that I might like to bring Polly back with me to Alconleigh, which I duly did. It was not a very good time for a visit there since everybody's nerves were upset by Linda's engagement, but Polly did not seem to notice the atmosphere and no doubt her presence restrained Uncle Matthew from giving vent to the full violence of his feelings while she was there. Indeed, she said to me as we drove back to Hampton together after the visit that she envied the Radlett children their upbringing in such a quiet, affectionate household, a remark which could only have been made by somebody who had inhabited the best spare room, out of range of Uncle Matthew's early morning gramophone concerts, and who had never happened to see that violent man in one of his tempers. Even so, I thought it strange, coming from Polly, because if anybody had been surrounded by affection all her life it was she; I did not yet fully understand how difficult the relations were beginning to be between her and her mother.

Chapter 8

P OLLY AND I were bridesmaids at Linda's wedding in February, and when it was over I motored down to Hampton with Polly and Lady Montdore to spend a few days there. I was grateful to Polly for suggesting this, as I remembered too well the horrible feeling of anti-climax there had been after Louisa's wedding, which would certainly be ten times multiplied after Linda's. Indeed, with Linda married, the first stage of my life no less than of hers was finished and I felt myself to be left in a horrid vacuum, with childhood over but married life not yet beginning.

As soon as Linda and Anthony had gone away, Lady Montdore sent for her car and we all three huddled onto the back seat. Polly and I were still in our bridesmaid's dresses (sweet pea tints, in chiffon) but well wrapped up in fur coats and each with a Shetland rug wound round our legs, like children going to a dancing class. The chauffeur spread a great bearskin over all of us and put a foot warmer under our silver kid shoes. It was not really cold, but shivery, pouring and pouring with rain as it had been all day, getting dark now. The inside of the motor car was like a dry little box, and as we splashed down the long wet shiny roads, with the rain beating against the windows, there was a specially delicious cosiness about being in this little box and knowing that so much light and warmth and solid comfort lay ahead.

"I love being so dry in here," as Lady Montdore put it, "and seeing all those poor people so wet."

She had done the journey twice that day, having driven up from Hampton in the morning, whereas Polly had gone up the day before with her father for a last fitting of her bridesmaid's dress and in order to go to a dinner-dance.

First of all we talked about the wedding. Lady Montdore was wonderful when it came to picking over an occasion of that sort. With her gimlet eye nothing escaped her, nor did any charitable inhibitions tone down her comments on what she had observed.

"How extraordinary Lady Kroesig looked, poor woman! I suppose somebody must have told her that the bridegroom's mother should have a bit of everything in her hat—for luck, perhaps. Fur, feathers, flowers and a scrap of lace—it was all there and a diamond brooch on top to finish it off nicely. Rose diamonds—I had a good look. It's a funny thing that these people who are supposed to be so rich never seem to have a decent jewel to put on. I've often noticed it. And did you see what mangy little things they gave poor Linda? A cheque—yes, that's all very well, but for how much, I wonder. Cultured pearls, at least I imagine so, or they would have been worth quite £10,000, and a hideous little bracelet. No tiara, no necklace—what will the poor child wear at Court? Linen, which we didn't see, all that modern silver and a horrible house in one of those squares by the Marble Arch. Hardly worth being called by that nasty German name, I should say. And Davey tells me there's no proper settlement. Really, Matthew Alconleigh isn't fit to have children if that's all he can do for them. Still, I'm bound to say he looked very handsome coming up the aisle, and Linda looked her very best too, really lovely."

I think she was feeling quite affectionately towards Linda for having removed herself betimes from competition, for, although not a great beauty like Polly, she was certainly far more popular with young men.

"Sadie, too, looked so nice, very young and handsome, and the little things so puddy." She pronounced the word pretty like that.

"Did you see our desert service, Fanny? Oh, did she? I'm glad. She could change it, as it came from Goods, but perhaps she won't want to. I was quite amused, weren't you, to see the difference between our side of the church and the Kroesig side. Bankers don't seem to be much to look at—so extraordinarily unsuitable having to know them at all, poor things, let alone marry them. But those sort of people have got megalomania nowadays, one can't get away from them. Did you notice the Kroesig sister? Oh, yes, of course, she was walking with you, Fanny. They'll have a job to get her off!"

"She's training to be a vet," I said.

"First sensible thing I've heard about any of them. No point in cluttering up the ballrooms with girls who look like that; it's simply not fair on anybody. Now, Polly, I want to hear exactly what you did, yesterday."

"Oh, nothing very much."

"Don't be so tiresome. You got to London at about twelve, I suppose?"

"Yes, we did," said Polly in a resigned voice. She would have to account for every minute of the day, she knew. Quicker to tell of her own accord than to have it pumped out of her. She began to fidget with her bridesmaid's wreath of silver leaves. "Wait a moment," she said. "I must take this off, it's giving me a headache."

It was twisted into her hair with wire. She tugged and pulled at it until finally she got it off and flung it down on the floor.

"Ow," she said, "that did hurt. Well, yes, then, let me think. We arrived, Daddy went straight to his appointment and I had an early luncheon at home."

"By yourself?"

"No, Boy was there. He'd looked in to return some books, and Bullitt said there was plenty of food so I made him stay."

"Well then, go on. After luncheon?"

"Hair."

"Washed and set?"

"Yes, naturally."

"You'd never think it. We really must find you a better hairdresser. No use asking Fanny, I'm afraid, her hair always looks like a mop."

Lady Montdore was becoming cross and like a cross child was seeking to hurt anybody within reach.

"It was quite all right until I had to put that wreath on it. Well then, tea with Daddy at the House, rest after tea, dinner you know about, and bed," she finished in one breath. "Is that all?"

She and her mother seemed to be thoroughly on each other's nerves, or perhaps it was having pulled her hair with the wreath that made her so snappy. She flashed a perfectly vicious look across me at Lady Montdore. It was suddenly illuminated by the head-lights of a passing motor. Lady Montdore neither saw it nor, apparently, noticed the edge in her voice and went on, "No, certainly not. You haven't told me about the party yet. Who sat next you at dinner?"

"Oh, Mummy, I can't remember their names."

"You never seem to remember anybody's name. It is too stupid. How can I invite your friends to the house if I don't know who they are?"

"But they're not my friends. They were the most dreadful, dreadful bores you can possibly imagine. I couldn't think of one thing to say to them."

Lady Montdore sighed deeply. "Then after dinner you danced?"

"Yes. Danced, and sat out and ate disgusting ices."

"I'm sure the ices were delicious. Sylvia Waterman always does things beautifully. I suppose there was champagne?"

"I hate champagne."

"And who took you home?"

"Lady Somebody. It was out of her way because she lives in Chelsea."

"How extraordinary," said Lady Montdore, rather cheered up by the idea that some poor ladies have to live in Chelsea. "Now who could she possibly have been?"

The Dougdales had also been at the wedding and were to dine at Hampton on their way home; they were there when we arrived, not having, like us, waited to see Linda go away. Polly went straight upstairs. She looked tired and sent a message by her maid to say that she would have her dinner in bed. The Dougdales, Lady Montdore and I dined, without changing, in the little morning room where they always had meals if there were fewer than eight people. This room was perhaps the most perfect thing at Hampton. It had been brought bodily from France and was entirely panelled in wood carved in a fine and elaborate pattern, painted blue and white; three china cupboards matched three French windows and contained a Sèvres dinner service made for Marie Antoinette; over cupboards, windows and doorways were decorative paintings by Boucher, framed in the panelling.

The talk, at dinner, was of the ball which Lady Montdore intended to give for Polly at Montdore House during the London season.

"May Day, I think," she said.

"That's good," said Boy. "It must either be the first or the last ball of the summer, if people are to remember it."

"Oh, not the last, on any account. I should have to invite all the girls whose dances Polly had been to, and nothing is so fatal to a ball as too many girls."

"But if you don't ask them," said Lady Patricia, "will they ask her?"

"Oh, yes," said Lady Montdore shortly. "They'll be dying to have her. I can pay them back in other ways. But, anyhow, I don't propose to take her about in the debutante world very much (all those awful parties, S.W. something). I don't see the point of it. She would become quite worn out and meet a lot of thoroughly unsuitable young men. I'm planning to let her go to not more than two dances a week, carefully chosen. Quite enough for a girl who's not very strong. I thought later on, if you'll help me, Boy, we could make a list of women to give dinners for my ball. Of course it must be perfectly understood that they are to ask the people I tell them to. Can't have them paying off their own friends and relations on me."

After dinner we sat in the Long Gallery. Boy settled down to his petit point while we three women sat with idle hands. He had a talent for needlework, had hemstitched some of the sheets for the Queen's doll's house and had covered many chairs at Silkin and at Hampton.

He was now engaged upon a fire screen for the Long Gallery, which he had designed himself in a sprawling Jacobean pattern. The theme of it was supposed to be flowers from Lady Montdore's garden, but the flowers looked more like horrid huge insects. Being young and deeply prejudiced, it never occurred to me to admire this work. I merely thought how too dreadful it was to see a man sewing and how hideous he looked, his grizzled head bent over the canvas into which he was deftly stitching various shades of khaki. He had the same sort of thick hair as mine and I knew that the waves in it, the little careless curls (boyish) must have been carefully wetted and pinched in before dinner.

Lady Montdore had sent for paper and a pencil in order to write down the names of dinner hostesses. "We'll put down all the possible ones and then weed," she said. But she soon gave up this occupation in order to complain about Polly, and though I had already heard her on the subject when she had been talking with Mrs. Chaddesley Corbett, the tone of her voice was now much sharper and more aggrieved.

"One does everything for these girls," she said. "Everything. You wouldn't believe it, perhaps, but I assure you I spend quite half my day making plans for Polly—appointments, clothes, parties, and so on. I haven't a minute to see my own friends, I've hardly had a game of cards for months, I've quite given up my painting—in the middle of that nude girl from Oxford, too—in fact, I devote myself entirely to the child. I keep the London house going simply for her convenience. I hate London in the winter as you know and Montdore would be quite happy in two rooms without a cook (all that cold food at the club), but I've got a huge staff there eating their heads off entirely on her account. You'd think she'd be grateful at least, wouldn't you? Not at all. Sulky and disagreeable, I can hardly get a word out of her."

The Dougdales said nothing. He was sorting out wools with great concentration, and Lady Patricia lay back, her eyes closed, suffering as she had suffered for so long, in silence. She was looking more than ever like some garden statue, her skin and her beige London dress exactly the same colour, while her poor face was lined with pain and sadness, the very expression of antique tragedy.

Lady Montdore went on with her piece, talking exactly as if I were not there.

"I take endless trouble so that she can go and stay in nice houses, but she never seems to enjoy herself a bit, she comes home full of complaints and the only ones she ever wants to go back to are Alconleigh and Emily Warbeck. Both pure waste of time! Alconleigh is a madhouse. . . . Of course, I love Sadie, everybody does, I think she's wonderful, poor dear, and it's not her fault if she has all those eccentric children. . . . She must have done what she can, but they are their father over again and no more need be said. Then I like the child to be with Fanny, and one has known Emily and Davey all one's life—Emily was our bridesmaid and Davey was an elf in the very first pageant I ever organized—but the fact remains Polly never meets anybody there and if she never meets people how can she marry them?"

"Is there so much hurry for her to marry?" said Lady Patricia.

"Well, you know she'll be twenty in May. She can't go on like this for ever. If she doesn't marry what will she do, with no interests in life, no occupation? She doesn't care for sketching or riding or society, she hardly has a friend in the world. . . . Oh, can you tell me how Montdore and I came to have a child like that? When I think of myself at her age! I remember so well Mr. Asquith saying he had never met anybody with such a genius for improvisation. . . ."

"Yes, you were wonderful," said Lady Patricia with a little smile. "But, after all, she may be slower at developing than you were and, as you say, she's not twenty yet. Surely it's rather nice to have her at home for another year or two?"

"The fact is," replied her sister-in-law, "girls are not nice. It's a perfectly horrid age. When they are children, so sweet and pretty, you think how delightful it will be to have their company later on, but what company is Polly to Montdore or to me? She moons about, always half-cross and half-tired and takes no interest in any mortal thing, and what she needs is a husband. Once she is married we shall be on excellent terms again. I've so often seen it happen. I was talking to Sadie the other day, and she agreed. She says she has had a most difficult time lately with Linda. Louisa, of course, was never any trouble. She had a nicer character and then she married straight out of the schoolroom. One thing you can say about the Radletts, no delay in marrying them off, though they might not be the sort of marriages one would like for one's own child. A banker and a dilapidated Scotch peer . . . Still, there it is— they are married. What can be the matter with Polly? So beautiful and no B.A. at all."

"S.A.," said Lady Patricia faintly, "or B.O."

"When we were young none of that existed, thank goodness. S.A. and B.O., perfect rubbish and bosh—one was a beauty or a *jolie-laide*, and that was that. All the same, now they have been invented I suppose it is better if the girls have them. Their partners seem to like it, and Polly hasn't a vestige, you can see that. But how differently," she said with a sigh, "how differently life turns out from what we expect! Ever since she was born, you know, I've worried and fussed over that child, and thought of the awful things that might happen to her—that Montdore might die before she was settled and we should have no proper home, that her looks would go (too beautiful at fourteen, I feared) or that she would have an accident and spend the rest of her days in a spinal chair—all sorts of things. I used to wake in the night and imagine them, but the one thing that never even crossed my mind was that she might end up an old maid."

There was a rising note of aggrieved hysteria in her voice.

"Come now, Sonia," said Lady Patricia rather sharply, "the poor girl is still in her teens. Do wait at least until she has had a London season before you call her an old maid. She'll find somebody she likes there soon enough, you can be quite sure."

"I only wish I could think it, but I have a strong feeling she won't, and that, what's more, they won't like her," said Lady Montdore. "She has no come-hither in her eye. Oh, it is really too bad. She leaves the light on in her bathroom night after night too, I see it shining out. . . ."

Lady Montdore was very mean about such small things as electric light.

Chapter 9

As her mother had predicted, summer came and went without any change in Polly's circumstances. The London season duly opened with a ball at Montdore House which cost £2000 or so Lady Montdore told everybody, and was certainly very brilliant. Polly wore a white-satin dress with pink roses at the bosom and a pink lining to the sash (touches of pink, as the *Tatler* said) chosen in Paris for her by Mrs. Chaddesley Corbett and brought over in the bag by some South American diplomat, a friend of Lady Montdore's, to save duty, a proceeding of which Lord Montdore knew nothing and which would have perfectly horrified him had he known. Enhanced by this dress, and by a little make-up, Polly's beauty was greatly remarked upon, especially by those of a former generation, who were all saying that since Lady Helen Vincent, since Lily Langtry, since the Wyndham sisters (according to taste), nothing so perfect had been seen in London. Her own contemporaries, however, were not so greatly excited by her. They admitted her beauty but said that she was dull, too large. What they really admired were the little skinny goggling copies of Mrs. Chaddesley Corbett which abounded that season. The many dislikers of Lady Montdore said that she kept Polly too much in the background, and this was not fair because, although it is true to say that Lady Montdore automatically filled the foreground of any picture in which she figured, she was only too anxious to push Polly in front of her, like a hostage, and it was not her fault if she was forever slipping back again.

On the occasion of this ball many of the royalties in Lady Montdore's bedroom had stepped from their silver frames and come to life, dustier and less glamorous, poor dears, when seen in all their dimensions; the huge reception rooms at Montdore House were scattered with them and the words Sir or Ma'am could be heard on every hand. The Ma'ams were really quite pathetic—you would almost say hungry-looking—so old, in such sad and crumpled clothes, while there were some blue-chinned Sirs of dreadfully foreign aspect. I particularly remember one of them because I was told that he was wanted by the police in France and not much wanted anywhere else, especially not, it seemed, in his native land where his cousin, the King, was daily expecting the crown to be blown off his head by a puff of east wind. This Prince smelt strongly, but not deliciously, of camellias and had a *fond de teint* of brilliant sunburn.

"I only ask him for the sake of dear old Princess Irene," Lady Montdore would explain, if people raised their eyebrows at seeing him in such a very respectable house. "I never shall forget what an angel she was to Montdore and me when we were touring the Balkans (one doesn't forget these things). I know people do say he's a daisy, whatever that may be, but if you listen to what everybody says about everybody, you'll end by never having anybody, and, besides, half these rumours are put about by anarchists, I'm positive."

Lady Montdore loved anybody royal. It was a genuine emotion, quite disinterested, since she loved them as much in exile as in power, and the act of curtseying was the consummation of this love. Her curtseys, owing to the solid quality of her frame, did not recall the graceful movement of wheat before the wind. She scrambled down like a camel, rising again backside foremost, like a cow, a strange performance, painful, it might be supposed, to the performer, the expression on whose face, however, belied this thought. Her knees cracked like revolver shots but her smile was heavenly.

I was the only unmarried woman to be asked to dine at Montdore House before the dance. There was a dinner party of forty people with a very grand Sir and Ma'am indeed, on account of whom everybody was punctual to the minute, so that all the guests arrived simultaneously and the large crowd in Park Lane was rewarded by good long stares into the queuing motor cars. Mine was the only cab.

Upstairs a long wait ensued, without cocktails, and even the most brassy people, even Mrs. Chaddesley Corbett, began to twitter with nerves, as though they were being subjected to an intolerable strain; they stood about piping stupidities in their fashionable voices. At last the butler came up to Lord Montdore and murmured something, upon which he and Lady Montdore went down into the hall to receive their guests, while the rest of us, directed by Boy, formed ourselves into a semi-circle. Very slowly Lady Montdore led this tremendous Sir and Ma'am round the semicircle, making presentations in the tone of voice, low, reverent but distinct which my aunts used for responses in church. Then, arm through exalted arm, the four of them moved off, still in slow motion, through the double doors into the dining room, leaving the rest of us to sort ourselves out and follow. It all went like clockwork.

Soon after dinner, which took a long time and was Hampton food at its climax, crest and top, people began to arrive for the ball. Lady Montdore in gold lamé, and many diamonds, including her famous pink-diamond tiara, Lord Montdore, genial, noble, his long thin legs in silk stockings and knee breeches, the Garter round one of them, its ribbon across his shirt front and a dozen miniatures dangling on his chest, and Polly, in her white dress and her beauty, stood shaking hands at the top of the stairs for quite an hour, and a very pretty sight it was to see the people streaming past them. Lady Montdore, true to her word, had invited very few girls and even fewer mammas. The guests were therefore neither too young nor too old to decorate but were all in their glittering prime.

Nobody asked me to dance. Just as no girls had been invited to the ball so also were there very few young men, except such as were firmly attached to the young married set, but I was quite happy looking on, and since there was not a soul I knew to see me no shame attached to my situation. All the same I was delighted when the Alconleighs, with Louisa and Linda and their husbands, Aunt Emily and Davey, who had all been dining together, appeared, as they always did at parties, nice and early. I became assimilated into their cheerful group and we took up a position, whence we could have a good view of the proceedings, in the picture gallery. This opened into the ballroom on one hand and the supper room on the other. There was a great deal of coming and going and at the same time never any crowd, so that we could see the dresses and jewels to their best advantage. Behind us hung a Correggio St. Sebastian with the habitual Buchmanite expression on his face.

"Awful tripe," said Uncle Matthew. "Fella wouldn't be grinning, he'd be dead with all those arrows in him."

On the opposite wall was the Montdore Botticelli which Uncle Matthew said he wouldn't give 7/6 for, and when Davey showed him a Leonardo drawing he said his fingers only itched for an india rubber.

"I saw a picture once," he said, "of shire horses in the snow. There was nothing else, just a bit of brokendown fence and three horses. It was dangerous good—Army and Navy Stores. If I'd been a rich man I'd have bought that—I mean you could see how cold those poor brutes must have felt. If all this rubbish is supposed to be valuable, that must be worth a fortune."

Uncle Matthew, who absolutely never went out in the evening, let alone to balls, would not hear of refusing an invitation to Montdore House, though Aunt Sadie, who knew how it tormented him to be kept awake after dinner, and how his poor eyes would turn back to front with sleepiness had said, "Really, darling, as we are between daughters, two married, and two not yet out, there's no occasion whatever for us to go, if you'd rather not. Sonia would understand perfectly—and be quite glad of our room, I daresay."

But Uncle Matthew had gloomily replied, "If Montdore asks us to his ball it is because he wants to see us there. I think we ought to go."

Accordingly, with many groans, he had squeezed himself into the knee breeches of his youth, now so perilously tight that he hardly dared sit down, but stood like a stork beside Aunt Sadie's chair, and Aunt Sadie had got all her diamonds out of the bank and lent some to Linda and some to Aunt Emily and even so had quite a nice lot left for herself, and here they were chatting away happily enough with their relations and with various county figures who came and went, and even Uncle Matthew seemed quite amused by it all until a dreadful fate befell him—he was made to take the German Ambassadress to supper. It happened like this. Lord Montdore, at Uncle Matthew's very elbow, suddenly exclaimed in horror, "Good heavens, the German Ambassadress is sitting there quite alone."

"Serve her right," said Uncle Matthew. It would have been more prudent to have held his tongue. Lord Montdore heard him speak, without taking in the meaning of his words, turned sharply round, saw who it was, seized him by the arm and said,

"My dear Matthew, just the very man—Baroness von Rumplemayer, may I present my neighbour, Lord Alconleigh? Supper is quite ready in the music room—you know the way, Matthew."

It was a measure of Lord Montdore's influence over Uncle Matthew that my uncle did not then and there turn tail and bolt for home. No other living person could have persuaded him to stay and shake hands with a Hun, let alone take it on his arm and feed it. He went off, throwing a mournful backward glance at his wife.

Lady Patricia now came and sat by Aunt Sadie, and they chatted, in rather a desultory way, about local affairs. Aunt Sadie, unlike her husband, really enjoyed going out so long as it was not too often, she did not have to stay up too late, and she was allowed to look on peacefully without feeling obliged to make any conversational effort. Strangers bored and fatigued her. She only liked the company of those people with whom she had day-to-day interests in common, such as country neighbours or members of her own family, and even with them she was generally rather absentminded. But on this occasion it was Lady Patricia who seemed half in the clouds, saying yes and no to Aunt Sadie, and what a monstrous thing it was to let the Skilton village idiot out again, specially now it was known what a fast runner he was, since he had won the asylum 100 yards.

"And he's always chasing people," Aunt Sadie said indignantly.

But Lady Patricia's mind was not on the idiot. She was thinking, I am sure, of parties in those very rooms when she was young, and how much she had worshipped the Lecturer, and what agony it had been when he had danced and flirted, she knew, with other people, and how perhaps it was almost sadder for her that now she could care about nothing any more but the condition of her liver.

I knew from Davey ("Oh, the luck," as Linda used to say, "that Dave is such an old gossip, poor simple us if it weren't for him!") that Lady Patricia had loved Boy for several years before he had finally proposed to her, and had indeed quite lost hope. And then how short-lived was her happiness, barely six months before she had found him in bed with a kitchen maid.

"Boy never went out for big stuff," I once heard Mrs. Chaddesley Corbett say. "He only liked bowling over the rabbits, and now, of course, he's a joke."

It must be hateful, being married to a joke.

Presently she said to Aunt Sadie, "When was the first ball you ever came to here?"

"It must have been the year I came out, in 1906. I well remember the excitement of actually seeing King Edward in the flesh and hearing his loud foreign laugh."

"Twenty-four years ago, fancy," said Lady Patricia. "Just before Boy and I were married. Do you remember how, in the war, people used to say we should never see this sort of thing again, and yet, look, only look at the jewels."

Presently, as Lady Montdore came into sight, she said,

"You know, Sonia really is phenomenal. I'm sure she's better looking and better dressed now than she has ever been in her life."

One of those middle-aged remarks I used to find incomprehensible. It did not seem to me that Lady Montdore could be described either as good-looking or as well-dressed; she was old and that was that. On the other hand, nobody could deny that on occasions of this sort she was impressive, almost literally covered with great big diamonds, tiara, necklace, earrings, a huge Maltese cross on her bosom, bracelets from wrist to elbow over her suede gloves and brooches wherever there was possible room for them. Dressed up in these tremendous jewels, surrounded by the exterior signs of "all this," her whole demeanor irradiated with the superiority she so deeply felt in herself, she appeared in her own house as a bull-fighter in his bull-ring, or an idol in its ark, the reason for and the very center of the spectacle.

Uncle Matthew, having made his escape from the Ambassadress with a deep bow, expressive of deep disgust, now came back to the family party.

"Old cannibal," he said. "She kept asking for more *Fleisch*. Can't have swallowed her dinner more than an hour ago—I pretended not to hear—wouldn't pander to the old ogress—after all who won the war? And what for, I should like to know? Wonderful public-spirited of Montdore to put up with all this foreign trash in his house—I'm blowed if I would. I ask you to look at that sewer!" He glared in the direction of a blue-chinned Sir who was heading for the supper room with Polly on his arm.

"Come now, Matthew," said Davey, "the Serbs were our allies, you know."

"Allies!" said Uncle Matthew, grinding his teeth. The word was as a red rag to a bull and naughty Davey knew this and was waving the rag for fun.

"So that's a Serb, is it? Well, just what one would expect. Needs a shave. Hogs, one and all. Of course Montdore only asks them for the sake of the country. I do admire that fella, he thinks of nothing but his duty—what an example to everybody!"

A gleam of amusement crossed Lady Patricia's sad face. She was not without a sense of humour and was one of the few people Uncle Matthew liked, though he could not bring himself to be polite to Boy and gazed furiously into space every time he passed our little colony, which he did quite often, squiring royal old ladies to the supper room. Of his many offences in the eyes of Uncle Matthew, the chief was that, having been A.D.C. to a general in the war, he was once discovered by my uncle sketching a château behind the lines. There must clearly be something wrong about a man who could waste his time sketching, or, indeed, undertake the duties of an A.D.C. at all when he might be slaughtering foreigners all day.

"Nothing but a blasted lady's maid," Uncle Matthew would say whenever Boy's name was mentioned. "I can't stick the sewer. Boy, indeed! Dougdale! What does it all mean? There used to be some perfectly respectable people called Blood at Silkin in the Old Lord's time. Major and Mrs. Blood."

The Old Lord was Lord Montdore's father. Jassy once said, opening enormous eyes, "He *must* have been old," upon which Aunt Sadie had remarked that people do not remain the same age all their lives, and he had no doubt been young in his time, just as one day, though she might not expect it, Jassy herself would become old.

It was not very logical of Uncle Matthew so exaggeratedly to despise Boy's military record, and was just another example of how those he liked could do no wrong and those he disliked no right, because Lord Montdore, his great hero, had never in his life heard the cheerful sound of musketry or been near a battle; he would have been rather elderly to have taken the field in the Great War, it is true, but his early years had vainly offered many a jolly fight, chances to hack away at native flesh, not to speak of Dutch flesh in that Boer war which had provided Uncle Matthew with such radiant memories, having given him his first experience of bivouac and battle.

"Four days in a bullock waggon," he used to tell us, "a hole as big as your fist in my stomach, and maggoty! Happiest time of my life. The only thing was, one got rather tired of the taste of mutton after a bit, no beef in that campaign, you know."

But Lord Montdore was a law unto himself and had even got away with the famous Montdore Letter to the *Morning Post* which suggested that the war had gone on long enough and might be brought to an end, several months before the cowardly capitulation of the Hun had made this boring adjournment necessary. Uncle Matthew found it difficult to condone such spoiling of sport but did so by saying that Lord Montdore must have had some good reason for writing it which nobody else knew anything about.

My thoughts were now concentrated upon the entrance to the ballroom door where I had suddenly perceived the back of somebody's head. So he had come, after all. The fact that I never thought he would (such a serious character) had in no way mitigated my disappointment that he had not; now, here he was. I must explain that the image of Sauveterre, having reigned in my hopeless heart for several months had recently been ousted and replaced by something more serious, with more reality and promise.

The back of a head, seen at a ball, can have a most agitating effect upon a young girl, so different from the backs of other heads that it might be surrounded by a halo. There is the question, will he turn round, will he see her, and, if so, will he merely give a polite good-evening or invite her to dance? Oh, how I wished I could have been whirling gaily round in the arms of some fascinator instead of sitting with my aunts and uncles, too obviously a wallflower. Not that it mattered. There were a few moments of horrible suspense before the head turned round, but when it did he saw me, came straight over, said good evening more than politely and danced me away. He thought he would never get here, it was a question of borrowed, but mislaid, knee breeches. Then he danced with Aunt Emily, again with me, and with Louisa, having engaged me to have supper after that.

"Who is that brute?" said Uncle Matthew, grinding his teeth as my young man went off with Louisa. "Why does he keep coming over here?"

"He's called Alfred Wincham," I said. "Shall I introduce him to you?"

"For pity's sake, Fanny!"

"What an old Pasha you are," said Davey. And, indeed, Uncle Matthew would clearly have preferred to keep all his female relations in a condition if not of virginity at any rate of exaggerated chastity and could never bear them to be approached by strange men.

When not dancing I went back and sat with my relations. I felt calmer now, having had two dances and the promise of supper and was quite happy to fill in the time by listening to my elders as they conversed.

Presently Aunt Sadie and Aunt Emily went off to have supper together. They always liked to do this at parties. Davey moved up to sit next Lady Patricia and Uncle Matthew stood by Davey's chair, sleeping on his feet as horses can, patiently waiting to be led back to his stable.

"It's this new man, Meyerstein," Davey was saying. "You simply must go to him Patricia. He does it all by salt elimination. You skip in order to sweat out all the salt in your organism and eat saltless meals, of course. Too disgusting. But it does break down the crystals."

"Do you mean skip with a skipping rope?"

"Yes, hundreds of times. You count. I can do three hundred at a go, as well as some fancy steps, now."

"But isn't it horribly tiring?"

"Nothing tires Davey—fella's as strong as a bull," said Uncle Matthew, opening one eye.

Davey cast a sad look at his brother-in-law and said that of course it was, desperately tiring, but well worth it for the results.

Polly was dancing now with her uncle, Boy. She did not look radiant and happy as such a spoilt darling should at her coming-out ball, but tired and pinched about the mouth, nor was she chattering away like the other women.

"I shouldn't care for one of my girls to look like that," Aunt Sadie said. "You'd think she had something on her mind."

And my new friend Mr. Wincham said, as we danced round before going to supper, "Of course she's a beauty. I quite see that she is, but she doesn't attract me, with that sulky expression. I'm sure she's very dull."

I began to deny that she was either sulky or dull when he said Fanny to me, the first time he ever had, and followed this up with a lot of things which I wanted to listen to very carefully so that I could think them over later on, when I was alone.

Mrs. Chaddesley Corbett shouted at me, from the arms of the Prince of Wales, "Hullo, my sweet! What news of the Bolter? Are you still in love?"

"What's all this?" said my partner. "Who is that woman? Who is the Bolter? And is it true that you are in love?"

"Mrs. Chaddesley Corbett," I said. I felt that the time was not yet ripe to begin explaining about the Bolter.

"And how about love?"

"Nothing," I said, rather pink. "Just a joke."

"Good. I should like you to be on the verge of love but not yet quite in it. That's a very nice state of mind, while it lasts."

But of course I had already dived over that verge and was swimming away in a blue sea of illusion towards, I supposed, the islands of the blest, but really towards domesticity, maternity and the usual lot of womankind.

A holy hush now fell upon the crowd as the Royals prepared to go home, the very grand Royals, serene in the knowledge that they would find the traditional cold roast chicken by their beds, not the pathetic Ma'ams and sinister Sirs who were stuffing away in the supper room as if they were far from sure they would ever see so much food again, nor the gay young Royals who were going to dance until morning with little neat women of the Chaddesley Corbett sort.

"How late they have stayed! What a triumph for Sonia!" I heard Boy saying to his wife.

The dancers divided like the Red Sea, forming a lane of bowing and curtsying subjects, down which Lord and Lady Montdore conducted their guests.

"Sweet of you to say so, Ma'am. Yes, at the next Court. Oh, how kind of you!"

The Montdores came back into the picture gallery, beaming happily and saying, to nobody in particular, "So simple, so easy, pleased with any little thing one can do for them, such wonderful manners, such a memory. Astounding how much they know about India, the Maharajah was amazed."

They spoke as though these Princes are so remote from life as we know it that the smallest sign of humanity, the mere fact even that they communicated by means of speech was worth noting and proclaiming.

The rest of the evening was spent by me in a happy trance, and I remember no more about the party, as such. I know that I was taken back to the Goring Hotel, where we were all staying, at five o'clock on a fine May morning by Mr. Wincham, who had clearly shown me, by then, that he was not at all averse to my company.

Chapter 10

So POLLY WAS now "out" in London society and played her part during the rest of the season, as she had at the ball, with a good enough grace, the performance only lacking vitality and temperament to make it perfect. She did all the things her mother arranged, went to the parties, wore the clothes and made the friends that Lady Montdore thought suitable for her, and never branched out on her own or gave any possible cause for complaint. She certainly did nothing to create an atmosphere of fun, but Lady Montdore was perhaps too much employed herself in that very direction to notice that Polly, though good and acquiescent, never for one moment entered into the spirit of the many entertainments they went to. Lady Montdore enjoyed it all prodigiously, appeared to be satisfied with Polly, and was delighted with the publicity that, as the most important and most beautiful debutante of the year, she was receiving. She was really too busy, in too much of a whirl of society while the season was going on to wonder whether Polly was being a success or not. When it was over, they went to Goodwood, Cowes, and Scotland, where, no doubt, among the mists and heather, she had time to take stock of the situation. They vanished from my life for many weeks.

By the time I saw them again, in the autumn, their relationship was back to what it had been before and they were clearly very much on each other's nerves. I was now living in London myself, Aunt Emily having taken a little house in St. Leonard's Terrace for the winter. It was a happy time in my life as presently I became engaged to Alfred Wincham, the same young man whose back view had so much disturbed me at the Montdore ball. During the weeks that preceded my engagement I saw a great deal of Polly.

She would telephone in the morning, "What are you up to, Fanny?"

"Aching," I would reply, meaning aching with boredom, a malaise from which girls, before national service came to relieve them, were apt to suffer considerably.

"Oh, good. So can I bend you to my will? You can't think how dull, but if you are aching anyway? Well, then, I've got to try on that blue velvet hat at Madame Rita, and go and fetch the gloves from Debenhams—they said they would have them to-day. Yes, but the worst is to come—I couldn't possibly bend you to have luncheon with my Aunt Edna at Hampton Court and afterwards to sit and chat while I have my hair done? No, forget I said anything so awful—anyway we'll see. I'll be round for you in half an hour."

I was quite pliable. I had nothing whatever to do and very much enjoyed bouncing round London in the big Daimler and watching Polly who, although such a simple character in many ways, was very conscious of being a beauty, as she went about the business which that demands. Although society, at present, had no charm for Polly, she was very much interested in her own appearance, and would never, I think, have given up bothering about it as Lady Patricia had.

So we went to Madame Rita, and I tried on all the hats in the shop while Polly had her fitting, and wondered why it was that hats never seemed to suit me, something to do with my heather-like hair, perhaps, and then we drove down to Hampton Court where

Polly's old great-aunt, the widow of a general, sat all day dealing out cards to herself as she waited for eternity.

"And yet I don't believe she aches, you know," said Polly.

"I've noticed," I said, "that married ladies, and even widows, never do seem to ache. There is something about marriage that seems to stop it for good. I wonder why?"

Polly did not answer. The very mention of the word marriage always shut her up like a clam, it was a thing that had to be remembered in her company.

The afternoon before my engagement was to be announced in the *Times*, Aunt Emily sent me round to Montdore House to tell them the news. It is not at all my nature to be one of those who "drop in." I like to be invited by people to their houses at a given time, so that when I arrive they are expecting me and have made their dispositions accordingly, but I saw Aunt Emily's point when she said that, after all Lady Montdore's kindness to me, and considering that Polly was such a very great friend, I could hardly allow them to become aware of my engagement by reading it casually, in the newspaper.

So round I went, trembling rather. Bullitt, the butler, always frightened me into a fit. He was like Frankenstein's monster and one had to follow his jerky footsteps as though through some huge museum before arriving at the little green room, the only room in the house which did not seem as if it had been cleared ready for a reception, and in which they always sat. Today, however, the front door was opened by a footman of more human aspect, and, furthermore, he told me the good news that Her Ladyship had not yet come in, but Lady Polly was there alone, so off we trudged and presently discovered her amid the usual five-o'clock paraphernalia of silver kettle on flame, silver tea pot, Crown Derby cups and plates, and enough sugary food to stock a pastrycook's shop. She was sitting on the arm of a chair reading the *Tatler*.

"Heavenly *Tatler* day," she said. "It really does help with the aching. I'm in and Linda's in, but not you this week. Faithful of you to come. I was just wishing somebody nice would—now we can have our tea."

I was uncertain how she would take my engagement. I had, in fact, never spoken to her of Alfred since I had begged her to get him asked to the ball. She always seemed so much against young men, or any talk of love. But when I told her the news she was enthusiastic and only reproached me with having been so secretive.

"I remember you made me ask him to the ball," she said. "But then you never mentioned him again, once."

"I didn't dare to talk about it," I said, "in case—well—it really was of too much importance."

"Oh, I do understand that. I'm so glad you were longing for it before he asked you. I never believe in the other sort, the ones who have to make up their minds, you know. How lucky you are! Oh, fancy being able to marry the person you love. You don't know your luck." Her eyes were full of tears, I saw. "Go on," she said. "Tell everything."

I was rather surprised at this show of feeling, so unusual with Polly, but in my selfish state of great new happiness did not pause to consider what it might mean, besides, I was, of course, longing to tell.

"He was terribly nice to me at your ball. I hadn't a bit expected that he would come to London for it because, for one thing, knee breeches. I knew how he wouldn't have any, and then he's so busy always and hates parties, so you can imagine when I saw him I was all excited. Then he asked me to dance, but he danced with old Louisa too and even Aunt Emily, so I thought oh, well, he doesn't know anybody else, it must be that. So then he took me to supper and said he liked my dress and he hoped I'd go and see him at Oxford, and then he said something which showed he'd remembered a conversation we had had before. You know how encouraging that always is. After that he asked me to Oxford, twice—once he had a luncheon party and once he was alone—but in the holidays he went to Greece. Oxford holidays are terribly long, you know. Not even a postcard, so I thought it was all off. Well, on Thursday

I went to Oxford again and this time he proposed to me and look . . ." I said, showing a pretty old ring, a garnet set in diamonds.

"Don't say he had it on him like in *The Making of a Marchioness*," said Polly.

"Just like, except that it's not a ruby."

"Quite the size of a pigeon's egg, though. You are lucky."

Lady Montdore now appeared. She bustled in, still wearing her outdoor clothes and seemed unusually mellow.

"Ah! The girls!" she said. "Talking balls, I suppose, as usual! Going to the Gravesend's tonight, Fanny? Give me some tea, I'm quite dead, such an afternoon with the Grand Duchess, I've just dropped her at Kensington Palace. You'd never believe that woman was nearly eighty. She could run us all off our feet, you know, and such a dear, so human, one doesn't mind what one says to her. We went to Woollands to get some woollens—she does feel the cold. Misses the double windows, so she tells me."

It must have been rather sad for Lady Montdore (though with her talent for ignoring disagreeable subjects she probably never even realized the fact) that friendship with royal personages only ever began for her when their days of glory were finished. Tsarskoe Selo, the Quirinal, Kotrocheny Palace, Miramar, Laecken and the island of Corfu knew her not, unless among an enormous crowd in the state apartments. If she went to a foreign capital with her husband she would, of course, be invited to official receptions, while foreign rulers who came to London would attend her big parties, but there was no intimacy. These potentates may not have had the sense to keep their power, but they were evidently not too stupid to realize that give Lady Montdore an inch and she would take an ell. As soon as they were exiled, however, they began to see her charm, another kingdom gone always meant a few more royal habitués at Montdore House, and when they were completely down and out, and had got through whatever money they had managed to salt away, she was allowed to act as lady-in-waiting and go with them to Woollands.

Polly handed her a cup of tea and told her my news. The happy afterglow from her royal outing immediately faded and she became intensely disagreeable.

"Engaged?" she said. "Well, I suppose that's very nice. Alfred what did you say? Who is he? What is that name?"

"He's a don, at Oxford."

"Oh, dear, how extraordinary. You don't want to go and live at Oxford, surely? I should think he had better go into politics and buy a place—I suppose he hasn't got one, by the way? No, or he wouldn't be a don, not an English don, at least. In Spain, of course, it's quite different—dons are somebody there, I believe. Let's think—yes, why shouldn't your father give you a place as a wedding present? You're the only child he's ever likely to have. I'll write to him at once—where is he now?"

I said vaguely that I believed in Jamaica, but did not know his address.

"Really, what a family! I'll find out from the Colonial Office and write by bag, that will be safest. Then this Mr. Thing can settle down and write books. It always gives a man status if he writes a book, Fanny. I advise you to start him off on that immediately."

"I'm afraid I haven't much influence with him," I said, uneasily.

"Oh, well, develop it, dear, quick. No use marrying a man you can't influence. Just look what I've done for Montdore, always seen that he takes an interest, made him accept things (jobs, I mean) and kept him up to the mark, never let him slide back. A wife must always be on the lookout, men are so lazy by nature. For example, Montdore is forever trying to have a little nap in the afternoon, but I won't hear of it. Once you begin that, I tell him, you are old, and people who are old find themselves losing interest, dropping out of things and then they might as well be dead. Montdore's only got me to thank if he's not in the same condition as most of his contemporaries, creeping about the Marlborough Club like dying flies and hardly able to drag themselves as far as the House of Lords. I make Montdore walk down there every day. Now, Fanny dear, the more I think of it the more it seems to me quite ridiculous for you to go marrying a don. What does Emily say?"

"She's awfully pleased."

"Emily and Sadie are hopeless. You must ask my advice about this sort of thing. I'm very glad indeed you came round; we must think how we can get you out of it. Could you ring him up now and say you've changed your mind? I believe it would be kindest in the long run to do it that way."

"Oh, no, I can't."

"Why not dear? It isn't in the paper yet."

"It will be tomorrow."

"That's where I can be so helpful. I'll send for Geoffrey Dawson now and have it stopped."

I was quite terrified. "Please," I said, "oh, please not!"

Polly came to my rescue. "But she wants to marry him, Mummy. She's in love, and look at her pretty ring!"

Lady Montdore looked and was confirmed in her opposition. "That's not a ruby," she said, as if I had been pretending it was. "And, as for love, I should have thought the example of your mother would have taught you something. Where has love landed her? Some ghastly white hunter. Love, indeed! Whoever invented love ought to be shot."

"Dons aren't a bit the same as white hunters," said Polly. "You know how fond Daddy is of them."

"Oh, I daresay they're all right for dinner, if you like that sort of thing. Montdore does have them over sometimes, I know, but that's no reason why they should go marrying people. So unsuitable, megalomania, I call it. No, Fanny, I'm very much distressed."

"Oh, please don't be," I said.

"However, if you say it's settled, I suppose there's no more I can do, except to try and help you make a success of it. Montdore can ask the Chief Whip if there's something for you to nurse. That will be best."

It was on the tip of my tongue to say that what I hoped to be nursing before long would be sent by God and not the Chief Whip, but I restrained myself, nor did I dare to tell her that Alfred was not a Tory.

The conversation now turned upon the subject of my trousseau, about which Lady Montdore was quite as bossy, though less embarrassing. I was not feeling much interest in clothes at that time, all my thoughts being of how to decorate and furnish a charming little old house which Alfred had taken me to see after placing the pigeon's egg on my finger and which, by a miracle of good luck, was to be let.

"The important thing, dear," she said, "is to have a really good fur coat, I mean a proper, dark one." To Lady Montdore, fur meant mink. She could imagine no other kind except sable, but that would be specified. "Not only will it make all the rest of your clothes look better than they are but you really needn't bother much about anything else as you need never take it off. Above all, don't go wasting money on underclothes; there is nothing stupider—I always borrow Montdore's myself. Now, for evening a diamond brooch is a great help, so long as it has good big stones. Oh, dear, when I think of the diamonds your father gave that woman, it really is too bad. All the same, he can't have got through everything, he was enormously rich when he succeeded. I must write to him. Now, dear, we're going to be very practical. No time like the present."

She rang for her secretary, and said my father's address must be found out.

"You could ring up the Under-Secretary for Colonies with my compliments, and will you make a note that I will write to Lord Logan tomorrow."

She also told her to make a list of places where linen, underclothes and house furnishings could be obtained at wholesale prices.

"Bring it straight back here for Miss Logan when it is ready."

When the secretary had gone, Lady Montdore turned to Polly and spoke to her exactly as if I had gone too, and they were alone. It was a habit she had, and I always found it very embarrassing as I never quite knew what she expected me to do, whether to interrupt her by saying good-bye or simply to look out of the window and pretend that my thoughts were far away. On this occasion, however, I was clearly expected to wait for the list of addresses, so I had no choice.

"Now, Polly, have you thought of a young man yet for me to ask down on the third?"

"Oh, how about John Coningsby?" said Polly, with an indifference which I could plainly see must be maddening to her mother. Lord Coningsby was her official young man, so to speak. She invited him to everything, and this had greatly pleased Lady Montdore to begin with, since he was rich, handsome, agreeable and an "eldest son," which meant, in Lady Montdore's parlance, the eldest son of a peer (never let Jones or Robinson major think of themselves for one moment as eldest sons). Too soon, however, she saw that he and Polly were excellent friends and would never be anything else, after which she regretfully lost all interest in him.

"Oh, I don't count John," she said.

"How d'you mean you don't count him?"

"He's only a friend. Now I was thinking in Woollands—I often do have good ideas in shops—how would it be to ask Joyce Fleetwood?"

Alas, the days when I, Albert Christian George Andrew Patrick David, was considered to be the only person worthy of taking thee, Leopoldina, must have become indeed remote if Joyce Fleetwood was to be put forward as a substitute. Perhaps it was in Lady Montdore's mind that, since Polly showed no inclination to marry an established, inherited position, the next best thing would be somebody who might achieve one by his own efforts. Joyce Fleetwood was a noisy, self-opinionated young Conservative M.P. who had mastered one or two of the drearier subjects of debate, agriculture, the Empire, and so on, and was always ready to hold forth upon them in the House. He had made up to Lady Montdore and she thought him much cleverer than he really was. His parents were known to her, they had a place in Norfolk.

"Well, Polly?"

"Yes, why not?" said Polly. "It's a shower bath when he talks, but do let's, he's so utterly fascinating, isn't he?"

Lady Montdore now lost her temper and her voice got quite out of control. I sympathised with her, really; it was too obvious that Polly was wilfully provoking her.

"It's perfectly stupid to go on like this."

Polly did not reply. She bent her head sideways and pretended to be deeply absorbed in the headlines, upside down, of the evening paper which lay on a chair by her mother. She might just as well have said out loud, "All right, you horrible vulgar woman, go on, I don't care. You are nothing to me," so plain was her meaning.

"Please, listen when I speak to you, Polly."

Polly continued to squint at the headlines.

"Polly, will you pay attention to what I'm saying?"

"What were you saying? Something about Mr. Fleetwood?"

"Let Mr. Fleetwood be, for the present. I want to know what, exactly, you are planning to do with your life. Do you intend to live at home and go mooning on like this for ever?"

"What else can I do? You haven't exactly trained me for a career, have you?"

"Oh, yes indeed, I have. I've trained you for marriage which, in my opinion (I may be old-fashioned) is by far the best career open to any woman."

"That's all very well, but how can I marry if nobody asks me?"

Of course that was really the sore point with Lady Montdore, nobody asking her. A Polly gay and flirtatious, surrounded by eligible suitors, playing one off against the others, withdrawing, teasing, desired by married men, breaking up her friends' romances, Lady Montdore would have been perfectly happy to watch her playing that game for several years, if need be, so long as it was quite obvious that she would finally choose some suitably important husband

and settle down with him. What her mother minded so dreadfully was that this acknowledged beauty should appear to have no attraction whatever for the male sex. The eldest sons had a look, said, "Isn't she lovely?" and went off with some chinless little creature from Cadogan Square. There had been three or four engagements of this sort lately which had upset Lady Montdore very much indeed.

"And why don't they ask you? It's only because you give them no encouragement. Can't you try to be a little jollier, nicer with them, no man cares to make love to a dummy, you know. It's too discouraging."

"Thank you, but I don't want to be made love to."

"Oh, dear, oh, dear! Then what is it you do want?"

"Leave me alone, Mother, please."

"To stay on here, with us, until you are old?"

"Daddy wouldn't mind a bit."

"Oh, yes, he would, make no mistake about that. Not for a year or two perhaps, but in the end he would. Nobody wants their girl to be hanging about forever, a sour old maid, and you'll be the sour kind, that's too obvious already, my dear, wizened up and sour."

I could hardly believe my ears. Could this be Lady Montdore speaking, in such frank and dreadful terms, to Polly, her beautiful paragon, whom she used to love so much that she was even reconciled to her being a daughter and not an heir? It seemed to me terrible. I went cold in my very backbone. There was a long and deeply embarrassing silence, broken by Frankenstein's monster who jerked into the room and said that the King of Portugal was on the telephone. Lady Montdore stumped off and I seized the opportunity to escape.

"I hate her," said Polly, kissing me good-bye. "I hate her and I wish she were dead. Oh, Fanny, the luck of not being brought up by your own mother—you've no idea what a horrible relationship it can be."

"Poor Polly," I said, very much upset. "How sad! But when you were little it wasn't horrible?"

"Always, always horrible. I've always hated her from the bottom of my heart."

I did not believe it.

"She isn't like this the whole time?" I said.

"More and more. Better make a dash for it, love, or you'll be caught again. I'll ring up very soon. . . ."

Chapter 11

I WAS MARRIED AT the beginning of the Christmas vacation and when Alfred and I returned from our honeymoon we went to stay at Alconleigh while our little house in Oxford was being got ready. This was an obvious and convenient arrangement as Alfred could go in to Oxford every day for his work, and I was at hand to supervise the decoration of the house, but, although Alconleigh had been a second home to me from my babyhood, it was not without misgivings that I accepted Aunt Sadie's invitation to take my husband there for a long visit, at the very outset of our married life. My Uncle Matthew's likes and dislikes were famous for their violence, for the predomination of the latter over the former, and for the fact that he never made the slightest attempt to conceal them from their object; I could see that he was already prejudiced against poor Alfred. It was an accepted fact in the family that he loathed me, furthermore, he also hated new people, hated men who married his female relations, hated and despised those who did not practise blood sports. I felt there was but little hope for Alfred, especially as, culmination of horror, "the fella reads books."

True, all this had applied to Davey when he had first appeared, engaged to Aunt Emily, but Uncle Matthew had taken an unreasoning fancy to Davey from the very beginning and it was not to be hoped that such a miracle could repeat itself. My fears, however, were not entirely realized. I think Aunt Sadie had probably read the riot act before our arrival. Meanwhile, I had been doing my best with Alfred. I made him have his hair cropped like a guardsman, explained to him that if he must open a book he should do so only in the privacy of his bedroom, and specially urged great punctuality at meal times. Uncle Matthew, as I told him, liked to get us all into the dining room at least five minutes before the meal was ready. "Come on," he would say, "we'll go and sit in." And in the family would sit, clasping hot plates to their bosoms (Aunt Sadie had once done this, absent-mindedly, with a plate of artichoke soup), all eyes upon the pantry door.

I tried to explain these things to Alfred, who listened patiently though uncomprehendingly. I also tried to prepare him for the tremendous impact of my uncle's rages, so that I got the poor man, really quite unnecessarily, into a panic.

"Do let's go to the Mitre," he kept saying.

"It may not be too bad," I replied, doubtfully.

And it was not, in the end, too bad at all. The fact is that Uncle Matthew's tremendous and classical hatred for me, which had begun when I was an infant and which had cast a shadow of fear over all my childhood, had now become more legend than actuality. I was such an habitual member of his household, and he such a conservative, that this hatred, in common with that which he used to nurture against Josh, the groom, and various other old intimates, had not only lost its force but I think had, with the passage of years, actually turned into love; such a lukewarm sentiment as ordinary avuncular affection being, of course, foreign to his experience. Be that as it may, he evidently had no wish to poison the beginning of my married life and made quite touching efforts to bottle up whatever irritation he felt at Alfred's shortcomings, his unmanly incompetence with his motor car, vagueness over time and fatal disposition to spill marmalade at breakfast. The fact that Alfred left for Oxford at nine o'clock, only returning in time for dinner, and that we spent Saturday to Monday of every week in Kent with Aunt Emily made our visit just endurable to Uncle Matthew, and, incidentally to Alfred himself, who did not share my unquestioning adoration for all members of the Radlett family.

The Radlett boys had gone back to their schools, and my cousin Linda, whom I loved best in the world after Alfred, was now living in London and expecting a baby, but, though Alconleigh was never quite the same without her, Jassy and Victoria were at home (none of the Radlett girls went to school) so the house resounded as usual with jingles, and jangles, and idiotic shrieks. There was always some joke being run to death at Alconleigh, and just now it was headlines from the Daily Express which the children had made into a chant and intoned to each other all day.

Jassy: "*Man's* long agony in a lift-*shaft*."

Victoria: "Slowly *crushed* to *death* in a *lift*."

Aunt Sadie became very cross about this, said they were really too old to be so heartless, that it wasn't a bit funny, only dull and disgusting and absolutely forbade them to sing it any more. After this they tapped it out to each other, on doors, under the dining-room table, clicking with their tongues or blinking with their eye-lids, and all the time in fits of naughty giggles. I could see that Alfred thought them terribly silly and he could hardly contain his indignation when he found out that they did no lessons of any sort.

"Thank heavens for your Aunt Emily," he said. "I really could not have married somebody quite illiterate."

So, of course, I too thanked heavens more than ever for dear Aunt Emily, but at the same time Jassy and Victoria made me laugh so much, and I loved them so much that it was impossible for me to wish them very different from what they were. Hardly had I arrived in the house than I was lugged off to their secret meeting place, the Hons' cupboard, to be asked what IT was like.

"Linda says it's not all it's cracked up to be," said Jassy, "and we don't wonder when we think of Tony."

"But Louisa says, once you get used to it, it's utter utter utter bliss-ikins," said Victoria, "and we do wonder, when we think of John."

"What's wrong with poor Tony and John?"

"Dull and old. Come on then Fanny—tell."

I said I agreed with Louisa but refused to enter into details.

"It is unfair, nobody ever tells. Sadie doesn't even know, that's quite obvious, and Louisa is an old prig, but we did think we could count on Linda and you. Very well then, we shall go to our marriage beds in ignorance, like Victorian ladies, and in the morning we shall be found stark, staring mad with horror, and live sixty more years in an expensive bin, and then perhaps you'll wish you had been more helpful."

"Weighted down with jewels and Valenciennes costing thousands," said Victoria. "The Lecturer was here last week and he was telling Sadie some very nice sexy stories about that kind of thing. Of course, we weren't meant to hear but you can just guess what happened. Sadie didn't listen and we did."

"I should ask the Lecturer for information," I said. "He'd tell."

"He'd show. No, thank you very much."

Polly came over to see me. She was pale and thinner, had rings under her eyes and seemed quite shut up in herself, though this may have been in contrast with the exuberant Radletts. When she was with Jassy and Victoria, she looked like a swan, swimming in the company of two funny little tumbling ducks. She was very fond of them. She had never got on very well with Linda, for some reason, but she loved everybody else at Alconleigh, especially Aunt Sadie, and was more at her ease with Uncle Matthew than anybody I ever knew, outside his own family circle. He, for his part, bestowed on her some of the deference he felt for Lord Montdore, called her Lady Polly, and smiled every time his eyes fell on her beautiful face.

"Now children," said Aunt Sadie, "leave Fanny and Polly to have a little chat. They don't want you all the time, you know."

"It is unfair—I suppose Fanny's going to *tell* Polly now. Well, back to the medical dictionary and the Bible. I only wish these things didn't look quite so sordid in cold print. What we need is some clean-minded married woman, to explain, but where are we to find her?"

Polly and I had a very desultory little chat, however. I showed her photographs of Alfred and me in the South of France where we had been so that he could meet my poor mother the Bolter, who was living there now with a nasty new husband. Polly said the Dougdales were off there next week, as Lady Patricia was feeling the cold so dreadfully that winter. She told me also that there had been a huge Christmas party at Hampton and that Joyce Fleetwood was in disgrace with her mother for not paying his bridge debts.

"So that's one comfort. We've still got the Grand Duchess, poor old thing. Goodness, she's dull—not that Mummy seems to think so. Veronica Chaddesley Corbett calls her and Mummy Ma'am and Super-Ma'am."

I did not like to ask if Polly and her mother were getting on any better, and Polly volunteered nothing on that subject, but she looked, I thought, very miserable. Presently she said she must go.

"Come over soon and bring Alfred."

But I dreaded the impact of Lady Montdore upon Alfred even more than that of Uncle Matthew, and said he was too busy but I would come alone sometime.

"I hear that she and Sonia are on very bad terms again," Aunt Sadie said when Polly had driven off.

"The hell-hag," said Uncle Matthew. "Drown her, if I were Montdore."

"Or he might cut her to pieces with nail scissors, like that French duke the Lecherous Lecturer was telling you all about, Sadie, when you weren't listening and we were."

"Don't call me Sadie, children, and don't call Mr. Dougdale the Lecherous Lecturer."

"Oh, dear. Well, we always do behind your backs so you see it's bound to slip out sometimes."

Davey arrived. He had come to stay for a week or so for treatment at the Radcliffe Infirmary. Aunt Emily was becoming more and more attached to all her animals and could seldom now be persuaded to leave them, for which, on this occasion, I was thankful, since our Sundays in Kent really were an indispensable refuge to Alfred and me.

"I met Polly in the drive," Davey said. "We stopped and had a word. I think she looks most dreadfully unwell."

"Nonsense," said Aunt Sadie, who believed in no illness except appendicitis. "There's nothing wrong with Polly. She needs a husband, that's all."

"Oh! How like a woman!" said Davey. "Sex, my dear Sadie, is not a sovereign cure for everything, you know. I only wish it were."

"I didn't mean sex at all," said my aunt, very much put out by this interpretation. Indeed, she was what the children called "against" sex, that is to say, it never entered into her calculations. "What I said, and what I meant, was she needs a husband. Girls of her age, living at home, are hardly ever happy and Polly is a specially bad case because she has nothing whatever to do. She doesn't care for hunting, or parties, or anything much that I can see, and she doesn't get on with her mother. It's true that Sonia teases and lectures her and sets about it all the wrong way. She's a tactless person, but she is perfectly right you know. Polly needs a life of her own, babies, occupations and interests — an establishment, in fact — and for all that she must have a husband."

"Or a lady of Llangollen," said Victoria.

"Time you went to bed, miss, now off you go, both of you."

"Not me, it's not nearly my bedtime yet."

"I said both of you, now begone."

They dragged themselves out of the room as slowly as they dared and went upstairs, stamping out "Man's long agony" on the bare boards of the nursery passage so that nobody in the whole house could fail to hear them.

"Those children read too much," said Aunt Sadie. "But I can't stop them. I honestly believe they'd rather read the label on a medicine bottle than nothing at all."

"Oh, but I love reading the labels of medicine bottles," said Davey. "They're madly enjoyable, you know."

Chapter 12

THE NEXT MORNING when I came down to breakfast I found everybody, even the children, looking grave. It seemed that by some mysterious local tom-tom Aunt Sadie had learnt that Lady Patricia Dougdale had died in the night. She had suddenly collapsed, Lord Montdore was sent for, but by the time he could arrive she had become unconscious, and an hour later was dead.

"Oh, poor Patricia," Aunt Sadie kept saying, very much upset, while Uncle Matthew, who cried easily, was mopping his eyes as he bent over the hot plate, taking a sausage, or, as he called it, a "banger" with less than his usual enthusiasm.

"I saw her only last week," he said, "at the Clarendon Yard."

"Yes," said Aunt Sadie, "I remember you told me. Poor Patricia, I always liked her so much, though of course all that about being delicate was tiresome."

"Well, now you can see for yourself that she was delicate," said Davey triumphantly. "She's dead. It killed her. Doesn't that show you? I do wish I could make you Radletts understand that there is no such thing as imaginary illness. Nobody who is quite well could possibly be bothered to do all the things that I, for instance, am obliged to, in order to keep my wretched frame on its feet."

The children began to giggle at this, and even Aunt Sadie smiled, because they all knew that so far from it being a bother to Davey it was his all-absorbing occupation and one which he enjoyed beyond words.

"Oh, of course I know you all think it's a great, great joke, and no doubt Jassy and Victoria will scream with laughter when I finally do conk out, but it's not a joke to me, let me tell you, and a liver in that state can't have been much of a joke to poor Patricia, what's more."

"Poor Patricia, and I fear she had a sad life with that boring old Lecturer."

This was so like Aunt Sadie. Having protested for years against the name Lecturer for Boy Dougdale, she was now using it herself. Very soon, no doubt, we should hear her chanting "Man's long agony."

"For some reason that I could never understand, she really loved him."

"Until lately," said Davey. "I think for the past year or two it has been the other way round, and he had begun to depend on her, and then it was too late, she had stopped bothering about him."

"Possibly. Anyway there it is, all very sad. We must send a wreath, darling, at once. What a time of year! It will have to come from Oxford I suppose. . . . Oh, the waste of money!"

"Send a wreath of frog spawn, frog spawn, frog spawn, lovely, lovely frog spawn, it is my favourite thing," sang Jassy.

"If you go on being so silly, children," said Aunt Sadie, who had caught a look of great disapproval on Alfred's face, "I shall be obliged to send you to school, you know."

"But can you afford to?" said Victoria. "You'd have to buy us plimsolls and gym tunics, underclothes in a decent state, and some good strong luggage. I've seen girls going off to school; they are covered with expensive things. Of course, we long for it, pashes for the prefects and rags in the dorm. School has a very sexy side, you know, Sadie. Why, the very word 'mistress,' Sadie, you know . . ."

But Aunt Sadie was not really listening; she was away in her cloud and merely said "Mm, very naughty and silly, and don't call me Sadie."

Aunt Sadie and Davey went off to the funeral together. Uncle Matthew had his Bench that day, and particularly wanted to attend in order to make quite sure that a certain ruffian who was to come up before it should be committed to the Assizes, where, it was very much to be hoped, he would get several years and the cat. One or two of Uncle Matthew's fellow beaks had curious, modern ideas about justice and he was obliged to carry on a strenuous war against them, in which he was greatly assisted by a retired Admiral of the neighbourhood.

So they had to go to the funeral without him, and came back in low spirits.

"It's the dropping off the perches," said Aunt Sadie. "I've always dreaded when that begins. Soon we shall all have gone. . . . Oh, well, never mind."

"Nonsense," Davey said, briskly. "Modern science will keep us alive, and young, too, for many a long day yet. Patricia's insides were a terrible mess. I had a word with Dr. Simpson while you were with Sonia and it's quite obviously a miracle she didn't die years ago. When the children have gone to bed I'll tell you."

"No, thank you," said Aunt Sadie, while the children implored him to go then and there with them to the Hons' cupboard and tell.

"It is unfair, Sadie doesn't want to hear the least bit, and we die to."

"How old was Patricia?" said Aunt Sadie.

"Older than we are," said Davey. "I remember when they married she was supposed to be quite a bit older than Boy."

"And he was looking a hundred in that bitter wind."

"I thought he seemed awfully cut up, poor Boy."

Aunt Sadie, during a little graveside chat with Lady Montdore, had gathered that the death had come as a shock and surprise to all of them, that, although they had known Lady Patricia to be far from well, they had no idea that she was in immediate danger; in fact, she had been greatly looking forward to her trip abroad the following week. Lady Montdore, who resented death, clearly thought it most inconsiderate of her sister-in-law to break up their little circle so suddenly, and Lord Montdore, devoted to his sister, was dreadfully shaken by the midnight drive with a death-bed at the end of it, but, surprisingly enough, the one who had taken it hardest was Polly. It seemed that she had been violently sick on hearing the news, completely prostrated for two days, and was still looking so unwell that her mother had refused to take her to the funeral.

"It seems rather funny," said Aunt Sadie, "in a way. I'd no idea she was so particularly devoted to Patricia, had you, Fanny?"

"Nervous shock," said Davey. "I don't suppose she's ever had a death so near to her before."

"Oh, yes, she has," said Jassy. "Ranger."

"Dogs aren't exactly the same as human beings, my dear Jassy."

But to the Radletts they were exactly the same, except that to them dogs, on the whole, had more reality than people.

"So tell me about the grave," said Victoria.

"Not very much to tell, really," said Aunt Sadie. "Just a grave, you know, lots of flowers and mud."

"They'd lined it with heather," said Davey, "from Craigside. Poor dear, she did love Scotland."

"And where was it?"

"In the graveyard, of course, at Silkin—between the Wellingtonia and the Blood Arms, if you see where I mean. In full view of Boy's bedroom window, incidentally."

Jassy began to talk fast and earnestly.

"You will promise to bury me here, whatever happens, won't you, won't you? There's one exact place I want. I note it every time I go to church—it's next door to that old lady who was nearly a hundred."

"That's not our part of the churchyard—miles away from grandfather."

"No, but it's the bit I want. I once saw a dear little dead baby vole there. Please, please, please, don't forget."

"You'll have married some sewer and gone to live in the Antipodes," said Uncle Matthew who had just come in. "They let that young hog off, said there was no evidence. Evidence be damned, you'd only got to look at his face to see who did it. Afternoon completely wasted. The Admiral and I are going to resign."

"Then bring me back," said Jassy, "pickled. I'll pay, I swear I will. Please, Fa, you must."

"Write it down," said Uncle Matthew, producing a piece of paper and a fountain pen. "If these things don't get written down, they are forgotten. And I'd like a deposit of ten bob, please."

"You can take it out of my birthday present," said Jassy, who was scribbling away with great concentration. "I've made a map like in Treasure Island," she said. "See?"

"Yes, thank you, that's quite clear," said Uncle Matthew. He went to the wall, took his master key from his pocket, opened a safe and put in the piece of paper. Every room at Alconleigh had one of these wall safes, whose contents would have amazed and discomfitted the burglar who managed to open them. Aunt Sadie's jewels, which had some very good stones, were never kept in them, but lay glittering about all over the house and garden, in any place where she might have taken them off and forgotten to put them on again—on the downstairs washbasin, by the flower bed she had been weeding, sent to the laundry pinning up a suspender. Her big party pieces were kept in the bank. Uncle Matthew himself possessed no jewels and despised all men who did. (Boy's signet ring and platinum-and-pearl evening watch chain were great causes for tooth grinding.) His own watch was a large loudly ticking object in gun metal, tested twice a day by Greenwich mean time on a chronometer in the business room, and said to gain three seconds a week, this was attached to his key ring across his moleskin waistcoat by an ordinary leather bootlace, in which Aunt Sadie often tied knots to remind herself of things.

The safes, nevertheless, were full of treasures, if not of valuables, for Uncle Matthew's treasures were objects of esoteric worth, such as a stone quarried on the estate and said to have imprisoned for two thousand years a living toad; Linda's first shoe; the skeleton of a mouse regurgitated by an owl; a tiny gun for shooting bluebottles; the hair of all his children made into a bracelet; a silhouette of Aunt Sadie done at a fair; a carved nut; a ship in a bottle; altogether a strange mixture of sentiment, natural history and little objects which from time to time had taken his fancy.

"Come on, do let's see," said Jassy and Victoria, making a dash at the door in the wall. There was always great excitement when the safes were opened, as they hardly ever were, and seeing inside was considered a treat.

"Oh! The dear little bit of shrapnel, may I have it?"

"No, you may not. It was once in my groin for a whole week."

"Talk about death," said Davey. "The greatest medical mystery of our times must be the fact that dear Matthew is still with us."

"It only shows," said Aunt Sadie, "that nothing really matters the least bit, so why make these fearful efforts to keep alive?"

"Oh, but it's the efforts that one enjoys so much," said Davey, and this time he was speaking the truth.

Chapter 13

I THINK IT WAS about a fortnight after Lady Patricia's funeral that Uncle Matthew stood, after luncheon, outside his front door, watch in hand, scowling fiercely, grinding his teeth and awaiting his greatest treat of all the year, an afternoon's chubb fuddling. The Chubb Fuddler was supposed to be there at half-past two.

"Twenty-three and a quarter minutes past," Uncle Matthew was saying furiously, "in precisely six and three-quarter minutes the damned fella will be late."

If people did not keep their appointments with him well before the specified time he always counted them as being late. He would begin to fidget quite half an hour too soon, and wasted, in this way, as much time as people do who have no regard for it, besides getting himself into a thoroughly bad temper.

The famous trout stream that ran through the valley below Alconleigh was one of Uncle Matthew's most cherished possessions. He was an excellent dry fly fisherman, and was never happier, in and out of the fishing season, than when messing about the river in waders and inventing glorious improvements for it. It was the small boy's dream come true. He built dams, he dug lashers, he cut the weeds and trimmed the banks, he shot the herons, he hunted the otters, and he restocked with young trout every year. But he had trouble with the coarse fish, and especially the chubb, which not only gobble up the baby trout, but also their food, and they were a great worry to him. Then, one day he came upon an advertisement in *Exchange and Mart.* "Send for the Chubb Fuddler."

The Radletts always said that their father had never learnt to read, but in fact he could read quite well, if really fascinated by his subject, and the proof is that he found the Chubb Fuddler like this all by himself. He sat down then and there and sent. It took him some time, breathing heavily over the writing paper and making, as he always did, several copies of the letter before finally sealing and stamping it.

"The fella says here to enclose a stamped and addressed envelope, but I don't think I shall pander to him. He can take it or leave it."

He took it. He came, he walked along the river bank, and sowed upon its waters some magic seed, which soon bore magic fruit for, up to the surface, flapping, swooning, fainting, choking, thoroughly and undoubtedly fuddled, came hundreds upon hundreds of chubb. The entire male population of the village, warned beforehand and armed with rakes and landing nets fell upon the fish, several wheelbarrows were filled and the contents taken off to be used as manure for cottage gardens or chubb pie, according to taste.

Henceforward chubb fuddling became an annual event at Alconleigh, the Fuddler appearing regularly with the snowdrops, and to watch him at his work was a pleasure which never palled. So here we all were, waiting for him, Uncle Matthew pacing up and down outside the front door, the rest of us just inside, on account of the bitter cold, but peering out of the window, while all the men on the estate were gathered in groups down at the river's edge. Nobody, not even Aunt Sadie, wanted to miss a moment of the fuddling except, it seemed, Davey, who had retired to his room saying, "It isn't madly me, you know, and certainly not in this weather."

A motor car was now heard approaching, the scrunch of wheels and a low, rich hoot, and Uncle Matthew, with a last look at his

watch, was just putting it back in his pocket, when down the drive
came, not at all the Chubb Fuddler's little Standard but the huge
black Daimler from Hampton Park containing both Lord and Lady
Montdore. This was indeed a sensation! Callers were unknown at
Alconleigh. Anybody rash enough to try that experiment would see
no sign of Aunt Sadie or the children, who would all be flat on the
floor out of sight, though Uncle Matthew, glaring most embarrass-
ingly, would stand at a window, in full view, while they were being
told "not at home." The neighbours had long ago given it up as a
bad job. Furthermore, the Montdores, who considered themselves
King and Queen of the neighbourhood, never called but expected
people to go to them, so from every point of view, it seemed most
peculiar. I am quite sure that if anybody else had broken in upon
the happy anticipation of an afternoon's chubb fuddling, Uncle
Matthew would have bellowed at them to "get out of it," possibly
even have hurled a stone at them. When he saw who it was, however, he had one moment of stunned surprise and then leapt forward to open the door of the motor, like a squire of olden times
leaping to the stirrup of his liege lord.

The hell-hag, we could all see at once, even through the window, was in a dreadful state. Her face was blotchy and swollen as
from hours of weeping. She seemed perfectly unaware of Uncle
Matthew and did not throw him either a word or a look as she struggled out of the car, angrily kicking at the rug round her feet. She
then tottered with the gait of a very old woman, legs all weak and
crooked, towards the house. Aunt Sadie, who had dashed forward,
put an arm round her waist and took her into the drawing room,
giving the door a great "keep out, children" bang. At the same time,
Lord Montdore and Uncle Matthew disappeared together into my
uncle's business room; Jassy, Victoria and I were left to goggle at
each other with eyes like saucers, struck dumb by this extraordinary
incident. Before we had time to begin speculating on what it could
all mean, the Fuddler drove up, punctual to the very minute.

"Damned fella," Uncle Matthew said afterwards, "if he hadn't been so late we should have started by the time they arrived."

He parked his little tin pot of a motor in line with the Daimler and bustled, all happy smiles, up to the front door. At his first visit he had gone modestly up the back drive, but the success of his magic had so put Uncle Matthew on his side that he had told him, in future, to come to the front door, and always gave him a glass of port before starting work. He would no doubt have given him Imperial Tokay if he had had any.

Jassy opened the door before the Fuddler had time to ring, and then we all hung about while he drank his port, saying, "Bitter, isn't it?" and not quite knowing what to be at.

"His Lordship's not ill, I hope?" he said, surprised, no doubt, not to have found my uncle champing up and down as usual, his choleric look clearing suddenly into one of hearty welcome as he hurried to slap the Fuddler's back and pour out his wine.

"No, no, we think he'll be here in a moment. He's busy."

"Not so like His Lordship to be late, is it?"

Presently a message came from Uncle Matthew that we were to go down to the river and begin. It seemed too cruel to have the treat without him, but the fuddling had, of course, to be concluded by daylight. So we shivered out of the house, into the temporary shelter of the Fuddler's Standard and out again into the full blast of a north wind which was cutting up the valley. While the Fuddler sprinkled his stuff on the water, we crept back into his car for warmth and began to speculate on the reason for the extraordinary visit now in progress. We were simply dying of curiosity.

"I guess the Government has fallen," said Jassy.

"Why should that make Lady Montdore cry?"

"Well, who would do all her little things for her?"

"There'd soon be another lot for her to fag—Conservatives this time, perhaps. She really likes that better."

"D'you think Polly is dead?"

"No, no, they'd be mourning o'er her lovely corpse, not driving about in motor cars and seeing people."

"Perhaps they've lost all their money and are coming to live with us," said Victoria. This idea cast a regular gloom, seeming as it did rather a likely explanation. In those days, when people were so rich and their fortunes so infinitely secure it was quite usual for them to think that they were on the verge of losing all their money, and the Radlett children had always lived under the shadow of the work-house, because Uncle Matthew, though really very comfortably off with about £10,000 a year, gross, had a financial crisis every two or three years and was quite certain in his own mind that he would end up on parish relief.

The Fuddler's work was done, his seed was sown and we got out of the motor with our landing nets. This was a moment that never failed to thrill. The river banks were dotted with people all gazing excitedly into the water, and very soon the poor fish began to squirm about the surface. I landed a couple of whales and then a smaller one, and just as I was shaking it out of the net, a well-known voice behind me, quivering with passion, said, "Put it back at once, you blasted idiot! Can't you see it's a greyling, Fanny? Oh, my God, women—incompetent—and isn't that my landing net you've got there? I've been looking for it all over the place."

I gave it up with some relief, ten minutes at the water's edge was quite enough in that wind. Jassy was saying, "Look look, they've gone," and there was the Daimler crossing the bridge, Lord Mont-dore sitting very upright in the back seat, bowing a little from side to side, almost like royalty. They overtook a butcher's van and I saw him lean forward and give the driver a gracious salute for having got out of the way. Lady Montdore was hardly visible, bundled up in her corner. They had gone, all right.

"Come on, Fanny," said my cousins, downing tools. "Home, don't you think? Too cold here," they shouted at their father, but he was busy cramming a giant chubb in its death throes into his hare pocket and took no notice.

"And now," said Jassy as we raced up the hill, "for worming it all out of Sadie."

IT WAS NOT, in fact, necessary to do any worming, Aunt Sadie was bursting with her news. She was more human and natural with her younger children than she had ever been with the elder ones. Her attitude of awe-inspiring vagueness alternating with sudden fits of severity, which had combined with Uncle Matthew's rages to drive Louisa and Linda and the boys underground, so that their real lives were led in the Hons' cupboard, was very much modified with regard to Jassy and Victoria. She was still quite as vague, but never very severe, and far more companionable. She had always been inclined to treat her children as if they were all exactly the same age, and the younger ones were now benefiting from the fact that Louisa and Linda were married women who could be spoken to, and in front of, without reserve.

We found her and Davey in the hall. She was quite pink with interest and, as for Davey, he was looking as much excited as if he had developed some fascinating new symptom.

"Come on," said the children, question marks all over their faces. "Tell."

"You'll never believe it," said Aunt Sadie, addressing herself to me. "Polly Hampton has informed her poor mother that she is going to marry Boy Dougdale. Her uncle, if you please! Did you ever hear such a thing? The wretched Patricia, not cold in her grave . . ."

"Well," said Jassy, aside, "cooling, in this weather . . ."

"Miserable old man!" Aunt Sadie spoke in tones of deep indignation and was clearly a hundred percent on Lady Montdore's side. "You see, Davey, how right Matthew has been about him all these years?"

"Oh, poor Boy, he's not so bad," Davey said, uncomfortably.

"I don't see how you can go on standing up for him after this, Davey."

"But, Sadie," said Victoria, "how can she marry him if he's her uncle?"

"Just exactly what I said. But it seems, with an uncle by marriage that you can. Would you believe that anything so disgustingly dreadful could be allowed?"

"I say," said Jassy. "Come on, Dave."

"Oh, no, dear, thank you. Marry one of you demons? Not for any money!"

"What a law!" said Aunt Sadie. "Whenever was it passed? Why it's the end of all family life, a thing like that."

"Except it's the beginning for Polly."

"Who told Lady Montdore?" Of course I was fascinated. This key-piece of the jig-saw made everything quite clear, and now I could not imagine how I could ever have been so stupid as to have missed it.

"Polly told her," said Aunt Sadie. "It happened like this. They hadn't seen Boy since the funeral because he caught a bad cold at it and stayed indoors. Sonia got an awful cold there too, and still has it, but he had spoken to Sonia every day on the telephone, as he always does. Well, yesterday they both felt a bit better, and he went over to Hampton with the letters he'd had about poor Patricia, from Infantas and things, and they had a good gloat over them, and then a long discussion about what to put on the tombstone. It seems they more or less settled on, 'She shall not grow old as we that are left grow old.'"

"Stupid!" said Jassy. "She had grown old already!"

"Old! A few years older than me," said Davey.

"Well . . . !" said Jassy.

"That's enough, miss. Sonia says he seemed terribly low and unhappy, talking about Patricia and what she'd always been to him, and how empty the house seems without her—just what you'd expect after twenty-three years, or something. Miserable old hypocrite! Well, he was supposed to stay for dinner, without dressing, because of his cold. Sonia and Lord Montdore went upstairs to change, and when Sonia came down again she found Polly, still in her day clothes, sitting on that white rug in front of the fire. She said, 'What are you doing, Polly? It's very late. Go up and dress. Where's Boy, then?' Polly got up and stretched herself and said, 'He's gone home and I've got something to tell you. Boy and I are going to be married.' At first, of course, Sonia didn't believe it, but Polly never jokes, as you know, and she very soon saw she was in deadly earnest and then she was so furious she went sort of mad— how well I can understand that!—and rushed at Polly and boxed her ears, and Polly gave her a great shove into an armchair and went upstairs. I imagine that Sonia was perfectly hysterical by then. Anyway, she rang for her maid who took her up and put her straight to bed. Meanwhile Polly dressed, came down again and calmly spent the evening with her father without saying a single word about it all to him, merely telling him that Sonia had a headache and wouldn't dine. So this morning poor Sonia had to tell him. She said it was terrible, because he so adores Polly. Then she tried to ring up Boy, but the wretched coward has gone away, or pretends to have, leaving no address. Did you ever hear such a story?"

I was speechless with interest. Davey said, "Personally, and speaking as an uncle, the one I feel for over all this is the unhappy Boy."

"Oh, no, Davey, nonsense. Just imagine the Montdores' feelings—while they were trying to argue her out of it this morning she told them she'd been in love with him since before they went to India, when she was a little girl of fourteen."

"Yes, very likely, but how do we know he wanted her to be in love with him? If you ask me, I don't suppose he had the very faintest idea of it."

"Come now, Davey, little girls of fourteen don't fall in love without any encouragement."

"Alas, they do," said Jassy. "Look at me and Mr. Fosdyke. Not one word, not one kindly glance has he ever thrown me and yet he is the light of my life."

Mr. Fosdyke was the local M.F.H.

I asked if Lady Montdore had had an inkling of all this before, knowing really quite well that she had not, as everything always came straight out with her and neither Polly nor Boy would have had one moment's peace.

"Simply no idea at all. It was a complete bolt from the blue. Poor Sonia, we know she has her faults, but I can't think she has deserved this. She said Boy had always been very kind about taking Polly off her hands when they were in London, to the Royal Academy and so on, and Sonia was pleased because the child never seemed to have anybody to amuse her. Polly wasn't a satisfactory girl to bring out, you know. I'm very fond of her myself, I always have been, but you could see that Sonia was having a difficult time in many ways. Oh, poor Sonia, I do feel . . . Now children, will you please go up and wash your fishy hands before tea?"

"This is the very limit. You're obviously going to say things while we're away. What about Fanny's fishy hands then?"

"Fanny's grown-up, she'll wash her hands when she feels like it. Off you go."

When they were safely out of the room, she said, in horror, to Davey and me, "Just imagine, Sonia, who had completely lost control of herself (not that I blame her), sort of hinted to me that Boy had once been her own lover."

"Darling Sadie, you are such an innocent," Davey said, laughing. "It's a famous, famous love affair which everybody except you has known all about for years. I sometimes think your children are right and you don't know the facts of life."

"Well, all I can say is, I'm thankful I don't. How perfectly hateful! Do you think Patricia knew?"

"Of course she did, and she was only too glad of it. Before his affair with Sonia began, Boy used to make Patricia chaperone all the dismal little debutantes that he fancied, and they would sob out broken hearts on her shoulder, and beg her to divorce him. Very last thing he wanted, naturally. She had a lot of trouble with him, you know."

"I remember a kitchen maid," Aunt Sadie said.

"Oh, yes, it was one thing after another before Sonia took him on, but she had some control over him, and Patricia's life became much easier and more agreeable, until her liver got so bad."

"All the same," I said, "we know he still went for little girls, because look at Linda."

"Did he?" said Aunt Sadie. "I have sometimes wondered. Ugh! What a man! How you can think there's anything to be said for him, Davey, and how can you pretend he hadn't the faintest idea Polly was in love with him? If he made up to Linda, of course he must have done the same to her."

"Well, Linda's not in love with him, is she? He can't be expected to guess that because he strokes the hair of a little girl when she's fourteen she's going to insist on marrying him when she grows up. Bad luck on a chap, I call it."

"Davey, you're hopeless! And if I didn't know quite well that you're only teasing me I should be very cross with you."

"Poor Sonia," said Davey. "I feel for her, her daughter and her lover at a go. . . . Well, it often happens, but it can't ever be very agreeable."

"I'm sure it's the daughter she minds," said Aunt Sadie. "She hardly mentioned Boy. She was moaning and groaning about Polly, so perfectly beautiful, being thrown away like that. I should be just the same. I couldn't bear it for any of mine. . . . That old fellow they've known all their lives, and it's worse for her, Polly being the only one."

"And such a treasure, so much the apple of their eye. Well, the more I see of life the more profoundly thankful I am not to have any children."

"Between two and six they are perfect," said my aunt, rather sadly, I thought. "After that, I must say they are a worry, the funny little things. Then another horror for Sonia is wondering what went on all those years between Polly and Boy. She says last night she couldn't sleep for thinking of times when Polly pretended to have been to the hairdresser and obviously hadn't—that sort of thing— she says it's driving her mad."

"It needn't," I said firmly. "I'm quite sure nothing ever happened. From various things I can remember Polly saying to me I'm quite sure her love for the Lecturer must always have seemed hopeless to her. Polly's very good, you know, and she was very fond of her aunt."

"I daresay you're right, Fanny. Sonia herself said that when she came down and found Polly sitting on the floor she thought at once, 'The girl looks as if she had been making love,' and said she'd never seen her look like that before, flushed, her eyes simply huge and a curl of tousled hair hanging over her forehead. She was absolutely struck by her appearance, and then Polly told her . . ."

I could so well imagine the scene, Polly sitting, it was a very characteristic attitude with her, on the rug, getting up slowly, stretching, and then carelessly and gracefully implanting the cruel banderillas, the first movement of a fight that could only end in death.

"What I guess," I said, "is that he stroked a bit when she was fourteen and she fell in love then without him having any idea of it. Polly always bottles things up, and I don't expect anything more happened between them until the other evening."

"Simply too dreadful," said Aunt Sadie.

"Anyhow, Boy can't have expected to get engaged there and then, or he wouldn't have had all that talk about the Infanta's letter and the gravestone, would he?" said Davey. "I expect what Fanny says is true."

"You've been telling—it is unfair—Fanny's hands are still foully fishy." The children were back, out of breath.

"I do wonder what Uncle Matthew and Lord Montdore talked about in the business-room," I said. I could not imagine such a tale being unfolded between those two, somehow.

"They topicked," said Aunt Sadie. "I told Matthew afterwards, I've never seen anybody so angry. But I haven't told you yet what it was that Sonia really came about. She's sending Polly here for a week or two."

"No!" we all cried in chorus.

"Oh, the utter fascination!" said Jassy. "But why?"

"Polly wants to come. It was her idea and Sonia can't endure the sight of her for the present, which I can well understand. I must say I hesitated at first, but I am very fond of that little girl, you know. I really love her, and if she stays at home her mother will have driven her into an elopement within a week. If she comes here we might be able to influence her against this horrible marriage—and I don't mean you, children. You'll please try and be tactful for once in your lives."

"I will be," said Jassy, earnestly. "It's dear little Vict you must speak to. There's no tack in her and, personally, I think it was a great mistake ever to have told her at all—ow—help—help— Sadie, she's killing me . . . !"

"I mean both of you," said Aunt Sadie, calmly, taking no notice whatever of the dog-fight in progress. "You can talk about the chubb at dinner. That ought to be a safe subject."

"What?" they said, stopping the fight. "She's not coming today?"

"Yes, she is. After tea."

"Oh, what a thrill. Do you think the Lecturer will have himself carried into the house dressed up as a sack of wood?"

"They shan't meet under my roof," Aunt Sadie said firmly. "I promised Sonia that, but of course I pointed out that I can't control what Polly does elsewhere. I can only leave that to her own sense of what is in good taste, while she is staying with me."

Chapter 14

POLLY SOON MADE it clear that Aunt Sadie need have no misgivings about her behaviour while at Alconleigh. Her self-possession was complete, the only exterior indication that her life was at a crisis being an aura of happiness, which transformed her whole aspect. Nothing she said or did was at all out of the usual or could have led anybody to suppose that she had recently been involved in scenes of such intensity. And it was obvious that she held no communication of any sort with Boy; she never went near the telephone, she did not sit all day scribbling letters, received very few, and none, so the children informed me, with a Silkin postmark. She hardly ever left the house and then only to get a breath of air with the rest of us, certainly not in order to go for long solitary walks which might end in lovers' meetings.

Jassy and Victoria, romantic like all the Radletts, found this incomprehensible and most disappointing. They had expected to be plunged into an atmosphere of light opera and had supposed that the Lecturer would hang, sighing but hopeful, about the precincts, that Polly would hang, sighing but expectant, out of a moonlit window, to be united and put on the first stage of their journey to Gretna Green, by the ingenuity and enterprise of their two young friends.

They lugged a mattress and stocks of food into the Hons' cupboard in case Boy wanted to hide there for a day or two. They had thought of everything, so they informed me, and were busy making a rope ladder. But Polly would not play.

"If you have any letters for the post, Polly, you know what I mean, a letter—we could easily run down to the village with it on our bikes."

"Darling, you are kind, but they'll go just as quickly if I put them on the hall table, won't they?"

"Oh, of course you can do that if you like, but everybody will read the envelope and I just thought . . . Or any messages? There's a telephone in the village post office, rather public, but you could talk in French."

"I don't know French very well. Isn't there a telephone here?"

"Oh, it's a brute, extensions all over the place. Now there's a hollow tree in the park quite big enough for a man to hide in—quite dry and comfy—shall we show you?"

"You must, one day. Too cold to go out to-day, I think."

"You know there's a frightfully nice little temple in a wood the other side of the river, would you like us to take you there?"

"Do you mean Faulkner's Folly, where they have the meets? But, Jassy, I know it quite well, I've often seen it. Very pretty."

"What I really mean is the key is kept under a stone, and we could show you exactly where, so that you could go inside."

"There's nothing to see inside except cobwebs," I said. "It was never finished, you know."

Jassy made a furious face at me. "Tackless," she muttered.

"Let's go there next summer, darlings," said Polly, "for a picnic. I can't enjoy anything out of doors in this weather my eyes water too much."

The children slouched away, discouraged.

Polly exploded with laughter. "Aren't they too heavenly? But I don't really see the point of making all these great efforts to spend a few minutes with Boy in freezing cold temples, or to write to him about nothing at all, when very soon I shall be with him for the whole rest of my life. Besides, I don't want to annoy Lady Alconleigh when she is being such an angel to have me here."

Aunt Sadie herself, while applauding Polly's attitude, which relieved her of any need to worry, found it most unnatural.

"Isn't it strange?" she said. "You can see by looking at her that she is very happy, but, if it weren't for that, nobody could guess that she was in love. My girls always get so moony, writing reams all day, jumping when the telephone bell rings and so on, but there's none of that with Polly. I was watching her last night when Matthew put *'Che Gelida Manina'* on the gramophone. She didn't look a bit sentimental. Do you remember what an awful time we had with Linda when Tony was in America — never out of floods?"

But Polly had been brought up in a harder school for the emotions than had the Radletts, with a mother determined to find out everything that was in her mind, and to mould her very thoughts to her own wishes. One could only admire the complete success with which she had countered both of these aims. Clearly her character had a steely quality, incomprehensible to my cousins, blown hither and thither as they were upon the winds of sentiment.

I managed to have a few long talks alone with Polly at this time, but it was not very easy. Jassy and Victoria hardly left us for a single minute, so frightened were they of missing something. Furthermore, they were shameless eavesdroppers, while hair-brushing chats at bedtime were ruled out by the fact of my so-recent marriage. Mercifully, the children went riding every day, when an hour or so of peace could be counted on, there was no hunting at this time because of foot-and-mouth disease.

Gradually, the whole thing came out. Polly's reserve, it is true, never really broke down, but every now and then the landscape was illuminated and its character exposed to view by flashes of startling frankness. It all seemed to have been very much as we had thought.

For instance, I said to her something about when Boy proposed, and she replied, quite carelessly, "Oh, Boy never proposed to me at all. I don't think he ever would have, being that kind of a person—I mean so wonderfully unselfish and thinking that it matters for me, not being left things in wills and all that rubbish. Besides, he knows Mummy so well and he knew just what a hullabaloo she would make. He couldn't face it for me. No, no, I always realized that I should have to do the proposing, and I did. It wasn't very difficult."

So Davey was right, no doubt, the idea of such a marriage would never have entered the Lecturer's head if it had not been put there by Polly herself. After that it would clearly have been beyond flesh and blood to resist such a prize, greatest beauty and greatest heiress of her generation, potential mother of the children, the little half-Hamptons, he had always longed for. He could never have said no once it all lay at his feet, waiting to be pocketed.

"After all, I've loved him ever since I can remember. Oh, Fanny—isn't being happy wonderful?"

I felt just the same myself and was able to agree with all my heart. But her happiness had a curiously staid quality, and her love seemed less like the usual enchanted rapture of the young girl, newly engaged, than a comfortable love of old establishment, love which does not need to assert itself by continually meeting, corresponding with and talking about its object, but which takes itself, as well as his response, for granted. The doubts and jealousies which can be so painful, and make a hell almost of a budding love affair did not seem to have occurred to Polly, who took the simple view that she and Boy had hitherto been kept apart by one insuperable barrier, and that this barrier having been removed, the path to life-long bliss lay at their feet.

"What can it matter if we have a few more weeks of horrid waiting when we are going to live together all the rest of our lives and be buried in the same grave?"

"Fancy being buried in the same grave with the Lecturer," Jassy said, coming into my bedroom before luncheon.

"Jassy, I think it's too awful the way you listen at doors."

"Don't tease, Fan, I intend to be a novelist (child novelist astounds the critics) and I'm studying human nature like mad."

"I really ought to tell Aunt Sadie."

"That's it. Join the revereds, now you are married, just like Louisa. No, but seriously, Fanny, think of sharing a grave with that old Lecturer. Isn't it disgusting? And anyway what about Lady Patricia?"

"Well, she's nice and snug in one all to herself, lined with heather. She's quite all right."

"I think it's shocking."

Meanwhile, Aunt Sadie was doing what she could to influence Polly, but as she was much too shy to speak to her directly on such intimate subjects as sex and marriage, she used an oblique method of letting fall an occasional reflection, hoping that Polly would apply it to her own particular case.

"Always remember, children, that marriage is a very intimate relationship. It's not just sitting and chatting to a person; there are other things, you know."

Boy Dougdale, to her, was physically repulsive, as I think he often was to those women who did not find him irresistible, and she thought that if Polly could be brought to a realization of the physical aspect of marriage she might be put off him for good.

As Jassy very truly observed, however, "Isn't Sadie a scream? She simply doesn't realize that what put Polly on the Lecturer's side in the first place must have been all those dreadful things he did to her, like he once tried to with Linda and me, and that now what she really wants most in the world is to roll and roll and roll about with him in a double bed."

"Yes, poor Sadie, she's not too hot on psychology," said Victoria. "Now I should say the only hope of curing Polly's uncle-fixation is to analyse her. Shall we see if she'd let us try?"

"Children, I absolutely forbid you to," I said firmly. "And if you do I promise I'll tell Aunt Sadie about the eavesdropping, so there."

I knew what dreadful questions they would ask Polly and that as she was rather prim she would be shocked and angry. They were very much taken up at this time with the study and practise of psycho-analysis. They got hold of a book on the subject ("Elliston's library, would you believe it?") and several days of peace had ensued while they read it out to each other in the Hons' cupboard, after which they proceeded to action.

"Come and be analysed," was their parrot cry. "Let us rid you of the poison that is clogging your mental processes, by telling you all about yourselves. Now, suppose we begin with Fa, he's the simplest proposition in the house."

"What d'you mean, simple?"

"A.B.C. to us. No, no, not your hand, you dear old thing, we're grown out of palmistry ages ago, this is science."

"All right, let's hear it."

"Well, so then you're a very straightforward case of frustration — wanted to be a gamekeeper, were obliged to be a lord — followed, as is usual, by the development of over-compensation, so that now you're a psychoneurotic of the obsessive and hysterical type engrafted on to a paranoid and schizoid personality."

"Children, you are not to say these things about your father."

"Scientific truths are nothing to object to, Sadie, and in our experience everybody enjoys learning about themselves. Would you care for us to test your intelligence level with an ink blot, Fa?"

"What's that?"

"We could do it to you all in turn and mark you, if you like. It's quite easy. You show the subject an ordinary blot of ink on white paper and, according to the picture it makes for each individual (you understand what I mean, does it look like a gum boil, or the Himalayas? everybody sees something different), a practised questioner can immediately assess his intelligence level."

"Are you practised questioners?"

"Well, we've practised on each other and all the Joshes and Mrs. Aster. And we've noted the results in our scientific notebook, so come on."

Uncle Matthew gazed at the blot for awhile and then said that it looked to him very much like an ordinary ink blot and reminded him of nothing so much as Stephen's Blue Black.

"It's just as I had feared," said Jassy, "and shows a positively subhuman level—even Baby Josh did better than that. Oh, dear, subhuman, that's bad. . . ."

Jassy had now overstepped the boundary in the perpetual game of Tom Tiddler's Ground that she played with her father. He roared at her in a sudden rage and sent her to bed. She went off chanting, "Paranoid *and* schizoid, paranoid *and* schizoid," which had taken the place of "Man's long agony." She said to me afterwards, "Of course, it's rather grave for all of us because whether you believe in heredity or environment, either way we are boiled, shut up here with this old subhuman of a father."

DAVEY NOW DECIDED that it would be only kind to go over and see his old friend Lady Montdore, so he rang her up and was invited to luncheon. He stayed until after tea, and, by good luck, when he got back Polly was lying down in her bedroom, so he was able to tell all.

"She is in a rage," he said. "A rage. Simply frightening. She has taken what the French call a *'coup de vieux.'* She looks a hundred. I wouldn't care to be hated by anyone as much as she hates Boy. After all, you never know. There may be something in Christian Science, and evil thoughts and so on, directed at us with great intensity may affect the body. How she hates him! Just imagine, she has had the tapestry he made for that fire screen cut out quite roughly with a pair of scissors, and the screen is there in front of the fire with a huge hole in it. It gave me quite a shock."

"Poor Sonia, how like her, somehow. And what does she feel about Polly?"

"She mourns her, and she's pretty cross with her too for being so underhand and keeping it a secret all these years. I said, 'You really couldn't expect that she would tell you?' but she didn't agree. She asked me a lot of questions about Polly and her state of mind. I was obliged to say that her state of mind is not revealed to me, but that she is looking twice as pretty as before, if possible, so it can therefore be presumed that she is happy."

"Yes, you can always tell by that, with girls," said Aunt Sadie. "If it weren't for that, I wouldn't have thought she cared a bit, one way or the other. What a strange character she must have, after all."

"Not so strange," said Davey. "Many women are rather enigmatic, very few laugh when they are happy and cry when they are sad to the extent that your children do, my dear Sadie, nor do we all see everything in black and white. Life is oversimplified at Alconleigh. It's part of the charm and I'm not complaining, but you mustn't suppose that all human beings are exactly like Radletts, because it is not so."

"You stayed very late."

"Poor Sonia, she's lonely. She must be, dreadfully, if you come to think of it. We talked about nothing else, too, round and round the subject, every aspect of it. She asked me to go over and see Boy to find out if there's any hope of his giving up the idea and going abroad for a bit. She says Montdore's lawyer has written and told him that the day Polly marries him she will be completely cut out of her father's will and also Montdore will stop Patricia's allowance which he was intending to give Boy for his life. Even so, she fears they will have enough to live on, but it might shake him, I suppose. I didn't promise to go, but I think perhaps I will, all the same."

"Oh, but you must," said Jassy. "There's us to consider."

"Children, do stop interrupting," said Aunt Sadie. "If you can't hold your tongues you will have to leave the room when we are having serious conversations. In fact," she said, becoming strict all of a sudden, just as she used to be when Linda and I were little, "I think you'd better go now. Go on, off with you."

They went. As they reached the door, Jassy said in a loud aside,

"This labile and indeterminate attitude to discipline may do permanent damage to our young psychology. I really think Sadie should be more careful."

"Oh, no, Jassy," Victoria said. "After all, it's our complexes that make us so fascinating and unusual."

When they had shut the door, Davey said, rather seriously, "You know, Sadie, you do spoil them."

"Oh, dear," said Aunt Sadie, "I'm afraid so. It comes of having so many children. One can force oneself to be strict for a few years, but after that it becomes too much of an effort. But, Davey, do you honestly imagine it makes the smallest difference when they are grown-up?"

"Probably not to your children, demons one and all. But look how well we brought up Fanny."

"Davey! You were never strict," I said. "Not the least bit. You spoilt me quite completely."

"Yes, now, that's true," said Aunt Sadie. "Fanny was allowed to do all sorts of dreadful things—specially after she came out. Powder her nose, travel alone, go in cabs with young men—didn't she once go to a night club? Fortunately for you she seems to have been born good, though why she should have been, with such parents, is beyond me."

Davey told Polly that he had seen her mother but she merely said, "How was Daddy?"

"In London, House of Lords, something about India. Your mother doesn't look at all well, Polly."

"Temper," said Polly, and left the room.

Davey's next visit was to Silkin. "Frankly, I can't resist it." He bustled off in his little motor car on the chance of finding the Lecturer at home. He still refused to come to the telephone, giving out that he was away for a few weeks, but all other evidence pointed to the fact that he was living in his house, and, indeed, this now proved to be the case.

"Puzzled and lonely and gloomy, poor old Boy, and he's still got an awful cold he can't get rid of. Sonia's evil thoughts, perhaps. He has aged, too. Says he has seen nobody since his engagement to Polly. Of course, he has cut himself off at Silkin, but he seems to think that the people he has run into, at the London Library, and so on, have been avoiding him as if they already knew about it. I expect it's really because he's in mourning—or perhaps they don't want to catch his cold—anyway, he's fearfully sensitive on the subject. Then he didn't say so, but you can see how much he is missing Sonia. Naturally, after seeing her every day all these years. Missing Patricia, too, I expect."

"Did you talk quite openly about Polly?" I asked.

"Oh, quite. He says the whole thing originated with her, wasn't his idea at all."

"Yes, that's true. She told me that herself."

"And if you ask me, it shocks him dreadfully. He can't resist it, of course, but it shocks him and he fully expects to be a social outcast as the result. Now that would have been the card for Sonia to have played, if she had been clever enough to foresee it all. Too late, once the words were spoken, of course, but if she could have warned Boy what was likely to happen and then rubbed in about how that would finish him for ever in the eyes of society I think she might have stopped it. After all, he's frightfully social, poor chap. He would hate to be ostracised. As a matter of fact, though I didn't say so to him, people will come round in no time once they are married."

"But you don't really think they will marry?" said Aunt Sadie.

"My dear Sadie, after ten days in the same house with Polly I don't doubt it for one single instant. What's more, Boy knows he's in for it, all right, whether he likes it or not—and of course he half likes it very much indeed. But he dreads the consequences, not that there'll be any. People have no memory about that sort of thing and, after all, there's nothing to forget except bad taste."

"*Détournement de jeunesse?*"

"It won't occur to the ordinary person that Boy could have made a pass at Polly when she was little. We would never have thought of it, except for what he did to Linda. In a couple of years nobody outside the family will even remember what all the fuss was about."

"I'm afraid you're right," said my aunt. "Look at the Bolter! Ghastly scandal after ghastly scandal, elopements, horse whippings, puts herself up as a prize in a lottery, cannibal kings—I don't know what all—headlines in the papers, libel actions, and yet she only has to appear in London and her friends queue up to give parties for her. But don't encourage Boy by telling him. Did you suggest he might chuck it and go abroad?"

"Yes, I did, but it's no good. He misses Sonia. He is horrified, in a way, by the whole thing, hates the idea of his money being stopped, though he's not penniless himself, you know. He's got an awful cold and is down in the dumps, but at the same time you can see that the prospect dazzles him and as long as Polly makes all the running I bet you he'll play. Oh, dear, fancy taking on a new young wife at our age—how exhausting! Boy, too, who is cut out to be a widower, I do pity him."

"Pity him, indeed! All he had to do was to leave little girls alone."

"You're so implacable, Sadie. It's a heavy price to pay for a bit of cuddling. I wish you could see the poor chap . . . !"

"Whatever does he do with himself all the time?"

"He's embroidering a counterpane," said Davey. "It's his wedding present for Polly. He calls it a bedspread."

"Oh, really!" Aunt Sadie shuddered. "He is the most dreadful man! Better not tell Matthew. In fact, I wouldn't tell him you've been over at all. He nearly has a fit every time he thinks of Boy now, and I don't blame him. Bedspread, indeed!"

Chapter 15

SOON AFTER THIS, Polly announced to Aunt Sadie that she would like to go to London the following day as she had an appointment there with Boy. We were sitting alone with Aunt Sadie in her little room. Although it was the first time that Polly had mentioned her uncle's name to anybody at Alconleigh, except me, she brought it out not only without a tremor of self-consciousness but as though she spoke of him all and every day. It was an admirable performance. There was a pause. Aunt Sadie was the one who blushed and found it difficult to control her voice and when at last she replied it did not sound natural at all, but hard and anxious.

"Would you care to tell me what your plans are, Polly?"

"Please—to catch the 9:30, if it's convenient."

"No, I don't mean your plans for tomorrow, but for your life."

"You see, that's what I must talk about, with Boy. Last time I saw him we made no plans, we simply became engaged to be married."

"And this marriage, Polly dear—your mind is made up?"

"Yes, quite. So I don't see any point in all this waiting. As we are going to be married whatever happens, what can it matter when? In fact, there is every reason why it should be very soon now. It's out of the question for me to go and live with my mother again, and I

can't foist myself on you indefinitely. You've been much too kind as
it is."

"Oh, my darling child, don't give that a thought. It never matters
having people here, so long as Matthew likes them. Look at Davey
and Fanny, they're in no hurry to go. They know quite well we love
having them."

"Oh, yes, I know, but they are family."

"So are you, almost, and quite as welcome as if you were. I have
got to go to London in a few weeks, as you know, for Linda's baby,
but that needn't make any difference to you, and you must stay on
for as long as ever you like. There'll be Fanny, and when Fanny
goes there are the children—they worship you, you are their hero-
ine, it's wonderful for them having you here. So don't think about
that again. Don't, for heaven's sake, rush into marriage because you
think you have nowhere to live, because for one thing it's not the
case at all, since you can live here, and, anyhow, it could never be a
sufficient reason for taking such a grave step."

"I'm not rushing," said Polly. "It's the only marriage I could ever
have made, and if it had continued to be impossible I should have
lived and died a spinster."

"Oh, no, you wouldn't," said Aunt Sadie. "You've no idea how
long life goes on and how many, many changes it brings. Young
people seem to imagine that it's over in a flash, that they do this
thing, or that thing, and then die, but I can assure you they are
quite wrong. I suppose it's no good saying this to you, Polly, as I can
see your mind is made up, but since you have the whole of your life
before you as a married woman, why not make the most of being a
girl? You'll never be one again. You're only twenty. Why be in such
a hurry to change?"

"I hate being a girl. I've hated it ever since I grew up," said Polly.
"And besides, do you really think a lifetime is too long for perfect
happiness? I don't. . . ."

Aunt Sadie gave a profound sigh.

"I wonder why it is that all girls suppose the married state to be one of perfect happiness? Is it just clever old Dame Nature's way of hurrying them into the trap?"

"Dear Lady Alconleigh, don't be so cynical."

"No, no, you are quite right, I mustn't be. You've settled upon your future, and nothing anybody can say will stop you, I'm sure, but I must tell you that I think you are making a terrible mistake. There, I won't say another word about it. I'll order the car for the 9:30, and will you be catching the 4:45 back or the 6:10?"

"4:45 please. I told Boy to meet me at the Ritz at one. I sent him a postcard yesterday."

And by a miracle the said postcard had lain about all day on the hall table without either Jassy or Victoria spotting it. Hunting had begun again, and although they were only allowed out three times a fortnight the sheer physical exhaustion which it induced did a great deal towards keeping their high spirits within bounds. As for Uncle Matthew, who went out four days a week, he hardly opened an eye after tea time, but nodded away, standing up in his business room, with the gramophone blaring his favourite tunes. Every few minutes he gave a great jump and rushed to change the needle and the disc.

That evening, before dinner, Boy rang up. We were all in the business room listening to *Lakmè* on the gramophone, new records which had just arrived from the Army and Navy Stores. My uncle ground his teeth when the temple bells were interrupted by a more penetrating peal, and gnashed them with anger when he heard Boy's voice asking for Polly, but he handed her the receiver and pushed up a chair for her with the old-fashioned courtesy which he used towards those he liked. He never treated Polly as if she were a very young person, and I believe he was really rather in awe of her.

Polly said, "Yes? Oh? Very well. Goodbye," and hung up the receiver. Even this ordeal had done nothing to shake her serenity.

She told us that Boy had changed the rendezvous, saying he thought it was pointless to go all the way to London, and suggesting the Mitre in Oxford as a more convenient meeting place.

"So perhaps we could go in together, Fanny darling."

I was going, anyhow, to visit my house.

"Ashamed of himself," said Davey, when Polly had gone upstairs. "Doesn't want to be seen. People are beginning to talk. You know how Sonia can never keep a secret, and once the Kensington Palace set gets hold of something it is all round London in a jiffy."

"Oh, dear," said Aunt Sadie. "But if they are seen at the Mitre it will look far worse. I feel rather worried. I only promised Sonia they shouldn't meet here, but ought I to tell her? What do you think?"

"Shall I go over to Silkin and shoot the sewer?" said Uncle Matthew, half-asleep.

"Oh, no, darling, please don't. What do you think, Davey?"

"Don't you worry about the old she-wolf. Good Lord, who cares a brass button for her?"

If Uncle Matthew had not hated Boy so much, he would have been quite as eager as his daughters were to aid and abet Polly in any enterprise that would fly in the face of Lady Montdore.

Davey said, "I wouldn't give it a thought. It so happens that Polly has been perfectly open and above board about the whole thing—but suppose she hadn't told you? She's always going in to Oxford with Fanny, isn't she? I should turn the blind eye."

So in the morning Polly and I motored to Oxford together, and I lunched, as I often did, with Alfred at the George. (If I never mention Alfred in this story, it is because he is so totally uninterested in other human beings and their lives that I think he was hardly aware of what was going on. He certainly did not enter into it with fascination like the rest of us. I suppose that I and his children and, perhaps, an occasional clever pupil seem real to him, but otherwise he lives in a world of shadows and abstract thought.)

After luncheon I spent a freezing, exhausting and discouraging hour in my little house, which seemed hopelessly haunted by builders. I noted, with something like despair, that they had now made one of the rooms cosy, a regular home from home, with blazing fire, stewing tea and film stars on the walls. As far as I could see, they never left it at all to ply their trade and, indeed, I could hardly blame them for that, so terrible were the damp and cold in the rest of the house. After a detailed inspection with the foreman, which merely revealed more exposed pipes and fewer floor boards than last time I had been there, I went to the window of what was supposed to be my drawing room, to fortify myself with the view of Christ Church, so beautiful against the black clouds. One day, I thought (it was an act of faith), I would sit by that very window, open wide, and there would be green trees and a blue sky behind the college. I gazed on, through glass which was almost opaque with dirt and whitewash, forcing myself to imagine that summer scene, when, battling their way down the street, the East wind in their faces, Polly and the Lecturer appeared to view. It was not a happy picture, but that may have been the fault of the climate. No aimless dalliance hand in hand beneath warm skies for poor English lovers who, if circumstances drive them to making love out of doors, are obliged to choose between the sharp brisk walk and the stupefying stuffiness of the cinema. They stumped on out of my sight, hands in pockets, heads bowed, plunged, one would have said, in gloom.

Before going home, I paid a visit to Woolworth, having been enjoined by Jassy to get her a goldfish bowl for her frog spawn. She had broken hers the day before and had only got the precious jelly to the spare-room bath just in time, she said, to save it. Alfred and I were obliged to use the nursery bathroom until Jassy got a new bowl. "So you see how it's to your own advantage, Fanny, not to forget."

Once inside Woolworth I found other things that I needed, as one always does, and presently I ran into Polly and Boy. He was holding a mouse trap, but I think it was really shelter from the wind that they sought.

"Home soon?" said Polly.

"Now, d'you think?" I was dead tired.

"Do let's."

So we all three went to the Clarendon Yard where our respective motor cars were waiting. The Lecturer still had a terrible cold, which made him most unappetizing, I thought, and he seemed very grumpy. When he took my hand to say good-bye he gave it no extra squeeze, nor did he stroke and tickle our legs when tucking us up in the rug, which he would certainly have done had he been in a normal state, and when we drove off he just walked gloomily away with no backward glance, jaunty wave or boyish shake of the curls. He was evidently at a low ebb.

Polly leaned forward, wound up the window between us and the chauffeur and said, "Well, everything's settled, thank goodness. A month from to-day if I can get my parents' consent. I shall still be under age, you see. So the next thing is a tussle with Mummy. I'll go over to Hampton tomorrow if she's there and point out that I shall be of age in May, after which she won't be able to stop me, so hadn't she better swallow the pill and have done with it. They won't be wanting to have birthday celebrations for me now, since, in any case, Daddy is cutting me off without a shilling."

"Do you think he really will?"

"As if I cared! The only thing I mind about is Hampton, and he can't leave me that even if he wants to. Then I shall say, 'Do you intend to put a good face on it and let me be married in the chapel (which Boy terribly wants for some reason, and I would rather like it, I must say) or must we sneak off and be done in London?' Poor Mummy—now I'm out of her clutches I feel awfully sorry for her, in a way. I think the sooner it's over the better for everybody."

Boy, it was clear, was still leaving all the dirty work to Polly. Perhaps his cold was sapping his will power, or perhaps the mere thought of a new young wife at his age was exhausting him already.

So Polly rang up her mother and asked if she could lunch at Hampton the following day and have a talk. I thought it would have been more sensible to have had the talk without the additional strain imposed by a meal, but Polly seemed unable to envisage a country house call which did not centre round food. Perhaps she was right, since Lady Montdore was very greedy and therefore more agreeable during and after meals than at other times. In any case, this is what she suggested; she also told her mother to send a motor as she did not like to ask the Alconleighs for one two days running. Lady Montdore said very well, but that she must bring me, Lord Montdore was still in London and I suppose she felt she could not bear to see Polly alone. Anyhow, she was one of those people who always avoid a tête-à-tête, if possible, even with their intimates. Polly said to me that she herself had just been going to ask if I could come too.

"I want a witness," she added. "If she says yes in front of you she won't be able to wriggle out of it again later."

Poor Lady Montdore, like Boy, was looking very much down. Not only old and ill (also like Boy, she was still afflicted with Lady Patricia's funeral cold which seemed to have been a specially viru-lent germ), but positively dirty. The fact that she had never, at the best of times, been very well groomed, had formerly been off-set by her flourish and swagger, radiant health, enjoyment of life, and the inward assurance of superiority bestowed upon her by "all this." These supports had been cut away by her cold as well as by the simultaneous defection of Polly, which must have taken much of the significance out of "all this" and of Boy, her constant compan-ion, the last lover, surely, that she would ever have. Life, in fact, had become sad and meaningless.

We began luncheon in silence. Polly turned her food over with a fork. Lady Montdore refused the first dish, while I munched away rather self-consciously alone, enjoying the change of cooking. Aunt Sadie's food, at that time, was very plain. After a glass or two of wine, Lady Montdore cheered up a bit and began to chat. She told us that the dear Grand Duchess had sent her such a puddy postcard from Cap d'Antibes where she was staying with other members of the Imperial family. She remarked that the Government really ought to make more effort to attract such important visitors to England.

"I was saying so only the other day to Ramsay," she complained. "And he quite agreed with me but, of course, one knows nothing will be done; it never is in this hopeless country. So annoying. All the Rajahs are at Survretta House again. . . . The King of Greece has gone to Nice. . . . The King of Sweden has gone to Cannes and the young Italians are doing winter sports. Perfectly ridiculous not to get them all here."

"Whatever for," said Polly, "when there's no snow?"

"Plenty in Scotland. Or teach them to hunt. They'd love it. They only want encouraging a little."

"No sun," I said.

"Never mind. Make it the fashion to do without sun, and they'll all come here. They came for my ball and Queen Alexandra's funeral—they love a binge, poor dears. The Government really ought to pay one to give a ball every year. It would restore confidence and bring important people to London."

"I can't see what good all these old royalties do when they are here," said Polly.

"Oh, yes, they do, they attract Americans, and so on," said Lady Montdore, vaguely. "Always good to have influential people around, you know. Good for a private family and also good for a country. I've always gone in for them myself and I can tell you it's a very great mistake not to. Look at poor dear Sadie, I've never heard of anybody important going to Alconleigh."

"Well," said Polly, "and what harm has it done her?"

"Harm! You can see the harm all round. First of all, the girls' husbands." On this point Lady Montdore did not lean, suddenly remembering, no doubt, her own situation in respect of daughters' husbands, but continued, "Poor Matthew has never got anything, has he? I don't only mean jobs, but not even a V.C. in the war and, goodness knows, he was brave enough. He may not be quite cut out to be a Governor, I grant you that, especially not where there are black people, but you don't tell me there's nothing he could have got, if Sadie had been a little cleverer about it. Something at Court, for instance. It would have calmed him down."

The idea of Uncle Matthew at Court made me choke into my pancake, but Lady Montdore took no notice and went on.

"And now I'm afraid it will be the same story with the boys. I'm told they were sent to the very worst house at Eton because Sadie had nobody to advise her or help her at all when the time came for them to go there. One must be able to pull strings in life. Everything depends on that in this world, I'm afraid. It's the only way to be successful. Luckily for me, I like important people best, and I get on with them like a house on fire, but even if they bored me I should have thought it my duty to cultivate them, for Montdore's sake."

When we had finished our meal we installed ourselves in the Long Gallery. The butler brought in a coffee tray which Lady Montdore told him to leave. She always had several cups of strong black coffee. As soon as he had gone she turned to Polly and said sharply, "So what is it you want to say to me?"

I made a half-hearted attempt to go, but they both insisted on me staying. I knew they would.

"I want to be married in a month from now," said Polly. "And to do that I must have your consent as I'm not of age until May. It seems to me that as it is only a question of nine weeks, when I shall marry anyhow, you might as well agree and get it over, don't you think?"

"I must say that's very puddy—your poor aunt—when the breath has hardly left her body."

"It doesn't make the slightest difference to Aunt Patricia whether she has been dead three months or three years, so let's leave her out of it. The facts are what they are. I can't live at Alconleigh much longer. I can't live here with you. Hadn't I better start my new life as soon as possible?"

"Do you quite realize, Polly, that the day you marry Boy Dougdale your father is going to alter his will?"

"Yes, yes, yes," said Polly impatiently. "The times you've told me!"

"I've only told you once before."

"I've had a letter about it. Boy has had a letter about it. We know."

"I wonder whether you also know that Boy Dougdale is a very poor man? They lived, really, on Patricia's allowance, which, of course, in the ordinary way your father would have continued during Boy's lifetime. That will also stop if he marries you."

"Yes. It was all in the letters."

"And don't count on your father changing his mind, because I've no intention of allowing him to."

"I'm quite sure you haven't."

"You think it doesn't matter being poor, but I wonder if you realize what it is like."

"The one who doesn't realize," said Polly, "is you."

"Not from experience, I'm glad to say, but from observation I do. One's only got to look at the hopeless, dreary expression on the faces of poor people to see what it must be."

"I don't agree at all. But anyhow we shan't be poor like poor people. Boy has £800 a year, besides what he makes from his books."

"The parson here and his wife have £800 a year," said Lady Montdore. "And look at their faces . . . !"

"They were born with those. I did better, thanks to you. In any case, Mummy, it's no good going on and on arguing about it, because everything is as much settled as if we were married already, so it's just pure waste of time."

"Then why have you come? What do you want me to do?"

"First, I want to have the wedding next month, for which I need your consent and then I also want to know what you and Daddy prefer about the actual marriage ceremony itself. Shall we be married here in the chapel or shall I go off without you to London for it? We naturally don't want anybody to be there except Fanny and Lady Alconleigh, and you, if you'd care to come. I must say, I would love to be given away by Daddy. . . ."

Lady Montdore thought for awhile and finally said, "I think it is quite intolerable of you to put us in this position and I shall have to talk it over with Montdore, but frankly I think that if you intend to go through with this indecent marriage at all costs, it will make the least talk if we have it here, and before your birthday. Then I shan't have to explain why there are to be no coming-of-age celebrations. The tenants have begun asking about that already. So I think you may take it that you can have the marriage here, and next month, after which, you incestuous little trollop, I never want to set eyes on either you or your uncle again, as long as I live. And please don't expect a wedding present from me."

Tears of self-pity were pouring down her cheeks. Perhaps she was thinking of the magnificent parure in its glass case against which, had things been otherwise, so many envious noses would have been pressed during the wedding reception at Montdore House. "From the Bride's Parents." Her dream of Polly's wedding, long and dearly cherished, had ended in a sad awakening indeed.

"Don't cry, Mummy, I'm so very, very happy."

"Well, I'm not," said Lady Montdore, and rushed furiously from the room.

Chapter 16

E XACTLY ONE MONTH later Davey, Aunt Sadie and I drove over to Hampton together for the wedding, our ears full of the lamentations of Jassy and Victoria, who had not been invited.

"Polly is a horrible Counter Hon and we hate her," they said. "After we made our fingers bleed over that rope ladder, not to speak of all the things we would have done for her, smuggling the Lecturer up to the Hons' cupboard—sharing our food with him—no risk we wouldn't have taken to give them a few brief moments of happiness together, only they were too cold-blooded to want it, and she doesn't even ask us to the wedding. Do admit, Fanny."

"I don't blame her for a single minute," I said. "A wedding is a very serious thing. Naturally she doesn't want gusts of giggles the whole way through it."

"And did we gust at yours?"

"I expect so, only it was a bigger church, and more people, and I didn't hear you."

Uncle Matthew, on the other hand, was asked and said that nothing would induce him to accept.

"Wouldn't be able to keep my hands off the sewer," he said. "Boy!" he went on, scornfully. "There's one thing, you'll hear his real name at last. Just note it down for me, please. I've always wanted to know what it is, to put in a drawer."

It was a favourite superstition of Uncle Matthew's that if you wrote somebody's name on a piece of paper and put it in a drawer, that person would die within the year. The drawers at Alconleigh were full of little slips bearing the names of those whom my uncle wanted out of the way, private hates of his and various public figures, such as Bernard Shaw, de Valera, Gandhi, Lloyd George and the Kaiser, while every single drawer in the whole house contained the name Labby, Linda's old dog. The spell hardly ever seemed to work, even Labby having lived far beyond the age usual in Labradors, but he went hopefully on, and if one of the characters did happen to be carried off in the course of nature he would look pleased, but guilty, for a day or two.

"I suppose we must all have heard his name when he married Patricia," Aunt Sadie said, looking at Davey. "But I can't remember it, can you? Such a thousand, thousand years ago. Poor Patricia, what can she be thinking now?"

"Was she married in the chapel at Hampton, too?" I said.

"No, in London, and I'm trying to remember where. Lord Montdore and Sonia were married in the Abbey, of course. I well remember that because Emily was a bridesmaid and I was so furiously jealous, and my Nanny took me, but outside, because Mamma thought we would see more like that than if we were stuck away behind a tomb. It was like a royal wedding, almost. Of course I was out by the time Patricia married. St. Margaret's, Westminster, I think—yes, I'm nearly sure it was. I know we all thought she was awfully old for a white wedding, thirty, or something terrible."

"But she was beautiful," said Davey.

"Very much like Polly, of course, but she never had that something extra, whatever it is, that makes Polly such a radiant beauty. I only wish I knew why these lovely women have both thrown themselves away on that old Lecturer—so unnatural."

"Poor Boy," said Davey, with a deeply sympathetic sigh.

Davey, who had been in Kent with Aunt Emily since finishing his cure, had come back to Alconleigh in order to be best man. He had accepted, so he said, for poor Patricia's sake, but really I think because he longed to go to the wedding. He also very much enjoyed the excuse it gave him to bustle about between Silkin and Hampton and see for himself all that was going on in those two stricken homes.

Polly had gone back to Hampton. She had taken no steps whatever towards getting a trousseau and, as the engagement and wedding were to be announced simultaneously in the *Times*, "took place very quietly, owing to deep mourning, at Hampton Park" (all these little details arranged by Davey), she had no letters to write, no presents to unpack and none of the business that usually precedes a wedding. Lord Montdore had insisted that she should have an interview with his lawyer, who came all the way from London to explain to her formally that everything hitherto set aside in her father's will, for her and her children, that is to say, Montdore House, Craigside Castle and their contents, the property in Northumberland, with its coal mines, the valuable and extensive house property in London, one or two docks and about two million pounds sterling would now all go to her father's only male heir, Cedric Hampton. In the ordinary course of events he would merely have inherited Hampton itself and Lord Montdore's titles, but as the result of this new will, Cedric Hampton was destined to be one of the five or six richest men in England.

"And how is Lord Montdore taking it?" Aunt Sadie asked Davey when he brought back this news from Hampton, via a visit to Boy at Silkin.

"Quite impossible to say. Sonia is wretched, Polly is nervous, but Montdore is just as usual, you couldn't guess that anything out of the ordinary was happening to him."

"I always knew he was an old stick. Had you realized he was so rich, Davey?"

"Oh, yes, one of the very richest."

"Funny when you think how stingy Sonia is, in little ways. How long d'you imagine he'll keep it up, cutting off Polly, I mean?"

"As long as Sonia is alive. I bet you she won't forgive, and, as you know, he is entirely under her thumb."

"Yes. So what does Boy say to living with a wife, on £800 a year?"

"Doesn't like it. He talks of letting Silkin and going to live somewhere cheap, abroad. I told him he'll have to write more books. He doesn't do so badly with them, you know, but he is very low, poor old fellow, very."

"I expect it will do him good to get away," I said.

"Well, yes," said Davey expressively. "But . . ."

"I do wonder what Cedric Hampton is like."

"So do we all. Boy was talking about it just now. It seems they don't really know where he is, even. The father was a bad lot. He went to Nova Scotia, fell ill there and married his nurse, an elderly Canadian woman, who had this one child, but he (the father) is dead and nothing more is known except the bare fact that there is this boy. Montdore gives him some small allowance, paid into a Canadian bank every year. Don't you think it's very odd he hasn't taken more interest in him, considering he will have his name, and is the only hope of this ancient family being carried on?"

"Probably he hated the father."

"I don't believe he ever knew him. They are quite a different generation—second cousins, once removed—something like that. No, I put it down to Sonia. I expect she couldn't bear the idea of Hampton going away from Polly, and so pretended to herself that this Cedric did not really exist. You know what a one she is for shutting her eyes to things she doesn't like. I should imagine she'll be obliged to face up to him now, Montdore is sure to want to see him, under these new circumstances."

"Sad, isn't it, the idea of some great lumping colonial at Hampton!"

"Simply tragic!" said Davey. "Poor Montdores, I do feel for them."

Somehow, the material side of the business had never been fully
born in upon me until Davey went into these facts and figures, but
now I realized that "all this" was indeed something tremendous, to
be so carelessly thrown into the lap of a total stranger.

When we arrived at Hampton, Aunt Sadie and I were shown
straight into the chapel, where we sat alone. Davey went off to find
Boy. The chapel was a Victorian building among the servants' quar-
ters. It had been constructed by the "old lord," and contained his
marble effigy, in Garter robes, with that of Alice, his wife. There
was some bright stained glass, a family pew designed like a box at
the opera, all red plush with curtains, and a very handsome organ.
Davey had engaged a first-class organist from Oxford, who now
regaled us with Bach preludes. None of the interested parties
seemed to have bothered to take a hand in any of the arrangements,
Davey had chosen all the music, and the gardener had evidently
been left to himself with the flowers, which were quite overwhelm-
ing in their magnificence—the exaggerated hot-house flowers
beloved of all gardeners and, it must be said, of Lady Montdore too,
arranged with typical florist's taste. I began to feel dreadfully sad.
The Bach and the flowers induced melancholy; besides, look at it
as you would, this marriage was a depressing business.

Boy and Davey came up the aisle, and Boy shook hands with us.
He had evidently got rid of his cold, at last, and was looking quite
well; his hair, I noticed, had received the attention of a damp comb
to induce little waves and a curl or two, and his figure, not bad at
all, especially from behind, was set off by his wedding clothes. He
wore a white carnation, and Davey a red one. But though he was in
the costume of a bridegroom, he had not the spirit to add this new
part to his repertory and his whole attitude was more appropriate to
a chief mourner. Davey even had to show him where to stand, by
the altar steps. I never saw a man look so hopeless.

The clergyman took up his position, a very disapproving expression on his face. Presently a movement at our left indicated that

Lady Montdore had come into the family pew, which had its own entrance. It was impossible to stare, but I could not resist a glance and saw that she looked as if she were going to be sick. Boy also glanced, after which his back view became eloquent of a desire to slink in beside her and have a good, long gossip. It was the first time he had seen her since they had read the Infanta's letter together.

The organist from Oxford stopped playing Bach, which he had been doing with less and less interest during the last few minutes, and paused. Looking around, I saw that Lord Montdore was standing at the entrance to the chapel. He was impassive, well preserved, a cardboard Earl, and might have been about to lead his daughter up the aisle of Westminster Abbey to marry the King of England for all that could be read into his look.

"Oh Perfect Love, all Human Thought Transcending" rang out, sung by an invisible choir in the gallery. And then, up the aisle, one large white hand on her father's arm, dispelling the gloomy embarrassment which hung like a fog in the chapel, came Polly, calm, confident and noble, radiating happiness. Somehow she had got herself a wedding dress (Did I recognize a ball dress of last season? No matter.) and was in a cloud of white tulle, and lilies of the valley, and joy. Most brides have difficulty with their expression as they go to the altar, looking affected, or soulful, or, worst of all, too eager, but Polly simply floated along on waves of bliss, creating one of the most beautiful moments I have ever experienced.

There was a dry, choking sound on our left, the door of the family pew was slammed, Lady Montdore had gone.

The clergyman began to intone the wedding service. "For-as-much," and so on, "Who giveth this woman to be married to this man?" Lord Montdore bowed, took Polly's bouquet from her and went into the nearest pew.

"Please say after me, 'I, Harvey, take thee, Leopoldina . . .'" A look from Aunt Sadie.

It was soon over. One more hymn, and I was left alone while they all went behind a screen to sign the register. Then the burst of Mendelssohn and Polly in her cloud of joy floated out again as she had come in, only on the arm of a different well-preserved old man.

While Polly and Boy changed into their going-away things, we waited in the Long Gallery to say good-bye and see them off. They were motoring to the Lord Warden at Dover for the night, and going abroad the following day. I half-expected that Polly would send for me to go upstairs and chat, but she did not, so I stayed with the others. I think she was so happy that she hardly noticed if people were with her or she was alone. Perhaps she really preferred the latter. Lady Montdore put in no further appearance. Lord Montdore talked to Davey, congratulating him upon an anthology he had recently published, called *In Sickness and in Health*. I heard him say that, to his mind, there was not quite enough Browning, but that apart from that it would all have been his own choice.

"But Browning was so healthy," objected Davey. The stress throughout the book was upon sickness.

A footman handed round glasses of champagne. Aunt Sadie and I settled down, as one always did, somehow, at Hampton, to a prolonged scrutiny of *Tatler*, *Sketch* and *Bystander*, and Polly took so long that I even got on to *Country Life* before she appeared. Aunt Sadie also loved these papers dearly, though it never would have occurred to her to buy them for herself.

Through my happy haze of Baronets' wives, their children, their dogs, their tweeds and their homes, or just their huge faces, wave of hair on the forehead held by a diamond clip, I was conscious that the atmosphere in the Long Gallery, like that in the chapel, was one of embarrassment and gloom.

When Boy reappeared, I saw him give a puzzled glance at the mutilated fire screen, and then, realizing what had happened to it, he turned his back on the room and stood gazing out of the window. Nobody spoke to him. Lord Montdore and Davey sipped champagne, having exhausted the topic of the anthology, in silence.

At last Polly came in, wearing her last year's mink coat and a tiny brown hat. Though the cloud of tulle had gone, the cloud of joy still enveloped her. She was perfectly unselfconscious, hugged her father, kissed us all, including Davey, took Boy by the arm and led him to the front door. We followed. The servants, looking sad, and the elder ones sniffing were gathered in the hall. She said good-bye to them, had some rice thrown over her, rather half-heartedly, by the youngest housemaid, got into the big Daimler, followed, very half-heartedly, by Boy, and was driven away.

We said good-bye politely to Lord Montdore and followed suit. As we went up the drive I looked back. The footmen had already shut the front door, and it seemed to me that beautiful Hampton, between the pale spring green of its lawns and the pale spring blue of the sky, lay deserted, empty and sad. Youth had gone from it and henceforward it was to be the home of two lonely old people.

ABOUT A MILE from Alconleigh the children met us and crammed into the motor car.

"So come on, tell what it was?"

"What was what?"

"The Lecturer's real name, of course. We've come all this way to hear."

"Harvey."

"Like Hervey the Handsome," said Jassy, "who married the beautiful Molly Lepel."

"If you call a dog Hervey I shall love him," said Victoria.

"No," said Davey, "AR. I specially looked on the register."

"Yes, I see," said Jassy. "More like Boy Nichols?"

PART TWO

Chapter 1

My real life as a married woman, that is to say, life with my husband in our own house, now began. One day I went to Oxford and a miracle seemed to have taken place. There was paper on all the walls of my house, the very paper I had chosen, too, and looking even prettier than I had hoped it would, the smell of cheap cigarettes, cement, stewed tea and dry rot had gone, and in its place there was a heavenly smell of new paint and cleanliness, the floor boards were all smooth and solid, and the windows so clean that they seemed to be glassless. The day was perfect. Spring had come and my home was ready; I felt too happy for words. To set the seal upon this happiness, the wife of a Professor had called, her card and her husband's two cards had carefully been put by the workmen on a chimney piece: Professor and Mrs. Cozens, 209 Banbury Road. Now, at last I was a proper, grown-up married lady, on whom people called. It was very thrilling.

I had at this time a romantic but very definite picture in my mind of what life was going to be like in Oxford. I imagined a sort of Little Gidding, a community of delightful, busy, cultivated people, bound together by shared intellectual tastes and by their single-minded exertions on behalf of the youth entrusted to their care. I supposed that the other wives of dons would be beautiful, quiet women, versed in all the womanly arts but that of coqueterie, a little worn with the effort of making a perfection of their homes at the same time as rearing large families of clever little children, and keeping up with things like Kafka, but never too tired or too busy for long, serious discussions on subjects of importance, whether intellectual or practical. I saw myself, in the day-time, running happily in and out of the houses of these charming creatures, old houses, with some important piece of architecture framed in the windows, as Christ Church was in mine, passionately sharing every detail of their lives, while the evenings would be spent listening to grave and scholarly talk between our husbands. In short, I saw them as a tribe of heavenly new relations, more mature, more intellectual Radletts. This happy intimacy seemed to be heralded by the cards of Professor and Mrs. Cozens. For one moment the fact that they lived in the Banbury Road struck a note of disillusionment, but then it occurred to me that of course the clever Cozens must have found some little old house in that unpromising neighbourhood, some nobleman's folly, sole reminder of long vanished pleasure grounds, and decided to put up with the Banbury Road for the sake of its doorways and cornices, the rococo detail of its ceilings and the excellent proportions of its rooms.

I never shall forget that happy, happy day. The house at last was mine, the workmen had gone, the Cozens had come, the daffodils were out in the garden, and a blackbird was singing fit to burst its lungs. Alfred looked in and seemed to find my sudden rush of high spirits quite irrational. He had always known, he said, that the house would be ready sooner or later, and had not, like me, alternated between faith and black moods of scepticism. As for the Cozens, in spite of the fact that I realized by now that one human being, in Alfred's eyes, was exactly the same as another, I did find his indifference with regard to them and their cards rather damping.

"It's so terrible," I wailed, "because I can't return the call, our cards haven't come yet. Oh, yes, they are promised for next week, but I long to go now, this very minute, don't you see?"

"Next week will do quite well," Alfred said, shortly.

Soon an even more blissful day dawned. I woke up in my own bed in my own bedroom, done up in my own taste and arranged entirely to suit me. True, it was freezing cold and pouring with rain on this occasion, and, since I had as yet no servant, I was obliged to get up very early and cook Alfred's breakfast, but I did not mind. He was my own husband, and the cooking took place in my own kitchen. It all seemed like heaven to me.

And now, I thought, for the happy sisterhood on which I had pinned my hopes. But alas, as so often happens in life, this turned out rather differently from what I had expected. I found myself landed with two sisters indeed, but they were very far removed from the charming companions of my dream. One was Lady Montdore and the other was Norma Cozens. At this time I was not only young, barely twenty, but extremely simple. Hitherto, my human relationships had been with members of my family or with other girls (school-fellows and debutantes) of my own age. They had been perfectly easy and straightforward and I had no idea that anything more complicated could exist. Even love, with me, had followed an exceptionally level path. I supposed, in my simplicity, that when people liked me I ought to like them back as much, and that whatever they expected of me, especially if they were older people, I was morally bound to perform. In the case of these two, I doubt if it ever occurred to me that they were eating up my time and energy in a perfectly shameless way. Before my children were born, I had time on my hands and I was lonely. Oxford is a place where social life, contrary to what I had imagined, is designed exclusively for celibate men; all the good talk, good food and good wine being reserved for those gatherings where there are no women; the whole tradition is in its essence monastic, and, as far as society goes, wives are quite superfluous.

I should never have chosen Norma Cozens to be an intimate

friend, but I suppose that her company must have seemed prefer-
able to hours of my own, while Lady Montdore did at least bring a
breath of air which, though it could not have been described as
fresh, had its origins in the great world outside our cloister, a world
where women count for something.

Mrs. Cozens' horizon also extended beyond Oxford, though in
another direction. Her maiden name was Boreley, and the Boreley
family was well known to me, since her grandfather's huge 1890 Eliz-
abethan house was situated not far from Alconleigh, and they were
the new rich of the neighbourhood. This grandfather, now Lord
Driersley, had made his money in foreign railroads. He had married
into the landed gentry and produced a huge family, all the members
of which, as they grew up and married, he settled on estates within
easy motoring distance of Driersley Manor. They, in their turns, all
became notable breeders, so that the Boreley tentacles had spread
by now over a great part of the West of England and there seemed to
be absolutely no end of Boreley cousins, aunts, uncles, brothers and
sisters and their respective in-laws. There was very little variety about
them; they all had the same cross, white guinea-pig look, thought
alike, and led the same sort of lives, sporting country lives, they seldom went to London. They were respected by their neighbours for
the conformity, to the fashion of the day, of their morals, for their
wealth and for their excellence at all kinds of sport. They did everything that they ought to do in the way of sitting on Benches and
County Councils, walking hound puppies and running Girl Guides,
one was an M.P., another an M.F.H. In short, they were the backbone of England. Uncle Matthew, who encountered them on local
business, loathed them all, and they were collectively in many drawers under the one name, Boreley, I never quite knew why. However,
like Gandhi, Bernard Shaw and Labby the Labrador, they continued to flourish, and no terrible Boreley holocaust ever took place.

MY FIRST EXPERIENCE of Oxford society, as the wife of a junior
don, was a dinner party given in my honour by the Cozens. The

Waynflete Professor of Pastoral Theology was the professor of Alfred's subject, and was, therefore, of importance in our lives and an influence upon Alfred's career. I understood this to be so without Alfred exactly putting it into words. In any case, I was, of course, anxious that my first Oxford appearance should be a success, anxious to look nice, make a good impression, and be a credit to my husband. My mother had given me an evening dress from Mainbocher which seemed specially designed for such an occasion. It had a white pleated chiffon skirt, and black silk jersey top with a high neck and long sleeves, which was tucked into a wide, black, patent-leather belt. Wearing this, and my only jewel, a diamond clip sent by my father, I thought I was not only nicely, but also suitably dressed. My father, incidentally, had turned a deaf ear to Lady Montdore's suggestion that he should buy me a place, declaring himself to be too utterly ruined even to increase my allowance on my marriage. He did, however, send a cheque and this pretty jewel.

The Cozens' house was not a nobleman's folly. It was the very worst kind of Banbury Road house, depressing, with laurels. The front door was opened by a slut. I had never seen a slut before but recognized the genus without difficulty as soon as I set eyes on this one. Inside the hall, Alfred and I and the slut got rather mixed up with a large pram, however we sorted ourselves out and put down our coats, and then she opened a door and shot us, without announcing our names, into the terrible Cozens' drawing room. All this to the accompaniment of shrill barking from four Border Terriers.

I saw at once that my dress would not do. Norma told me afterwards, when pointing out the many fearful gaffes which I was supposed to have made during the course of the evening, that as a bride I would have been expected to wear my wedding dress at our first dinner party. But, even apart from that blunder, a jersey top, however Parisian, was obviously unacceptable for evening wear in high Oxford society The other women present were either in lace or marocain, décolleté to the waist, behind, and with bare arms.

Their dresses were in shades of biscuit, and so were they. It was a cold evening following upon a chilly day, the Cozens' hearth was not laid for a fire, but had a piece of pleated paper in the grate, and yet these naked ladies did not seem to be cold. They were not blue and goosey as I should have been, nor did they shiver. I was soon to learn that in donnish circles the Oxford summer is considered to be horribly hot, and the Oxford winter nice and bracing, but that no account is taken of the between seasons or of the findings of the thermometer; cold is never felt. Apart from there being no fire, the room was terribly cheerless. The hard little sofa, the few and hard little armchairs were upholstered in a cretonne of so dim and dismal a pattern that it was hard to imagine anybody, even a Boreley, actually choosing it, to imagine them going into a shop, and taking a seat, and having cretonnes thrown over a screen one after another, and suddenly saying, all excited, "That's the very thing for me — stop!" The lights were unshaded and held in chromium-plated fittings. There was no carpet on the floor, just a few slippery rugs; the walls were of shiny cream paint, and there were no pictures, objects or flowers to relieve the bareness.

Mrs. Cozens, whose cross, creased Boreley face I recognized from my hunting days, greeted us heartily enough, and the Professor came forward with a shadow of Lord Montdore's manner, an unctuous geniality which may have orginated with the Church, though his version of it was as that of a curate to Lord Montdore's cardinal. There were three other couples to whom I was introduced, all dons and their wives. I was perfectly fascinated to see these people among whom I was henceforward to live. They were ugly and not specially friendly, but no doubt, I supposed, very brilliant.

The food at dinner, served by the slut in a gaunt dining room, was so terrible that I felt deeply sorry for Mrs. Cozens, thinking that something must have gone wrong. I have had so many such meals since then that I do not remember exactly what it was, I guess, however, that it began with tinned soup and ended with dry sardines on dry toast, and that we drank a few drops of white wine. I do remember that the conversation was far from brilliant, a fact which, at the time, I attributed to the horrible stuff we were trying to swallow, but which I now know was more likely to have been due to the presence of females; dons are quite used to bad food but become paralized in mixed company. As soon as the last sardine tail had been got down, Mrs. Cozens rose to her feet, and we went into the drawing room, leaving the men to enjoy the one good item of the whole menu, excellent vintage port. They only reappeared just before it was time to go home.

Over the coffee, sitting round the pleated paper in the fireplace, the other women talked of Lady Montdore and Polly's amazing marriage. It seemed that, while their husbands all knew Lord Montdore slightly, none of them knew Lady Montdore, not even Norma Cozens, though, as a member of an important county family, she had been inside Hampton once or twice to various big functions. They all spoke, however, not only as if they knew her quite well, but as if she had done each of them personally some terrible wrong. Lady Montdore was not popular in the county, and the reason was that she turned up her nose at the local squires and their wives as well as at the local tradesmen and their wares, ruthlessly importing both her guests and her groceries from London.

It is always interesting, and usually irritating, to hear what people have to say about somebody whom they do not know but we do. On this occasion I positively squirmed with interest and irritation. Nobody asked for my opinion, so I sat in silence, listening. The dominant thought of the discussion was that Lady Montdore, wicked as hell, had been envious of Polly, her youth and her beauty, ever since she grew up, had snubbed her and squashed her and kept her out of sight as much as possible, and that, furthermore, as soon as Polly got an admirer, Lady Montdore had somehow managed to send him about his business, finally driving her into the arms of her uncle as the only escape from an unhappy home.

"Now I happen to know for a fact that Polly," (they all called her
Polly, though none of them knew her) "was on the point of getting
engaged to Joyce Fleetwood, only just the other day too, he stayed
at Hampton for Christmas and it was all going like a house on fire.
His own sister told me. Well, Lady Montdore got rid of him in double quick time, you see."

"Yes, and wasn't it just the same with John Coningsby? Polly was
madly in love with him, and no doubt he'd have come up to scratch
in the end, but when Lady Montdore twigged what was going on
she had him out on his ear."

"And in India too it happened several times. Polly only had to
fancy a young man for him to vanish mysteriously." They spoke as if
Lady Montdore were an enchantress in a fairy tale.

"She was jealous, you know, of her being supposed to be such a
beauty (never could see it myself, don't admire that flat fish look)."

"You'd think she'd want to get her off all the quicker."

"You can't tell how jealousy is going to take people."

"But I've always heard that Dougdale was Lady Montdore's own
lover."

"Of course he was, and that's exactly why she never imagined
there could be anything between him and Polly. Serves her jolly
well right, she ought to have let the poor girl marry all those others
when she wanted to."

"What a sly little thing though, under the very noses of her
mother and her aunt like that."

"I don't expect there's much to choose between them. The one
I'm sorry for is poor old Lord Montdore, he's such a wonderful old
man and she's led him the most awful dance, you know, for years,
ever since they married. Daddy says she utterly ruined his career,
and if it hadn't been for her he could have been Prime Minister or
anything."

"Well, but he was Viceroy," I said, putting in my oar at last. I felt
thoroughly on Lady Montdore's side against these hideous people.

"Yes, he was, and everybody knows she nearly lost us India. I believe the harm she did there was something terrible. Daddy has a great friend, an Indian judge, you should hear his stories! Her rudeness . . . !"

"Of course lots of people say Polly isn't Lord Montdore's child at all. King Edward, I've heard."

"It doesn't seem to make much difference now, whose child she is, because he's cut her out of his will and some American gets it all."

"And the whole thing is that old woman's fault, the old tart. That's all she is when you come to think of it. Needn't give herself such airs. . . ."

I suddenly became very furious. I was well aware of Lady Montdore's faults, I knew that she was deplorable in many ways, but it seemed to me wrong of people who had never even met her and knew nothing at first hand, to speak of her like this. I had a feeling that they did so out of an obscure jealousy, and that she only had to take any of these women up and bestow a flicker of her charm upon them for them to become her grovelling toadies.

"I hear she made a ghastly scene at the wedding," said the don's wife whose Daddy knew an Indian judge. "Screamed and yelled and had hysterics."

"She didn't," I said.

"Why, how do you know?"

"Because I was there."

They looked at me curiously and rather angrily, as though I ought to have spoken up sooner, and changed the subject to the eternal ones of children's illnesses and servants' misdeeds.

I hoped that at my next dinner party I should be meeting the noble, thoughtful, intellectual women of my Oxford dream, if, indeed, they existed.

After this Norma Cozens took a fancy to me for some reason, and used to drop into my house on her way to or from the huge walks she went for every day with the Border Terriers. I think she was the crossest person I ever met, nothing was ever right for her, and her conversation, which consisted of lectures, advice and criticism, was punctuated with furious sighs, but she was not a bad old thing, good-natured at heart, and often did me little kindnesses. I came to like her in the end the best of all the dons' wives. She was at least natural and unpretentious and brought her children up in an ordinary way. Those I found impossible to get on with were the arty-crafty ones with modern ideas, and ghastly children who had never been thwarted or cleaned up by the hand of a nanny. Norma was a type with which I was more familiar, one of those women in brown with whom the English countryside teems, who possess no talents, and especially not those it is nice for a woman to have, such as for housekeeping and dress, and no sense of humour, but who, nevertheless, are not exactly stupid and not at all nasty. Anyhow, there she was, self-constituted part of my new life, and accepted by me as such without question.

Chapter 2

Amore difficult and exacting relationship was the one which now developed between me and Lady Montdore. She haunted my house, coming at much odder and more inconvenient times than Norma (who was very conventional in such ways), and proceeded to turn me into a lady in waiting. It was quite easy. Nobody has ever sapped my will power as she did, and, like Lord Montdore, but unlike Polly, I was completely under her thumb. Even Alfred lifted his eyes for a moment from pastoral theology and saw what was going on. He said he could not understand my attitude, and that it made him impatient.

"You don't really like her, you're always complaining about her, why not say you are out when she comes?"

Why not, indeed? The fact was that I had never got over the physical feeling of terror which Lady Montdore had inspired in me from childhood, and though with my reason I knew now what she was, and did not care for what I knew, though the idol was down from its pedestal, the bullfighter back in his ready-made suit, and she was revealed as nothing more or less than a selfish old woman, still I remained in awe of her. When Alfred told me to pretend to be out when she came I knew that this would be impossible for me.

"Oh no, darling, I don't think I could do that."

He shrugged his shoulders and said no more. He never tried to influence me, and very rarely commented on, or even appeared to notice, my behaviour and the conduct of my life.

Lady Montdore's plan was to descend upon me without warning, either on her way to or from London or on shopping expeditions to Oxford, when she would take me round with her to fetch and carry and check her list. She would engage all my attention for an hour or two, tiring me out, exactly as small children can, with the demands she made of concentration upon her, and then vanish again, leaving me dissatisfied with life. As she was down on her own luck, but would have considered it a weakness to admit it, even to herself, she was obliged to bolster up "all this," to make it seem a perfect compensation for what she had lost, by denigrating the circumstances of other people. It was even a help to her, I suppose, because otherwise I cannot account for her beastliness, to run down my poor little house, so unpretentious, and my dull little life, and she did so with such conviction that, since I am easily discouraged, it often took days before everything seemed all right again.

Days, or a visit from some member of the Radlett family. The Radletts had the exactly opposite effect, and always made me feel wonderful, owing to a habit known in the family as "exclaiming."

"Fanny's shoes . . . ! Where? Lilley and Skinner? I must dash. And the lovely new skirt! Not a new suit, let's see—not lined with silk—Fanny! You are lucky, it is unfair!"

"Oh, dear, why doesn't my hair curl like that? Oh, the bliss of Fanny altogether—her eyelashes! You are lucky, it is unfair!"

These exclamations, which I remember from my very earliest childhood, now also embraced my house and household arrangements.

"The wallpaper! Fanny! Your bed—it can't be true! Oh, look at the darling little bit of Belleek—where did you find it? No! Do let's go there. And a new cushion! Oh, it is unfair, you are lucky to be you."

"I say, Fanny's food! Toast at every meal! Not Yorkshire pudding! Why can't we live with Fanny always—the heaven of it here! Why can't I be you?"

Fortunately for my peace of mind Jassy and Victoria came to see me whenever there was a motor car going to Oxford, which was quite often, and the elder ones always looked in if they were on their way to Alconleigh.

As I got to know Lady Montdore more intimately, I began to realize that her selfishness was monumental. She had no thoughts except in relation to herself, could discuss no subject without cleverly edging it round to something directly pertaining to her. The only thing she ever wanted to know about people was what impression did she make on them, and she would do anything to find this out, sometimes digging traps for the unwary, into which, in my innocence, I was very apt to tumble.

"I suppose your husband is a clever man, at least so Montdore tells me. Of course it's a thousand pities he is so dreadfully poor, I hate to see you living in this horrid little hovel—so unsuitable—and not more important, but Montdore says he has the reputation of being clever."

She had dropped in just as I was having my tea, which consisted of a few rather broken digestive biscuits with a kitchen pot on a tray and without a plate. I was so busy that afternoon, and Mrs. Heathery, my maid of all work, was so busy too, that I had dashed into the kitchen and taken the tray myself, like that. Unfortunately, it never seemed to be chocolate cake and silver tea-pot day when Lady Montdore came, though, such were the vagaries of my housekeeping while I was a raw beginner, that these days did quite often, though quite unaccountably, occur.

"Is that your tea? All right dear, yes, just a cup, please. How weak you have it! No, no, this will do quite well. Yes, as I was saying, Montdore spoke of your husband to-day at luncheon, with the Bishop. They had read something of his and seem to have been quite impressed, so I suppose he really is clever, after all."

"Oh, he is the cleverest man I ever met," I said, happily. I loved to talk about Alfred, it was the next best thing to being with him.

"So of course I suppose he thinks I'm a very stupid person." She looked with distaste at the bits of digestives, and then took one.

"Oh, no, he doesn't," I said, inventing, because Alfred had never put forward any opinion on the subject one way or another.

"I'm sure he must, really. You don't mean to tell me he thinks I'm clever?"

"Yes, very clever. He p'raps doesn't look upon you as an intellectual. . . ."

Crash! I was in the trap.

"Oh, indeed! Not an intellectual!"

I could see at once that she was terribly offended and thrashed about unhappily in my trap trying to extricate myself, to no avail, however. I was in it up to the neck.

"You see, he doesn't believe that women ever are intellectuals, hardly, hardly ever, perhaps one in ten million. . . . Virginia Woolf, perhaps . . ."

"I suppose he thinks I never read. Many people think that, because they see me leading this active life, wearing myself out for others. Perhaps I might prefer to sit in a chair all day and read some book, very likely I would, but I shouldn't think it right, in my position, to do so. I can't only be thinking of myself, you see. I never do read books in the daytime, that's perfectly true, I simply haven't a moment, but your husband doesn't know, and nor do you, what I do at night. I don't sleep well, not well at all, and at night I read volumes."

Old volumes of the *Tatler*, I guessed. She had them all bound up from the beginning, and very fascinating they were.

"You know, Fanny," she went on, "it's all very well for funny little people like you to read books the whole time. You only have yourselves to consider, whereas Montdore and I are public servants, in a way, we have something to live up to, tradition and so on, duties to perform, you know. It's a very different matter. A great deal is expected of us, I think and hope not in vain. It's a hard life, make no mistake about that; hard and tiring, but occasionally we have our reward—when people get a chance to show how they worship us. For instance, when we came back from India and the dear villagers pulled our motor car up the drive. Really touching! Now all you intellectual people never have moments like that. Well," she rose to leave, "one lives and learns. I know now that I am outside the pale, intellectually. Of course, my dear child, we must remember that all those women students probably give your husband a very funny notion of what the female sex is really like. I wonder whether he realizes that it's only the ones who can't hope for anything better that come here. Perhaps he finds them very fascinating—one never sees him in his own home, I notice." She was working herself up into a tremendous temper now. "And if I might offer you a little advice, Fanny, it would be to read fewer books, dear, and make your house slightly more comfortable. That is what a man appreciates, in the long run."

She cast a meaning look at the plateless digestives, and went away without saying good-bye.

I was really upset to have annoyed her so stupidly and tactlessly, and felt certain that she would never come and see me again; funnily enough, instead of being relieved by this thought, I minded.

I had no time to brood over it however, for hardly was she out of the house than Jassy and Victoria bundled in.

"Not digestives! Vict—look, digestives! Isn't Fanny wonderful? You can always count on something heavenly—weeks since I tasted digestives, my favourite food too."

Mrs. Heathery, who adored the children and had heard their shrieks as they came in, brought up some fresh tea and a Fuller's cake, which elicited more exclamations.

"Oh, Mrs. Heathery, you angel on earth, not Fuller's walnut? How can you afford it, Fanny? We haven't had it at home since Fa's last financial crisis. But things are better, you know. We are back to Bromo again now and the good writing paper. When the loo paper gets thicker and the writing paper thinner it's always a bad sign, at home."

"Fa had to come about some harness, so he brought us in to see you, only ten minutes, though. The thing is, we've got a funny story about Sadie for you, so are you listening? Well, Sadie was telling how some people, before their babies are born, gaze at Greuze so that the babies shall look like it, and she said, 'You never know about these things, because when I was a little girl in Suffolk a baby was born in the village with a bear's head. And what do you think? Exactly nine months before a dancing bear had been in that neighbourhood.' So Vict said, 'But I can quite understand that. I always think bears are simply terribly attractive,' and Sadie gave the most tremendous jump I ever saw and said, 'You awful child, that's not what I mean at all.' So are you shrieking, Fanny?"

"We saw your new friend Mrs. Cozens just now and her blissful Borders. You are so lucky to have new friends. It is unfair—we never do. Really, you know, we are the Lady of Shalott with our pathetic lives we lead. Even Davey never comes, now horrible Polly's marriage is over. Oh, by the way, we had a postcard from horrible Polly, but it's no use her bombarding us with these post-cards—we can never, never forgive."

"Where was it from?"

"Seville. That's in Spain."

"Did she sound happy?"

"Do people ever sound unhappy on postcards, Fanny? Isn't it always lovely weather and everything wonderful, on postcards? This one was a picture of a glorious girl called La Macarena, and the funny thing is this La Macarena is the literal image of horrible Polly herself. Do you think Lady Montdore gazed a bit before H. P. was born?"

"You mustn't say horrible Polly to me when I love her so much."

"Well, we'll have to see. We love her in a way, in spite of all, and in a few years, possibly, we might forgive, though I doubt if we can ever forget her deep, base treachery. Has she written to you?"

"Only postcards," I said. "One from Paris and one from St. Jean de Luz."

Polly had never been much of a letter writer.

"I wonder if it's as nice as she thought, being in bed with that old Lecturer."

"Marriage isn't only bed," I said, primly. "There are other things."

"You go and tell that to Sadie. There's Fa's horn, we must dash or he'll never bring us again if we keep him waiting, and we promised we would the very second he blew. Oh, dear, back to the fields of barley and of rye. You are so lucky to live in this sweet little house in a glamorous town. Good-bye Mrs. Heathery—the cake!"

They were still cramming it into their mouths as they went downstairs.

"Come in and have some tea," I said to Uncle Matthew, who was at the wheel of his new big Wolseley. When my uncle had a financial crisis he always bought a new motor car.

"No, thank you, Fanny. Very kind of you, but there's a perfectly good cup of tea waiting for me at home, and you know I never go inside other people's houses if I can possibly avoid it. Good-bye."

He put on his green hat, called a bramble, which he always wore, and drove away.

My next caller was Norma Cozens, who came in for a glass of sherry, but her conversation was so dull that I have not the heart to record it. It was a compound of an abscess between the toes of the mother Border Terrier, the things the laundry does to sheets, how it looked to her as if the slut had been at her store cupboard, so she was planning to replace her by an Austrian at 2/- a week cheaper wages, and how lucky I was to have Mrs. Heathery, but I must look out because new brooms sweep clean and Mrs. Heathery was sure not to be nearly as nice as she seemed.

I WAS VERY much mistaken if I thought that Lady Montdore was now out of my life for good. In less than a week she was back again.

The door of my house was always kept on the latch, like a country-house door, and she never bothered to ring but just stumped upstairs. On this occasion it was five minutes to one and I plainly saw that I would have to share the little bit of salmon I had ordered for myself, as a treat, with her.

"And where is your husband to-day?"

She showed her disapproval of my marriage by always referring to Alfred like this and never by his name. He was still Mr. Thing in her eyes.

"Lunching in college."

"Ah, yes? Just as well, so he won't be obliged to endure my unin-tellectual conversation."

I was afraid it would all start over again, including the working herself up into a temper, but apparently she had decided to treat my unlucky remark as a great joke.

"I told Merlin," she said, "that in Oxford circles I am not thought an intellectual, and I only wish you could have seen his face!"

When Mrs. Heathery offered the fish to Lady Montdore she scooped up the whole thing. No tiresome inhibitions caused her to ask what I would eat, and, in fact, I had some potatoes and salad. She was good enough to say that the quality of the food in my house seemed to be improving.

"Oh, yes, I know what I wanted to ask you," she said. "Who is this Virginia Woolf you mentioned to me? Merlin was talking about her, too, the other day at Maggie Greville's."

"She's a writer," I said. "A novelist, really."

"Yes, I see. And as she's so intellectual, no doubt she writes about nothing but stationmasters."

"Well, no," I said, "she doesn't."

"I must confess that I prefer books about society people, not being myself a highbrow."

"She did write a fascinating book about a society person," I said, "called *Mrs. Dalloway.*"

"Perhaps I'll read it, then. Oh, of course I'd forgotten—I never read, according to you—don't know how. Never mind. In case I have a little time this week, Fanny, you might lend it to me, will you? Excellent cheese—don't tell me you get this in Oxford?"

She was in an unusually good temper that day. I believe the fall of the Spanish throne had cheered her up. She probably foresaw a perfect swarm of Infantas winging its way towards Montdore House, besides, she was greatly enjoying all the details from Madrid. She said that the Duke of Barbarossa (this may not be the name, but it sounded like it) had told her the inside story, in which case he must also have told it to the *Daily Express*, where I had read word for word what she now kindly passed on to me, and several days before. She remembered to ask for *Mrs. Dalloway* before leaving, and went off with the book in her hand, a first edition. I felt sure that I had seen the last of it, but she brought it back the following week, saying that she really must write a book herself, as she knew she could do much better than that.

"Couldn't read it," she said. "I did try, but it is too boring. And I never got to that society person you told me of. Now, have you read the Grand Duchess' *Memoirs*? I won't lend you mine, you must buy them for yourself, Fanny, and that will help the dear Duchess with another guinea. They are wonderful. There is a great deal, nearly a whole chapter, about Montdore and me in India—she stayed with us at Viceroy's House, you know. She has really captured the spirit of the place quite amazingly. She was only there a week, but one couldn't have done it better oneself. She describes a garden party I gave, and visits to the Ranees in their harems, and she tells what a lot I was able to do for those poor women of India, and how they worshipped me. Personally, I find memoirs so very much more interesting than any novel because they are true. I may not be an intellectual, but I do like to read the truth about things. Now in a book like the Grand Duchess' you can see history in the very making, and if you love history as I do (but don't tell your husband I said so, dear, he would never believe it), if you love history, you must be interested to know the inside story, and it's only people like the Grand Duchess who are in a position to tell us that. And this reminds me, Fanny dear, will you put a call through to Downing Street for me, please, and get hold of the P.M. or his secretary? I will speak myself when he is on the line. I'm arranging a little dinner for the Grand Duchess, to give her book a good start. Of course I don't ask you, dear—it wouldn't be intellectual enough—just a few politicians and writers, I thought. Here is the number, Fanny."

I was trying at this time to economize in every direction, having overspent myself on doing up the house, and I had made a rule never to telephone, even to Aunt Emily's house or Alconleigh, if a letter would do as well, so it was most unwillingly that I did as she asked. There was a long wait on the line before I got the Prime Minister himself, after which Lady Montdore spoke for ages, the pip-pip-pips going at least five times—I could hear them—every pip an agony to me. First of all, she fixed a date for her dinner party; this took a long time, with many pauses while he consulted his secretary, and two pip-pip-pips. Then she asked if there were anything new from Madrid.

"Yes," she said. "Badly advised, poor man (pip-pip-pip), I fear. I saw Freddy Barbarossa last night (they are being so brave about it, by the way, quite stoical. Yes, at Claridge's), and he told me . . ." Here a flood of *Daily Express* news and views. "But Montdore and I are very much worried about our own special Infanta—yes, a close friend of ours—oh, Prime Minister, if you could hear anything I should be so more than grateful. Will you, really? You know, there is a whole chapter on Madrid in the Grand Duchess' book. It makes it very topical, rather splendid for her. Yes, a near relation. She describes the view (pip-pip-pip) from the Royal Palace—yes, very bleak—I've been there, wonderful sunsets, though. I know, poor woman. Oh, she hated them at first, she had special opera glasses with black spots for the cruel moments. Have you heard where they are going? Yes, Barbara Barbarossa told me that too, but I wonder they don't come here. You ought to try and persuade them. Yes, I see. Well, we'll talk about all that. Meanwhile, dear

Prime Minister, I won't keep you any longer (pip-pip-pip), but we'll see you on the tenth. So do I. I'll send your secretary a reminder, of course. Good-bye."

She turned to me, beaming, and said, "I have the most wonderful effect on that man, you know. It's quite touching how he dotes on me. I really think I could do anything with him, anything at all."

She never spoke of Polly. At first I supposed that the reason why she liked to see so much of me was that I was associated in her mind with Polly, and that sooner or later she would unburden herself to me, or even try and use me as go-between in a reconciliation. I soon realized, however, that Polly and Boy were dead to her. She had no further use for them, since Boy could never be her lover again, and Polly could never now, it seemed, do her credit in the eyes of the world. She simply dismissed them from her thoughts. Her visits to me were partly the outcome of loneliness and partly due to the fact that I was a convenient halfway house between London and Hampton, and that she could use me as restaurant, cloakroom and telephone booth when in Oxford.

She was horribly lonely, you could see that. She filled Hampton every week end with important people, with smart people, even just with people, but, although so great is the English predilection for country life, she generally managed to get these visits extended from Friday to Tuesday, even so she was left with two empty days in the middle of the week. She went less and less to London. She had always preferred Hampton, where she reigned alone, to London where she faced a certain degree of competition, and life there without Polly to entertain for and without Boy to help her plot the social game, had evidently become meaningless and dull.

Chapter 3

I T WAS NO doubt the dullness of her life which now deflected
her thoughts towards Cedric Hampton, Lord Montdore's heir.
They still knew nothing about him beyond the mere fact of his existence, which had hitherto been regarded as extremely superfluous
since but for him the whole of "all this," including Hampton,
would have gone to Polly, and, although the other things she had
been going to inherit were worth more money, it was Hampton
they all loved so much. I have never made out his exact relationship to Lord Montdore, but I know that when Linda and I used to
"look him up" to see if he was the right age for us to marry, it always
took ages to find him, breathing heavily over the peerage, pointing,
and going back and back.

. . . HAVING HAD ISSUE,
- HENRY, B. 1875, WHO M. DORA, DAU. OF
  STANLEY BOOTER ESQ. OF ANNAPOLIS, NOVA
  SCOTIA, AND D. 1913 LEAVING ISSUE,
- CEDRIC, HEIR PRES., B. 1907.

Just the right age, but what of Nova Scotia? An atlas, hastily consulted, showed it to be horribly marine. "A transatlantic Isle of
Wight," as Linda put it. "No, thanks." Sea breezes, in so far as they
are good for the complexion, were regarded by us as a means and
not an end, for at that time it was our idea to live in capital cities
and go to the opera alight with diamonds—"Who is that lovely
woman?"—and Nova Scotia was clearly not a suitable venue for
such doings. It never seemed to occur to us that Cedric could perhaps have been transplanted from his native heath to Paris, London
or Rome. Colonial, we thought, ignorantly. It ruled him out. I
believe Lady Montdore knew very little more about him than we
did. She had never felt interest or curiosity towards those unsuitable people in Canada. They were one of the unpleasant things of
life and she preferred to ignore them. Now, however, left alone
with an "all this" which would one day, and one day fairly soon, by
the look of Lord Montdore, be Cedric's, she thought and spoke of
him continually, and presently had the idea that it would amuse
her to see him.

Of course no sooner had she conceived this idea than she
wanted him to be there the very next minute, and was infuriated by
the delays that ensued. For Cedric could not be found.

I was kept informed of every stage in the search for him, as Lady
Montdore could now think of nothing else.

"That idiotic woman has changed her address," she told me.
"Montdore's lawyer has had the most terrible time getting in touch
with her at all. Now, fancy moving in Canada. You'd think one
place there would be exactly the same as another, wouldn't you?
Sheer waste of money, you'd think. Well, they've found her at last,
and now it seems that Cedric isn't with her at all, but somewhere in
Europe. Very odd of him not to have called on us, in that case. So
now, of course, there'll be more delays. Oh, dear, people are too
inconsiderate! It's nothing but self, self, self, nowadays, nothing . . . !"

In the end, Cedric was traced to Paris ("Simply extraordinary," she said. "Whatever could a Canadian be doing in Paris? I don't quite like it."), and an invitation to Hampton was given and accepted.

"He comes next Tuesday, for a fortnight. I wrote out the dates very carefully indeed. I always do when it is a question of a country-house visit, then there is no awkwardness about the length of it. People know exactly when they are expected to leave. If we like him he can come again, now we know that he lives in Paris, such an easy journey. But what do you suppose he is doing there, dear? I hope he's not an artist. Well, if he is, we shall simply have to get him out of it—he must learn to behave suitably, now. We are sending to Dover for him, so that he'll arrive just in time for dinner. Montdore and I have decided not to dress that evening, as most likely he has no evening clothes, and one doesn't wish to make him feel shy at the very beginning of his visit, poor boy."

This seemed most unlike Lady Montdore, who usually loved making people feel shy, it was well known to be one of her favourite diversions. No doubt Cedric was to be her new toy, and until such time as, inevitably, I felt, just as Norma felt about Mrs. Heathery, disillusionment set in, nothing was to be too good for him, and no line of conduct too much calculated to charm him.

I began to think a great deal about Cedric. It was such an inter-esting situation and I longed to know how he would take it, this young man from the West suddenly confronted with aristocratic England in full decadence, the cardboard Earl, with his empty nobility of look and manner, the huge luxurious houses, the terrify-ing servants, the atmosphere of bottomless wealth. I remembered how exaggerated it had all seemed to me as a child, and supposed that he would see it with very much the same eyes and find it equally overpowering.

I thought, however, that he might feel at home with Lady Mont-dore, especially as she desired to please, there was something spon-taneous and almost childlike about her which could accord with a transatlantic outlook. It was the only hope, otherwise, if he were at all timid, I thought he would find himself submerged. Words dimly associated with Canada kept on occurring to me, the word lumber, the word shack, staking a claim. (Uncle Matthew had once staked a claim, I knew, in Ontario, in his wild young poker-playing days, with Harry Oakes.) How I wished I could be present at Hampton when this lumberjack arrived to stake his claim to that shack. Hardly had I formed the wish than it was granted, Lady Montdore ringing up to ask if I would go over for the night. She thought it would make things easier to have another young person there when Cedric arrived.

This was a wonderful reward, as I duly remarked to Alfred, for having been a lady-in-waiting.

Alfred said, "If you have been putting yourself out all this time with a reward in view, I don't mind at all. I objected because I thought you were drifting along in the wake of that old woman merely from a lazy good-nature, and with no particular motive. That is what I found degrading. Of course, if you were working for a wage it is quite a different matter, so long, of course," he said, with a disapproving look, "as the wage seems to you worth while."

It did.

The Montdores sent a motor car to Oxford for me. When I arrived at Hampton I was taken straight upstairs to my room, where I had a bath and changed, according to instructions brought me by Lady Montdore's maid, into a day dress. I had not spent a night at Hampton since my marriage. Knowing that Alfred would not want to go, I had always refused Lady Montdore's invitations, but my bedroom there was still deeply familiar to me. I knew every inch of it by heart. Nothing in it ever changed, the very books, between their mahogany book-ends, were the same collection that I had known and read there now for twelve years, or more than half my life: novels by Robert Hitchens and W. J. Locke, Napoleon, *The Last Phase* by Lord Rosebery, *The House of Mirth* by Edith Wharton, Hare's *Two Noble Lives*, *Dracula*, and a book on dog management. In front of them on a mahogany tall-boy was a Japanese bronze tea-kettle with embossed water lilies. On the walls, besides the two country-house old masters, despised of Davey, were a Mor-land print "The Higglers Preparing for Market," a Richmond water colour of the "old lord" in a kilt, and an oil painting of Toledo either by Boy or Lady Montdore, whose styles were indistinguish-able. It was in their early manner, and had probably hung there for twenty years. This room had a womb-like quality in my mind, partly because it was so red and warm and velvety and enclosed, and partly because of the terror with which I always used to be assailed by the idea of leaving it and venturing downstairs. This evening as I dressed I thought how lovely it was to be grown-up, a married woman, and no longer frightened of people. Of Lord Merlin a lit-tle, of the Warden of Wadham perhaps, but these were not panicky, indiscriminate social terrors. They could rather be classed as whole-some, awe inspired by gifted elders.

When I was ready I went down to the Long Gallery, where Lord and Lady Montdore were sitting in their usual chairs one on each side of the chimney piece, but not at all in their usual frame of mind. They were both, and especially Lady Montdore, in a twitter of nerves, and looked up quite startled when I came into the room, relaxing again when they saw that it was only me. I thought that from the point of view of a stranger, a backwoodsman from the American continent, they struck exactly the right note. Lord Mont-dore, in an informal green-velvet smoking jacket, was impressive with his white hair and carved unchanging face, while Lady Mont-dore's very dowdiness was an indication that she was too grand to bother about clothes, and this too would surely impress. She wore printed black-and-white crepe-de-chine, her only jewels the enor-mous half-hoop rings which flashed from her strong old woman's fingers, and sat, as she always did, her knees well apart, her feet in their large buckled shoes firmly planted on the ground, her hands folded in her lap.

"We lit this little fire," she said, "thinking that he may feel cold after the journey." It was unusual for her to refer to any arrange-ment in her house, people being expected to like what they found there, or else to lump it. "Do you think we shall hear the motor when it comes up the drive? We generally can if the wind is in the west."

"I expect I shall," I said, tactlessly. "I hear everything."

"Oh, we're not stone deaf ourselves. Show Fanny what you have got for Cedric, Montdore."

He held out a little book in green morocco, Gray's *Poems*.

"If you look at the fly leaf," he said, "you will see that it was given to my grandfather by the late Lord Palmerston the day that Cedric's grandfather was born. They evidently happened to be dining together. We think that it should please him."

I did so hope it would. I suddenly felt very sorry for these two old people, and longed for Cedric's visit to be a success and cheer them up.

"Canadians," he went on, "should know all about the poet Gray, because General Woolf, at the taking of Quebec . . ."

There were footsteps now in the red drawing room, so we had not heard the motor, after all. Lord and Lady Montdore got up and stood together in front of the fireplace as the butler opened the door and announced, "Mr. Cedric Hampton."

There was a glitter of blue and gold across the parquet, and a human dragon-fly was kneeling on the fur rug in front of the Montdores, one long white hand extended towards each. He was a tall, thin young man, supple as a girl, dressed in rather a bright blue suit; his hair was the gold of a brass bed knob, and his insect appearance came from the fact that the upper part of the face was concealed by blue goggles set in gold rims quite an inch thick.

He was flashing a smile of unearthly perfection. Relaxed and happy, he knelt there bestowing this smile upon each Montdore in turn.

"Don't speak," he said, "just for a moment. Just let me go on looking at you—wonderful, wonderful people!"

I could see at once that Lady Montdore was very highly gratified. She beamed with pleasure. Lord Montdore gave her a hasty glance to see how she was taking it, and when he saw that beaming was the note he beamed too.

"Welcome," she said, "to Hampton."

"The beauty," Cedric went on, floating jointlessly to his feet. "I can only say that I am drunk with it. England, so much more beautiful than I had imagined (I have never had very good accounts of England, somehow), this house, so romantic, such a repository of treasures, and, above all, you—the two most beautiful people I have ever seen!"

He spoke with rather a curious accent, neither French nor Canadian, but peculiar to himself, in which every syllable received rather more emphasis than is given by the ordinary Englishman. Also he spoke, as it were, through his smile, which would fade a little, then flash out again, but which never altogether left his face.

"Won't you take off your spectacles?" said Lady Montdore. "I should like to see your eyes."

"Later, dear Lady Montdore, later. When my dreadful, paralyzing shyness (a disease with me) has quite worn off. They give me confidence, you see, when I am dreadfully nervous, just as a mask would. In a mask one can face anything. I should like my life to be a perpetual *bal masqué*, Lady Montdore, don't you agree? I long to know who the Man in the Iron Mask was, don't you, Lord Montdore? Do you remember when Louis XVIII first saw the Duchesse d'Angoulême after the Restoration? Before saying anything else, you know—wasn't it all awful, or anything?—he asked if poor Louis XVI had ever told her who the Man in the Iron Mask was? I love Louis XVIII for that—so like *one*."

Lady Montdore indicated me. "This is our cousin—and a distant relation of yours, Cedric—Fanny Wincham."

He took my hand and looked long into my face, saying, "I am enchanted to meet you," as if he really was. He turned again to the Montdores, and said, "I am so happy to be here."

"My dear boy, we are so happy to have you. You should have

come before. We had no idea—we thought you were always in Nova Scotia, you see."

Cedric was gazing at the big French map table. "Riesener," he said. "This is a very strange thing, Lady Montdore, and you will hardly believe it, but where I live in France we have its pair. Is that not a coincidence? Only this morning, at Chèvres, I was leaning upon that very table."

"What is Chèvres?"

"Chèvres—Fontaine, where I live, in the Seine et Oise."

"But it must be quite a large house," said Lady Montdore, "if that table is in it?"

"A little larger, in every dimension, than the central block at Versailles, and with much more water. At Versailles there only remain seven hundred *bouches*. (How is *bouche* in English? Jets?) At Chèvres we have one thousand five hundred, and they play all the time."

Dinner was announced. As we moved towards the dining room, Cedric stopped to examine various objects and touched them lovingly.

"Weisweiller—Boule—Riesener—Jacob . . . How is it you come to have these marvels, Lord Montdore, such important pieces?"

"My great-grandfather (your great-great-grandfather), who was himself half-French, collected it all his life. Some of it he bought during the great sales of royal furniture after the Revolution and some came to him through his mother's family, the Montdores."

"And the *boiseries*!" said Cedric. "First quality Louis XV. There is nothing to equal this at Chèvres. It's like jewellery when it is so fine."

We were now in the little dining room.

"He brought them over too, and built the house round them." Lord Montdore was evidently much pleased by Cedric's enthusiasm. He loved French furniture himself but seldom found anybody in England to share his taste.

"Porcelain with Marie Antoinette's cypher—delightful. At Chèvres we have the Meissen service she brought with her from Vienna. We have many relics of Marie Antoinette, poor dear, at Chèvres."

"Who lives there?" asked Lady Montdore.

"I do," he replied carelessly, "when I wish to be in the country. In Paris I have a pavilion of all beauty, *one's* idea of heaven." Cedric made great use of the word "one," which he pronounced with peculiar emphasis. Lady Montdore had always been a one for one, but she said it quite differently—"w'n." "It stands between court-yard and garden. It was built for Madame du Barry. Tiny, you know, but all one needs, that is to say, a bedroom and a bed-ballroom. You must come and stay with me there, dear Lady Montdore. You will live in my bedroom, which has comfort, and I in the bed-ballroom. Promise me that you will come."

"We shall have to see. Personally, I have never been very fond of France. The people are so frivolous. I greatly prefer the Germans."

"Germans!" said Cedric earnestly, leaning across the table and gazing at her through his goggles. "The frivolity of the Germans terrifies even one. I have a German friend in Paris, and a more friv-olous creature, Lady Montdore, does not exist. This frivolity has caused me many a heartache, I must tell you."

"I hope you will make some suitable English friends now, Cedric."

"Yes, yes, that is what I long for. But please, can my chief English friend be you, dear, dearest Lady Montdore?"

"I think you should call us Aunt Sonia and Uncle Montdore."

"May I, really? How charming you are to me! How happy I am to be here. You seem, Aunt Sonia, to shower happiness around you."

"Yes, I do. I live for others, I suppose that's why. The sad thing is that people have not always appreciated it. They are so selfish themselves."

"Oh, yes, aren't they selfish? I too have been a victim to the selfishness of people all my life. This German friend I mentioned just now, his selfishness passes comprehension. How one does suffer!"

"It's a he, is it?" Lady Montdore seemed glad of this.

"A boy called Klugge. I hope to forget all about him while I am here. Now, Lady Montdore—dearest Aunt Sonia—after dinner I want you to do me a great, great favour. Will you put on your jewels so that I can see you sparkling in them? I do so long for that."

"Really, my dear boy, they are down in the strong room. I don't think they've been cleaned for ages."

"Oh, don't say no, don't shake your head! Ever since I set eyes on you I have been thinking of nothing else, you must look so truly glorious in them. Mrs. Wincham (you are Mrs. I hope, aren't you? Yes, yes, I can tell that you are not a spinster), when did you last see Aunt Sonia laden with jewels?"

"It was at the ball for . . ." I stopped awkwardly, jibbing at the name, which was never now mentioned, but Cedric saved me from embarrassment by exclaiming, "A ball! Aunt Sonia, how I would love to see you at a ball. I can so well imagine you at all the great English functions, coronations, Lords, balls, Ascot, Henley. What is Henley? No matter. . . . And I can see you, above all, in India, riding on your elephant like a goddess. How they must have worshipped you there."

"Well, you know, they did," said Lady Montdore, delighted. "They really worshipped us. It was quite touching. And, of course, we deserved it. We did a very great deal for them. I think I may say we put India on the map. Hardly any of one's friends in England had ever even heard of India before we went there, you know."

"I'm sure. What a wonderful and fascinating life you lead, Aunt Sonia. Did you keep a journal when you were in the East? Oh! please say yes, I would so love to read it."

This was a very lucky shot. They had indeed filled a huge folio, whose morocco label, surmounted by an earl's coronet, announced "Pages from Our Indian Diary. M. and S. M."

"It's really a sort of scrapbook," Lord Montdore said. "Accounts of our journeys up-country, photographs, sketches by Sonia and our brother-in . . . That is to say, a brother-in-law we had then, letters of appreciation from rajahs. . . ."

"And Indian poytry translated by Montdore . . . 'Prayer of a Widow before Suttee,' 'Death of an Old Mahout,' and so on, touching, it makes you cry."

"Oh, I must read it all, every word, I can hardly wait."

Lady Montdore was radiant. How many and many a time had she led her guests to "Pages from Our Indian Diary," like horses to water, and watched them straying off after one half-hearted sip. Never before, I guess, had anybody so eagerly demanded to read it.

"Now, you must tell us about your life, my dear boy," said Lady Montdore. "When did you leave Canada? Your home is in Nova Scotia, is it not?"

"I lived there until I was eighteen."

"Montdore and I have never been in Canada. The States, of course—we spent a month once in New York and Washington and we saw Niagara Falls, but then we were obliged to come home. I only wish we could have gone on, they were quite touchingly anxious to have us, but Montdore and I cannot always do as we should like. We have our duties. Of course that was a long time ago, twenty-five years, I should think, but I daresay Nova Scotia doesn't alter much?"

"I am very very happy to say that kindly Nature has allowed a great sea-fog of oblivion to rise between me and Nova Scotia, so that I hardly remember one single thing about it."

"What a strange boy you are!" she said indulgently, but she was very well suited by the fact of the sea-fog, since the last thing she wanted would have been long-winded reminiscences of Cedric's family life in Canada. It was all, no doubt, much better forgotten, and especially the fact that Cedric had a mother. "So you came to Europe when you were eighteen?"

"Paris. Yes, I was sent to Paris by my guardian, a banker, to learn some horrid sort of job, I quite forget what, as I never had to go near it. It is not necessary to have jobs, in Paris. One's friends are so very, very kind."

"Really, how funny. I always thought the French were so mean."

"Certainly not to *one*. My needs are simple, admittedly, but such as they are they have all been satisfied over and over again."

"What are your needs?"

"I need a very great deal of beauty round me, beautiful objects wherever I look, and beautiful people who see the point of *one*. And speaking of beautiful people, Aunt Sonia, after dinner, the jewels? Don't, don't, please, say no!"

"Very well then," she said. "But now, Cedric, won't you take off your glasses?"

"Perhaps I could. Yes, I really think the last vestige of my shyness has gone."

He took them off, and the eyes which were now disclosed, blinking a little in the light, were the eyes of Polly, large, blue, and rather blank. They quite startled me, but I do not think the Montdores were specially struck by the resemblance, though Lady Montdore said, "Anybody can tell that you are a Hampton, Cedric. Please never let's see those horrid spectacles again."

"My goggles? Specially designed by Van Cleef for *one*?"

"I hate spectacles," said Lady Montdore firmly.

Lady Montdore's maid was now sent for, given the key of the safe from Lord Montdore's key ring and told to bring up all the jewel cases. When dinner was over and we got back to the Long Gallery, leaving Lord Montdore to his port, but accompanied by Cedric, who was evidently unaware of the English custom which keeps the men in the dining room after dinner, and who followed Lady Montdore like a dog, we found the map table covered with blue velvet trays, each of which contained a parure of large and beautiful jewels. Cedric gave a cry of happiness and got down to work at once.

"In the first place, dear Aunt Sonia," he said, "this dress won't do.

Let me see . . . ah, yes . . ." He took a piece of red brocade off the piano and draped her in it very cleverly, pinning it in place on one shoulder with a huge diamond brooch. "Have you some maquillage in this bag, dear? And a comb?"

Lady Montdore rummaged about and produced a cheap lipstick and a small green comb with a tooth out.

"Naughty, naughty you," he said, carefully painting her face. "It cakes! Never mind, that will do for now. Not pulling your hair, am I? We've got to show the bone structure, so beautiful on you. I think you'll have to find a new coiffeur, Aunt Sonia. We'll see about that. . . . Anyway it must go up—up—like this. Do you realize what a difference that makes? Now, Mrs. Wincham, will you please put out the top lights for me, and bring the lamp from that bureau over here. Thank you."

He placed the lamp on the floor at Lady Montdore's feet and began to hang her with diamonds, so that the brocade was covered with them to her waist, finally poising the crown of pink diamonds on the top of her head.

"Now," he said. "Look!" and he led her to a looking glass on the wall. She was entranced by the effect, which was indeed very splendid.

"My turn," he said.

Although Lady Montdore seemed to be almost solid with diamonds, the cases on the table still held many huge jewels. He took off his coat, his collar and tie, pulled open his shirt and clasped a great necklace of diamonds and sapphires round his neck, wound up another piece of silk into a turban, stuck a diamond feather in it and put it on his head. He went on talking all the time.

"You really must pat your face more, Aunt Sonia."

"Pat?"

"With nourishing creams. I'll show you. Such a wonderful face, but uncultivated, neglected and starved. We must feed it up, exercise it and look after it better from now on. You'll soon see what a lot can be done. Twice a week you must sleep in a mask."

"A mask?"

"Yes, back to masks, but this time I mean the sort you paint on at night. It goes quite hard, so that you look like Commandeur in Don Juan, and in the morning you can't smile, not a glimmer, so you mustn't telephone until you've removed it with the remover, because you know how if you telephone smilelessly you sound cross, and if it happened to be *one* at the other end, *one* couldn't bear that."

"Oh, my dear boy, I don't know about this mask. What would Griffith say?"

"If Griffith is your maid, she won't notice a thing, they never do. We shall notice, though, your great new beauty. Those cruel lines!"

They were absorbed in each other and themselves, and when Lord Montdore came in from the dining room they did not even notice. He sat for a while in his usual attitude, the fingers of both hands pressed together, looking into the fire, and very soon crept off to bed. In the months which had passed since Polly's marriage he had turned into an old man. He was smaller, his clothes hung sadly on him, his voice quavered and complained. Before he went, he gave the little book of poems to Cedric, who took it with a charming show of appreciation and looked at it until Lord Montdore was out of sight, when he quickly turned back to the jewels.

I was pregnant at this time and began to feel sleepy very soon after dinner. I had a look at the picture papers, and then followed Lord Montdore's example.

"Good night," I said, making for the door. They hardly bothered to answer. They were now standing each in front of a looking glass, a lamp at their feet, happily gazing at their own images.

"Do you think it is better like that?" one would say.

"Much better," the other would reply, without looking.

From time to time they exchanged a jewel ("Give me the rubies, dear boy." "May I have the emeralds, if you've finished with them?"), and he was now wearing the pink tiara, jewels lay all around them, tumbled onto the chairs and tables, even on the floor.

"I have a confession to make to you, Cedric," she said, as I was leaving the room. "I really rather like amethysts."

"Oh, but I love amethysts," he replied, "so long as they are nice, large, dark stones, set in diamonds. They suit *one* so well."

THE NEXT MORNING when I went to Lady Montdore's room to say good-bye, I found Cedric, in a pale mauve silk dressing gown, sitting on her bed. They were both rubbing cream into their faces out of a large pink pot. It smelt delicious, and certainly belonged to him.

"And after that," he was saying, "until the end of her life she wore a thick black veil."

"And what did he do?"

"He left cards on all Paris, on which he had written '*mille regrets.*'"

Chapter 4

———————————————

FROM THE MOMENT that the Montdores first set eyes on Cedric, there was no more question of his having come to Hampton for a fortnight. He was obviously there for good and all. They both took him to their hearts and loved him, almost at once, better than they had loved Polly for years, ever since she was a small child. The tremendous vacuum created by her departure was happily filled again, and filled by somebody who was able to give more than Polly had ever given in the way of companionship. Cedric could talk intelligently to Lord Montdore about the objects of art at Hampton. He knew an enormous amount about such things, though in the ordinary sense of the word he was uneducated, ill-read, incapable of the simplest calculation, and curiously ignorant of many quite elementary subjects. He was one of those people who take in the world through eye and ear, his intellect was probably worth very little, but his love of beauty was genuine. The librarian at Hampton was astounded at his bibliographical knowledge. It seemed, for instance, that he could tell at a glance whom a book had been bound for and by whom, and he said that Cedric knew much more than he did himself about eighteenth-century French editions. Lord Montdore had seldom seen his own cherished belongings so intelligently appreciated, and it was a great pleasure to him to spend hours with Cedric going over them. He had doted on Polly, she had been the apple of his eye, in theory, but in practice she had never been in any respect a companion to him.

As for Lady Montdore, she became transformed with happiness during the months that followed, transformed, too, in other ways, Cedric taking her appearance in hand with extraordinary results. Just as Boy (it was the hold he had over her) had filled her days with society and painting, Cedric filled them with the pursuit of her own beauty, and to such an egotist this was a more satisfactory hobby. Facial operations, slimming cures, exercises, massage, diet, make-up, new clothes, jewels reset, a blue rinse for her grey hair, pink bows and diamond daisies in the blue curls; it kept her very busy. I saw her less and less, but each time I did she looked more unnaturally modish. Her movements, formerly so ponderous, became smart, spry and birdlike. She never sat now with her two legs planted on the ground, but threw one over the other, legs which, daily massaged and steamed, gradually lost their flesh and became little more than bone. Her face was lifted, plucked and trimmed, and looked as tidy as Mrs. Chaddesley Corbett's, and she learnt to flash a smile brilliant as Cedric's own.

"I make her say 'brush' before she comes into a room," he told me. "It's a thing I got out of an old book on deportment and it fixes at once this very gay smile on one's face. Somebody ought to tell Lord Alconleigh about it."

Since she had never hitherto made the smallest effort to appear younger than she was, but had remained fundamentally Edwardian-looking, as though conscious of her own superiority to the little smart ephemeral types, the Chaddesley Corbetts and so on, Cedric's production of her was revolutionary. In my opinion it was not successful, for she made the sacrifice of a grand and characteristic appearance without really gaining in prettiness, but no doubt the effort which it involved made her perfectly happy.

Cedric and I became great friends and he visited me constantly in Oxford, just as Lady Montdore used to before she became so busy, and I must say that I greatly preferred his company to hers. During the later stages of my pregnancy, and after the baby was born, he would come and sit with me for hours on end, and I felt completely at my ease with him. I could go on with my sewing, or mending, without bothering about what I looked like, exactly as if he were one of my Radlett cousins. He was kind and thoughtful and affectionate, like a charming woman friend, better, because our friendship was marred by no tinge of jealousy.

Later on, when I had got my figure back after the baby, I began to dress and make myself up with a view to gaining Cedric's approbation, but I soon found that, with the means at my disposal, it was not much use. He knew too much about women and their accessories to be impressed by anything I could manage. For instance, if I made a great effort and changed into silk stockings when I expected him, he could see at once that they were Elliston, 5/11, all I could afford, and it really seemed more sensible to stick to lisle. Indeed, he once said to me, "You know, Fanny, it doesn't matter a bit that you're not able to dress up in expensive clothes, there'd be no point in it anyway. You are like the Royal Family, my darling, whatever you wear you look exactly the same, just as they do."

I was not very much pleased, but I knew that he was right. I could never look fashionable, even if I tried as hard as Lady Montdore, with my heather-hair and round salubrious face.

I remember that my mother, during one of her rare visits to England, brought me a little jacket in scarlet cloth from Schiaparelli. It seemed to me quite plain and uninteresting, except for the label in its lining, and I longed to put this on the outside so that people would know where it came from. I was wearing it, instead of a cardigan, in my house when Cedric happened to call, and the first thing he said was, "Aha! so now we dress at Schiaparelli, I see! Whatever next?"

"Cedric! How can you tell?"

"My dear, one can always tell. Things have a signature, if you use your eyes, and mine seem to be trained over a greater range of objects than yours, Schiaparelli—Reboux—Fabergé—Viollet le Duc—I can tell at a glance, literally a glance. So your wicked mother, the Bolter, has been here since last I saw you?"

"Might I not have bought it for myself?"

"No, no, my love, you are saving up to educate your twelve brilliant sons, how could you possibly afford £25 for a little jacket?"

"Don't tell me!" I said. "£25 for this?"

"Quite that, I should guess."

"Simply silly. Why, I could have made it myself."

"But could you? And if you had, would I have come into the room and said Schiaparelli?"

"There's only a yard of stuff in it, worth a pound, if that," I went on, horrified by the waste of money.

"And how many yards of canvas in a Fragonard? And how much do planks of wood cost, or the skin of a darling goat before some clever person turns them into commodes and morocco? Art is more than yards, just as *one* is more than flesh and bones. By the way, I must warn you that Sonia will be here in a minute, in search of strong tea. I took the liberty of having a word with Mrs. Heathery, the love of whose life I am, on my way up, and I also brought some scones from the Cadena which I deposited with her."

"What is Lady Montdore doing now?" I said, beginning to tidy up the room.

"Now this very minute? She is at Parker's, buying a birthday present for me. It is to be a great surprise, but I went to Parker's and prepared the ground and I shall be greatly surprised if the great surprise is not Ackerman's *Repository*."

"I thought you turned up your nose at English furniture?" I said.

"Less and less. Provincial but charming is now my attitude, and Ackerman's *Repository is* such an amusing book. I saw a copy the other day when Sonia and I went over to Lord Merlin's, and I long to possess it. I expect it will be all right. Sonia loves to give me these large presents, impossible to carry about. She thinks they anchor me to Hampton. I don't blame her, her life there must have been too dull for words, without me."

"But are you anchored?" I said. "It always seems to me that the place where you really belong is Paris. I can't imagine you staying here for ever."

"I can't imagine it, either, but the fact is, my darling, that the news from Paris is not too good. I told you, didn't I, that I left my German friend Klugge to look after my pavilion and keep it warm for me? Now what do I hear? The Baron came last week with a *camion* and took all the furniture, every stick, leaving poor Klugge to sleep on bare boards. I daresay he doesn't notice, he is always quite drunk by bedtime, but for waking up it can't be very nice, and meanwhile I am mourning my commodes. Louis XV — a pair — such *marqueterie*, such bronzes, really important pieces, *objets de musée* — well, often have I told you about them. Gone! The Baron, during one fatal afternoon, took everything. Bitter work!"

"What Baron?" I asked.

I knew all about Klugge, how hideous and drunken and brutal and German and unlettered he was, so that Cedric never could explain why he put up with his vagaries for a single moment, but the Baron was a new figure to me. Cedric was evasive, however. He was better than anybody I have ever known at not answering questions if he did not want to.

"Just another friend. The first night I was in Paris I went to the Opera, and I don't mind telling you, my darling, that all eyes were upon me, in my box, the poor *artistes* might just as well not have been on the stage at all. Well, one of the eyes belonged to the Baron."

"Two of the eyes, you mean," I said.

"No, dear, one. He wears a patch to make himself look sinister and fascinating. Nobody knows how much I hate barons. I feel exactly like King John whenever I think of them."

"But, Cedric, I don't understand. How could he take your furniture away?"

"How could he? How, indeed? Alas, he has, and that is that. My Savonnerie, my Sèvres, my sanguines, all my treasures gone, and I confess I am very low about it, because, although they cannot compare in quality with what I see every day round me at Hampton, one does so love one's own things which one has bought and chosen oneself. I must say the Boule at Hampton is the best I have ever seen — even at Chèvres we had no Boule like that. Sensational. Have you been over since we began to clean the bronzes? Oh, you must come. I have taught my friend Archie how to unscrew the bits, scrub them with ammonia, and pour boiling water on them from a kettle so that they dry at once with no moisture left to turn them green. He does it all day, and when he has finished it glitters like the cave of Aladdin."

This Archie was a nice handsome boy, a lorry driver, whom Cedric had found with his lorry broken down near the gates of Hampton.

"For your ear alone, my darling, it was a stroke of thunder when I saw him. What one does so love about love is the time before they find out what *one is* like."

"And it's also very nice," I said, disloyally, "before *one* finds out what they are like."

Archie had now left his lorry for ever, and gone to live at Hampton to do odd jobs. Lady Montdore was enthusiastic about him.

"So willing," she would say. "So clever of Cedric to think of having him. Cedric always does such original things."

Cedric went on, "But I suppose you would think it more hideous than ever, Fanny. I know that you like a room to sparkle with freshness, whereas I like it to glitter with richness. That is where we differ at present, but you'll change. Your taste is really good, and it is bound to mature one day."

It was true that my taste at this time, like that of the other young people I knew who cared at all about their houses, favoured pickled or painted furniture with a great deal of white, and upholstery in pale cheerful colours. French furniture with its finely chiselled ormolu (what Cedric called bronzes), its severe lines and perfect proportions was far above my head in those days, while Louis XIV needlework, of which there was a great amount at Hampton, seemed dark and stuffy, I frankly preferred a cheerful chintz.

Cedric's word with Mrs. Heathery had excellent results, and even Lady Montdore showed no signs of despising the tea which arrived at the same time as she did. In any case, now that she was happy again, she was much more good-natured about the attempts of the humble, such as myself, to regale her.

Her appearance still gave me quite a jump, though by now I really should have been getting accustomed to her flashing smile, her supple movements, and the pale-blue curls, a little sparse upon the head, not unattractively so, but like a baby's curls. To-day she was hatless, and wore a tartan ribbon to keep her hair in place. She was dressed in a plain but beautifully made grey coat and skirt, and as she came into the room, which was full of sun, she took her coat off with a curious, swift, double-jointed movement, revealing a piqué blouse and a positively girlish waistline. It was warm spring weather just then, and I knew that she and Cedric did a lot of sun bathing in a summer house specially designed by him, as a result of which her skin had gone rather a horrid yellow, and looked as if it had to be soaked in oil to prevent it from falling into a thousand tiny cracks. Her nails were varnished dark red, and this was an improvement, since formerly they had been furrowed and not always quite clean. The old-fashioned hoops of enormous diamonds set in gold which used so stiffly to encircle her stiff fingers were replaced by square-cut diamonds in clusters of cabuchon emeralds and rubies, her diamond earrings too had been reset, in the shape of cockle shells, and more large diamonds sparkled in a fashionable pair of clips, at her throat. The whole thing was stunning.

But although her aspect was so much changed, her personality remained the same, and the flashing (brush) smile was followed by the well-known up and down look.

"Is that your baby, making that horrid noise, Fanny?"

"Yes. He never cries, as a rule, but his teeth are upsetting him."

"Poor thing," said Cedric. "Couldn't he go to the dentist?"

"Well, I've got your birthday present, Cedric. It can't be a surprise though, because it's all over the floor of the motor. They seemed to think, at Parker's, that you would like it—a book called Ackerman's *Suppository*, or something."

"Not Ackerman's *Suppository*—not really!" said Cedric, clasping his hands under his chin in a very characteristic gesture. "How kind you are to me! How could you have guessed? Where did you find it? But, dearest, it's bad about the surprise. Birthday presents really ought to be surprises. I can't get Sonia to enter into the true spirit of birthdays, Fanny, what can *one* do about it?"

I thought *one* had done pretty well. Lady Montdore was famous for never giving presents at all, either for birthdays or at Christmas, and had never even relaxed this rule in favour of the adored Polly, though Lord Montdore used to make up for that by giving her several. But she showered presents, and valuable presents too, on Cedric, snatching at the smallest excuse to do so, and I quite saw that with somebody so intensely appreciative this must be a great pleasure.

"But I have got a surprise for you, as well as the books, something I bought in London," she said, looking at him fondly

"No!" said Cedric. I had the feeling he knew all about that, too. "I shan't have one moment's peace until I've wormed it out of you—how I wish you hadn't told me."

"You've only got to wait until to-morrow."

"Well, I warn you I shall wake you up for it at six. Now finish your tea, dear, and come, we ought to be getting back. I'm in a little bit of a fuss to see what Archie has been up to with all those bronzes. He's doing the Boule to-day and I have had a horrid idea—suppose he has re-assembled it into a lorry by mistake? What would dearest Uncle Montdore say if he suddenly came upon a huge Boule lorry in the middle of the Long Gallery?"

No doubt, I thought, but that both Lord and Lady Montdore would happily have got into it and been taken for a ride by Cedric. He had completely mesmerized them, and nothing that he could do ever seemed otherwise to them than perfection.

Chapter 5

C EDRIC'S ADVENT AT Hampton naturally created quite a
stir in the world outside. London society was not at first given the
chance to form an opinion on him, because this was the year following the Financial Crisis. In fact, Cedric and the Crisis had
arrived at about the same time, and Lady Montdore, though herself
unaffected by it, thought that as there was no entertaining in London it was hardly worth while to keep Montdore House open, she
had it shrouded in dust sheets except for two rooms where Lord
Montdore could put up if he wanted to go to the House of Lords.

Lady Montdore and Cedric never stayed there. They sometimes
went to London, but only for the day. She no longer invited large
house parties to Hampton. She said people could talk about nothing but money any more and it was too boring, but I thought there
was another reason, and that she really wanted to keep Cedric to
herself.

The county, however, hummed and buzzed with Cedric, and little else was talked of. I need hardly say that Uncle Matthew, after
one look, found that the word sewer had become obsolete and
inadequate. Scowling, growling flashing of eyes and grinding of
teeth, to a degree hitherto reserved for Boy Dougdale, were intensi-

fied a hundredfold at the mere thought of Cedric, and accompanied by swelling veins and apoplectic noises. The drawers at Alconleigh were emptied of the yellowing slips of paper on which my uncle's hates had mouldered all these years, and each now contained a clean new slip with the name, carefully printed in black ink, Cedric Hampton. There was a terrible scene on Oxford platform one day. Cedric went to the bookstall to buy *Vogue*, having mislaid his own copy. Uncle Matthew, who was waiting there for a train, happened to notice that the seams of his coat were piped in a contrasting shade. This was too much for his self-control. He fell upon Cedric and began to shake him like a rat. Just then, very fortunately, the train came in, whereupon my uncle, who suffered terribly from train fever, dropped Cedric and rushed to catch it. "You'd never think," as Cedric said afterwards, "that buying *Vogue* magazine could be so dangerous. It was well worth it though, lovely Spring modes."

The children, however, were in love with Cedric and furious because I would not allow them to meet him in my house. But Aunt Sadie, who seldom took a strong line about anything, had solemnly begged me to keep them apart, and her word with me was law. Besides, from my pinnacle of sophistication as wife and mother, I also considered Cedric to be unsuitable company for the very young, and when I knew he was coming to see me I took great care to shoo away any undergraduates who might happen to be sitting about in my drawing room.

Uncle Matthew and his neighbours seldom agreed on any subject. He despised their opinions, and they, in their turn, found his violent likes and dislikes quite incomprehensible, taking their cue as a rule from the balanced Boreleys. Over Cedric, however, all were united. Though the Boreleys were not haters in the Uncle Matthew class, they had their own prejudices, things they "could not stick," foreigners, for example, well-dressed women and the Labour Party. But the thing they could stick least in the world were "Aesthetes—you know—those awful effeminate creatures—pansies."

When, therefore, Lady Montdore, whom anyhow they could not stick much, installed the awful effeminate pansy Cedric at Hampton, and it became borne in upon them that he was henceforth to be their neighbour for ever, quite an important one at that, the future Lord Montdore, hatred really did burgeon in their souls. At the same time they took a morbid interest in every detail of the situation, and these details were supplied to them by Norma, who got her facts, I am ashamed to say, from me. It tickled me so much to make Norma gasp and stretch her eyes with horror that I kept back nothing that might tease her and infuriate the Boreleys.

I soon found out that the most annoying feature of the whole thing to them was the radiant happiness of Lady Montdore. They had all been delighted by Polly's marriage, even those people who might have been expected wholeheartedly to take Lady Montdore's side over it, such as the parents of pretty young daughters, having said with smug satisfaction "Serve her right." They hated her and were glad to see her downed. Now, it seemed, the few remaining days of this wicked woman, who never invited them to her parties, were being suitably darkened with a sorrow which must soon bring her grey hairs to the grave. The curtain rises for the last act and the stalls are filled with Boreleys all agog to witness the agony, the dissolution, the muffled drum, the catafalque, the procession to the vault, the lowering to the tomb, the darkness. But what is this? Onto the stage in a dazzling glare, springs Lady Montdore, supple as a young cat and her grey hair now a curious shade of blue, with a partner, a terrible creature from Sodom, from Gomorrah, from Paris, and with him proceeds to dance a wild fandango of delight. No wonder they were cross.

On the other hand, I thought the whole thing simply splendid, since I like my fellow-beings to be happy and the new state of affairs at Hampton had so greatly increased the sum of human happiness. An old lady, a selfish old creature admittedly, who deserved nothing at the end but trouble and sickness (but which of us will deserve better?) is suddenly presented with one of life's bonuses, and is rejuvenated, occupied and amused; a charming boy with a great love of beauty and of luxury, a little venal, perhaps (but which of us is not if we get the opportunity to be?), whose life hitherto depended upon the whims of Barons, suddenly and respectably acquires two doting parents and a vast heritage of wealth, another bonus; Archie, the lorry driver, taken from long cold nights on the road, long oily hours under his lorry, and put to polish ormolu in a warm and scented room; Polly married to the love of her life; Boy married to the greatest beauty of the age, five bonuses, five happy people, and yet the Boreleys were disgusted. They must indeed be against the human race, I thought, so to hate happiness.

I said all this to Davey, and he winced a little.

"I wish you needn't go on about Sonia being an old, old woman on the brink of the grave," he said. "She is barely sixty, you know, only about ten years older than your Aunt Emily."

"Davey, she's forty years older than I am; it must seem old to me. I bet people forty years older than you are seem old to you, now do admit."

Davey admitted. He also agreed that it is nice to see people happy, but made the reservation that it is only very nice if you happen to like them, and that although he was, in a way, quite fond of Lady Montdore, he did not happen to like Cedric.

"You don't like Cedric?" I said, amazed. "How couldn't you, Dave? I absolutely love him."

He replied that, whereas to an English rosebud like myself Cedric must appear as a being from another, darkly glamorous world, he, Davey, in the course of his own wild cosmopolitan wanderings, before he had met and settled down with Aunt Emily, had known too many Cedrics.

"You are lucky," I said. "I couldn't know too many. And if you think I find him darkly glamorous you've got hold of the wrong end of the stick, my dear Dave. He seems to me like a darling Nanny."

"Darling Nanny! Polar bear—tiger—puma—something that can never be tamed. They always turn nasty in the end. Just you wait, Fanny, all this ormolu radiance will soon blacken, and the last state of Sonia will be worse than her first, I prophesy. I've seen this sort of thing too often."

"I don't believe it. Cedric loves Lady Montdore."

"Cedric," said Davey, "loves Cedric, and, furthermore, he comes from the jungle, and just as soon as it suits him he will tear her to pieces and slink back into the undergrowth—you mark my words."

"Well," I said, "if so, the Boreleys will be pleased."

Cedric himself now sauntered into the room and Davey prepared to leave. I think after all the horrid things he had just been saying he was afraid of seeming too cordial to him in front of me. It was very difficult not to be cordial to Cedric, he was so disarming.

"I shan't see you again, Fanny," Davey said, "until I get back from my cruise."

"Oh, are you going for a cruise? How delicious! Where?"

"In search of a little sun. I give a few lectures on Minoan things and go cheap."

"I do wish Aunt Emily would go too," I said. "It would be so good for her."

"She'll never move until after Siegfried's death," said Davey. "You know what she is."

When he had gone I said to Cedric, "What d'you think, he may be able to go and see Polly and Boy in Sicily—wouldn't it be interesting?"

Cedric of course was deeply fascinated by anything to do with Polly. "The absent influence, so boring and so overdone in literature, but I see now that in real life it can eat you with curiosity."

"When did you last hear from her, Fanny?" he said.

"Oh, months ago, and then it was only a postcard. I'm so delighted about Dave seeing them because he's always so good at telling. We really shall hear how they are getting on, from him."

"Sonia has still never mentioned her to me," said Cedric, "never once."

"That's because she never thinks of her then."

"I'm sure she doesn't. This Polly can't be much of a personality, to have left such a small dent where she used to live?"

"Personality . . ." I said. "I don't know. The thing about Polly is her beauty."

"Describe it."

"Oh, Cedric I've described it to you hundreds of times." It rather amused me to do so though, because I knew that it teased him.

"Well," I said, "as I've often told you before, she is so beautiful that it's difficult to pay much attention to what she is saying, or to make out what she's really like as a person, because all you want to do is just gaze and gaze."

Cedric looked sulky, as he always did when I talked like this.

"More beautiful than *one*?" he said.

"Very much like you, Cedric."

"So you say, but I don't find that you gaze and gaze at *one*. On the contrary, you listen intently, with your eye out of the window."

"She is very much like you, but all the same," I said firmly, "she must be more beautiful because there is that thing about the gazing."

This was perfectly true, and not said to annoy poor Cedric or make him jealous. He was like Polly, and very good-looking, but not an irresistible magnet to the eye as she was.

"I know exactly why," he said. "It's my beard, all that horrible shaving. I shall send to New York this very day for some wax—you can't conceive the agony it is, but if it will make you gaze, Fanny, it will be worth it."

"Don't bother to do that," I said. "It's not the shaving. You do look like Polly, but you are not as beautiful. Lady Patricia also looked like her, but it wasn't the same thing. It's something extra that Polly has, which I can't explain, I can only tell you that it is so."

"What extra can she possibly have except beardlessness?"

"Lady Patricia was quite beardless."

"You are horrid. Never mind, I shall try it and you'll see. People used to gaze before my beard grew, like mad, even in Nova Scotia.

You are so fortunate not to be a beauty, Fanny, you'll never know the agony of losing your looks."

"Thank you," I said.

"And as talking about pretty Polly makes us both so disagreeable let's get onto the subject of Boy."

"Ah, now, nobody could say that Boy was pretty. No gazing there. Boy is old and grizzled and hideous."

"Now, Fanny, that's not true, dear. Descriptions of people are only interesting if they happen to be true, you know. I've seen many photographs of Boy. Sonia's books are full of them, from Boy playing diabolo, Boy in puttees for the war, to Boy with his bearer Boosee. After India I think she lost her Brownie, in the move, perhaps, because 'Pages from Our Indian Diary' seems to be the last book, but that was only three years ago and Boy was still ravishing then, the kind of looks I adore, stocky and with deep attractive furrows all over his face—dependable."

"Dependable!"

"Why do you hate him so much, Fanny?"

"Oh, I don't know, he gives me the creeps. He's such a snob, for one thing."

"I like that," said Cedric. "I am one myself."

"Such a snob that living people aren't enough for him, he has to get to know the dead, as well—the titled dead, of course, I mean. He dives about in their memoirs so that he can talk about his 'dear Duchesse de Dino,' or 'as Lady Bessborough so truly says.' He can reel off pedigrees; he always knows just how everybody was related, Royal families and things I mean. Then he writes books about all these people, and, after that, anybody would think they were his own personal property. Ugh!"

"Exactly as I had supposed," said Cedric. "A handsome, cultivated man, the sort of person I like the best. Gifted too. His needlework is marvellous and the dozens of *toiles* by him in the squash court are worthy of the Douanier himself, landscapes with gorillas. Original and bold."

"Gorillas! Lord and Lady Montdore, and anybody else who would pose."

"Well, it is original and bold to depict my aunt and uncle as gorillas. I wouldn't dare. I think Polly is a very lucky girl."

"The Boreleys think you will end by marrying Polly, Cedric." Norma had propounded this thrilling theory to me the day before. They thought that it would be a deathblow to Lady Montdore, and longed for it to happen.

"Very silly of them, dear, I should have thought they only had to look at *one* to see how unlikely that is. What else do the Boreleys say about me?"

"Cedric, do come and meet Norma one day—I simply long to see you together."

"I think not, dear, thank you."

"But why? You're always asking what she says and she's always asking what you say, you'd much better ask each other and do without the middleman."

"The thing is, I believe she would remind me of Nova Scotia, and when that happens my spirits go down, down, past *grande pluie* to *tempête*. The house carpenter at Hampton reminds me, don't ask me why, but he does, and I have to rudely look away every time I meet him. I believe that's why Paris suits me so well, there's not a shade of Nova Scotia there, and perhaps it's also why I put up with the Baron all those years. The Baron could have come from many a land of spices, but from Nova Scotia he could not have come. Whereas Boreleys abound there. But though I don't want to meet them I always like hearing about them, so do go on with what they think about *one*."

"Well, so then Norma was full of you just now, when I met her out shopping, because it seems you travelled down from London with her brother Jock yesterday, and now he can literally think of nothing else."

"Oh, how exciting. How did he know it was me?"

"Lots of ways. The goggles, the piping, your name on your luggage. There is nothing anonymous about you, Cedric."

"Oh, good!"

"So according to Norma he was in a perfect panic, sat with one eye on you and the other on the communication cord, because he expected you to pounce at any minute."

"Heavens! What does he look like?"

"You ought to know. It seems you were quite alone together after Reading."

"Well, darling, I only remember a dreadful moustachio'd murderer sitting in a corner. I remember him particularly, because I kept thinking, 'Oh, the luck of being *one* and not somebody like that.'"

"I expect that was Jock. Sandy and white."

"That's it. Oh, so that's a Boreley, is it? And do you imagine people often make advances to him, in trains?"

"He says you gave him hypnotic stares through your glasses."

"The thing is he did have rather a pretty tweed on."

"And then apparently you made him get your suitcase off the rack at Oxford, saying you are not allowed to lift things."

"No, and nor I am. It was very heavy, not a sign of a porter, as usual. I might have hurt myself. Anyway it was all right because he terribly sweetly got it down for me.

"Yes, and now he's simply furious that he did. He says you hypnotised him."

"Oh, poor him, I do so know the feeling."

'Whatever had you got in it, Cedric? He says it simply weighed a ton."

"*Complets*," Cedric said. "And a few small things for my face. I have found a lovely new resting cream, by the way. Very little, really."

"And now they are all saying, 'There you are—if he even fixed old Jock, no wonder he has got round the Montdores.'"

"But why on earth should I want to get round the Montdores?"

"Wills and things. Living at Hampton."

"My dear, come to that, Chèvres-Fontaine is twenty times more beautiful than Hampton."

"But could you go back there now, Cedric?" I said.

Cedric gave me rather a nasty look and went on, "But in any case, I wish people would understand that there's never much point in hanging about for wills. It's just not worth it. I have a friend who used to spend months of every year with an old uncle in the Sarthe so as to stay in his will. It was torture to him, because he knew the person he loved was being unfaithful to him in Paris, and anyhow the Sarthe is utterly lugubrious, you know. But all the same he went pegging away at it. Then what occurs? The uncle dies, my poor friend inherits the house in the Sarthe, and now he feels obliged to live a living death there so as to make himself believe that there was some point after all in having wasted months of his youth in the Sarthe. You see my argument? It's a vicious circle, and there is nothing vicious about me. The thing is, I love Sonia, that's why I stay."

I believed him, really. Cedric lived in the present, it would not be like him to bother about such things as wills. If ever there were a grasshopper, a lily of the field, it was he.

WHEN DAVEY GOT back from his cruise he rang me up and said he would come over to luncheon and tell me about Polly. I thought Cedric might as well come and hear it at first hand. Davey was always better with an audience even if he did not much like its component parts, so I rang up Hampton, and Cedric accepted to lunch with pleasure, and then said could he possibly stay with me for a night or two?

"Sonia has gone for this orange cure—yes, total starvation, except for orange juice, but don't mind too much for her, I know she'll cheat, and Uncle Montdore is in London for the House and I feel sad, all alone here. I'd love to be with you and to do some serious Oxford sightseeing, which there's never time for when I've got Sonia with me. That will be charming, Fanny, thank you, dear. One o'clock then."

Alfred was very busy just then and I was delighted to think I should have Cedric's company for a day or two. I cleared the decks by warning Aunt Sadie that he would be there, and telling my undergraduate friends that I should not be wanting them around for the present.

"Who is that spotty child?" Cedric had once said, when a boy who had been crouching by my fireplace got up and vanished at a look from me.

"I see him as the young Shelley," I answered, sententiously, no doubt.

"And *I* see him as the young Woodley."

Davey arrived first.

"Cedric is coming," I said, "so you mustn't begin without him." I could see he was bursting with his news.

"Oh, Cedric—I never come without finding that monster here. He seems to live in your house. What does Alfred think of him?"

"Doubt if he knows him by sight, to tell you the truth. Come and see the baby, Dave."

"Sorry if I'm late, darlings," Cedric said, floating in. "One has to drive so slowly in England, because of the walking *Herrschaften*. Why are the English roads always so covered with these tweeded stumpers?"

"They are colonels," I said. "Don't French colonels go for walks?"

"Much too ill. They have always lost a leg or two and been terribly gassed. I can see that French wars must have been far bloodier than English ones, though I do know a colonel, in Paris, who walks to the antique shops sometimes."

"How do they take their exercise?" I asked.

"Quite another way, darling. You haven't started about Boy, have you? Oh, how loyal. I was delayed by Sonia, too, on the telephone. She's in a terrible do. . . . It seems they've had her up for stealing the nurses' breakfast—well, had her up in front of the principal, who spoke quite cruelly to her, and said that if she does it again, or gets one more bite of illicit food, he'll give her the sack. Just imagine, no dinner, one orange juice at midnight, and woken up by the smell of kippers. So naturally the poor darling sneaked out and pinched one, and they caught her with it under her dressing gown. I'm glad to say she'd eaten most of it before they got it away from her. The thing is she started off demoralized by finding your name in the visitors' book, Davey, apparently she gave a scream and said, 'But he's a living skeleton, whatever was he doing here?' and they said you had gone there to put on weight. What's the idea?"

"The idea," said Davey, impatiently, "is health. If you are too fat you lose and if you are too thin you gain. I should have thought a child could understand that. But Sonia won't stick it for a day. No self-discipline."

"Just like *one*," said Cedric. "But then what are we to do to get rid of those kilos? Vichy, perhaps?"

"My dear, look at the kilos she's lost already," I said. "She's really so thin, ought she to get any thinner?"

"It's just that little extra round the hips," said Cedric. "A jersey and skirt is the test, and she doesn't look quite right in that yet. And there's a weeny roll round her ribs. Besides, they say the orange juice clears the skin. Oh, I do hope she sticks it for a few more days, for her own sake, you know. She says another patient told her of a place in the village where you can have Devonshire teas, but I begged her to be careful. After what happened this morning they're sure to be on the lookout and one more slip may be fatal. What d'you think, Davey?"

"Yes, they're madly strict," said Davey. "There'd be no point, otherwise."

We sat down to our luncheon and begged Davey to begin his story.

"I may as well start by telling you that I don't think they are at all happy."

Davey, I knew, was never a one for seeing things through rose-coloured spectacles, but he spoke so definitely and with so grave an emphasis, that I felt I must believe him.

"Oh, Dave, don't say that. How dreadful!"

Cedric, who, since he did not know and love Polly, was rather indifferent as to whether she was happy or not, said, "Now, Davey dear, you're going much too fast. New readers begin here. You left your boat . . ."

"I left my ship at Syracuse, having wired them from Athens that I would be arriving for one night, and they met me on the quay with a village taxi. They have no motor car of their own."

"Every detail. They were dressed?"

"Polly wore a plain blue-cotton frock and Boy was in shorts."

"Wouldn't care to see Boy's knees," I said.

"They're all right," said Davey, standing up for Boy, as usual.

"Well then, Polly? Beautiful?"

"Less beautiful" (Cedric looked delighted to hear this news) "and peevish. Nothing right for her. Hates living abroad, can't learn the language, talks Hindustanee to the servants, complains that they steal her stockings . . ."

"You're going much too fast, we're still in the taxi. You can't skip to stockings like this—how far from Syracuse?"

"About an hour's drive, and beautiful beyond words—the situation, I mean. The villa is on a southeasterly slope looking over olive trees, umbrella pines and vineyards to the sea—you know, the regular Mediterranean view that you can never get tired of. They've taken the house, furnished, from Italians and complain about it ceaselessly. It seems to be on their minds, in fact. I do see that it can't be very nice in winter—no heating, except open fireplaces which smoke, bath water never hot, none of the windows fit, and so on, you know. Italian houses are always made for the heat, and of course it can be jolly cold in Sicily. The inside is hideous, all khaki and bog oak, depressing, if you had to be indoors much. But at this time of year it's ideal, you live on a terrace, roofed-in with vines and bougainvillaea—I never saw such a perfect spot—huge tubs of geraniums everywhere—simply divine."

"Oh, dear, as I seem to have taken their place in life I do wish we could swop over sometimes," said Cedric. "I do so love Sicily."

"I think they'd be all for it," said Davey. "They struck me as being very homesick. Well, we arrived in time for luncheon and I struggled away with the food (Italian cooking, so oily)."

"What did you talk about?"

"Well, you know, really, it was one long wail from them about how difficult everything is, more expensive than they thought it would be and how the people—village people, I mean—don't really help but say yes, yes, the whole time and nothing gets done, and how they are supposed to have vegetables out of the garden in return for paying the gardener's wages but actually they have to buy everything and as they are sure he sells the vegetables in the village they suppose that it's their own that they buy back again; how when they first came there wasn't a kettle in the place and the blankets were as hard as boards, and none of the electric-light switches worked and no lamps by the beds—you know, the usual complaints of people who take furnished houses. I've heard them a hundred times. After luncheon it got very hot, which Polly doesn't like, and she went off to her room with everything drawn and I had a session with Boy on the terrace, and then I really saw how the land lay. Well, all I can say is, I know it is wrong, not right, to arouse the sexual instincts of little girls so that they fall madly in love with you, but the fact is, poor old Boy is taking a fearful punishment. You see, he has literally nothing to do from morning to night, except water his geraniums, and you know how bad it is for them to have too much water. Of course they are all leaf as a result, I told him so. He has nobody to talk to, no club, no London Library, no neighbours, and, of course, above all, no Sonia to keep him on the run. I don't expect he ever realized what a lot of his time used to be taken up by Sonia. Polly's no company for him, really. You can see that, and in many ways she seems dreadfully on his nerves. She's so insular, you know, nothing is right for her, she hates the place, hates the people, even hates the climate. Boy, at least, is very cosmopolitan, speaks beautiful Italian, prepared to be interested in the local folklore, and things like that, but you can't be interested quite alone and Polly is so discouraging. Everything seems rot to her and she only longs for England."

"Funny," I said, "that she should be quite so narrow-mindedly English when you think that she spent five years in India."

"Oh, my dear child, the butler was grander and the weather was hotter but otherwise there wouldn't be much to choose between Hampton and Viceroy's House. If anything, Viceroy's House was the less cosmopolitan of the two, I should say, and certainly it was no preparation for Sicilian housekeeping. No, she simply loathes it. So there is the poor fellow, shut up month after month with a cross little girl he has known from a baby. Not much cop, you must admit."

"I thought," said Cedric, "that he was so fond of dukes? Sicily is full of heavenly dukes, you know."

"Fairly heavenly, and they're nearly always away. Anyhow, he doesn't count them the same as French or English dukes."

"Well, that's nonsense, nobody could be grander than Monte Pincio. But if he doesn't count them (I do see some of the others are a bit unreal), and if he's got to live abroad, I can't imagine why he doesn't choose Paris. Plenty of proper dukes there—fifty, to be exact—Souppes told me so once. You know how they can only talk about each other, in that trade."

"My dear Cedric, they are very poor—they can't afford to live in England, let alone Paris. That's why they are still in Sicily. If it wasn't for that they'd come home now like a shot. Boy lost money in the crash last autumn, and he told me that if he hadn't got a very good let for Silkin they would really be almost penniless. Oh, dear, and when you think how rich Polly would have been . . ."

"No cruel looks at *one*," said Cedric. "Fair's fair, you know."

"Anyway it's a shocking business and only shows where dear old sex can land a person. I never saw anybody so pleased as he was when I appeared—like a dog let off a lead. Wanted to hear every single thing that's been going on. You could just see how lonely and bored he feels, poor chap."

But I was thinking of Polly. If Boy was bored and lonely, she was not likely to be very happy, either. The success or failure of all human relationships lies in the atmosphere each person is aware of creating for the other. What atmosphere could a disillusioned Polly feel that she was creating for a bored and lonely Boy? Her charm, apart from her beauty, and husbands, we know, get accustomed to the beauty of their wives so that it ceases to strike them at the heart, her charm used to derive from the sphinx-like quality which came from her secret dream of Boy. In the early days of that dream coming true, at Alconleigh, happiness had made her irresistible. But I quite saw that with the riddle solved, and with the happiness dissolved, Polly, without her own little daily round of Madame Rita, Debenhams and the hairdresser to occupy her, and too low in vitality to invent new interests for herself, might easily sink into sulky dumps. She was not at all likely to find consolation in Sicilian folklore, I knew, and probably not, not yet anyhow, in Sicilian noblemen.

"Oh, dear," I said. "If Boy isn't happy I don't suppose Polly can be, either. Oh, poor Polly."

"Poor Polly—m'm—but at least it was her idea," said Davey. "My heart bleeds for poor Boy. Well, he can't say I didn't warn him, over and over again."

"What about a baby?" I asked. "Any signs?"

"None that I could see, but, after all, how long have they been married? Eighteen months? Sonia was eighteen years before she had Polly."

"Oh, goodness!" I said. "I shouldn't imagine the Lecturer, in eighteen years time, will be able . . ."

I was stopped by a well-known hurt look on Davey's face.

"Perhaps that is what makes them sad," I ended rather lamely.

"Possibly. Anyhow I can't say that I formed a happy impression."

At this point Cedric was called to the telephone, and Davey said to me in a lowered voice, "Entirely between you and me, Fanny, and this is not to go any further, I think Polly is having trouble with Boy."

"Oh, dear," I said, "kitchen maids?"

"No," said Davey, "not kitchen maids."

"Don't tell me!" I said, horrified.

Cedric came back and said that Lady Montdore had been caught red-handed having elevenses in the Devonshire tea-rooms and had been given the sack. She told him that the motor would call for him on its way, so that she would have a companion for the drive home.

"There now," he said gloomily. "I shan't have my little visit to you, after all, and I had so been looking forward to it."

It struck me that Cedric had arranged the orange cure less with a view to getting rid of kilos than to getting rid of Lady Montdore for a week or two. Life with her must be wearing work, even to Cedric, with his unflagging spirits and abounding energy, and he may well have felt that he had earned a short holiday after nearly a year of it.

Chapter 6

CEDRIC HAMPTON AND Norma Cozens met at last, but though the meeting took place in my garden it was none of my arranging—a pure chance. I was sitting, one afternoon of Indian summer, on my lawn, where the baby was crawling about stark naked and so brown that he looked like a little Topsy, when Cedric's golden head appeared over the fence, accompanied by another head, that of a thin and ancient horse.

"I'm coming to explain," he said, "but I won't bring my friend. I'll attach him to your fence, darling. He's so sad and good, he won't do any harm, I promise."

A moment later he joined me in the garden. I put the baby back in its pram and was turning to Cedric to ask what this was all about, when Norma came up the lane which passes my garden, on her afternoon trudge with her dogs. Now the Boreley family consider that they have a special mandate, bestowed from on high, to deal with everything that regards the horse. They feel it to be their duty, no less than their right, and therefore the moment she saw Cedric's friend, sad and good, standing by my fence, Norma unhesitatingly came into the garden to see what she could do about it. I introduced Cedric to her.

"I don't want to interrupt you," she said, her eye upon the famous piping of the seams, brown to-day upon a green linen coat, vaguely Tyrolean in aspect, "but there's a very old mare, Fanny, tied up to your fence. Do you know anything about it? Whom does she belong to?"

"Don't, dear Mrs. Cozens, tell me that the first horse I have ever owned is a female!" said Cedric, with a glittering (brush) smile.

"The animal is a mare," said Norma, "and if she is yours I must tell you that you ought to be ashamed of yourself for keeping her in that dreadful condition."

"Oh, but I only began keeping her ten minutes ago. My intention is to build her up. I hope that when you see her again, in a few months time, you simply won't know her."

"Do you mean to say that you bought that creature? She ought to go straight away to the kennels."

"The kennels? But why? She's not a dog!"

"The knacker, the horse butcher," said Norma impatiently, "she must be put down immediately, or I shall ring up the R.S.P.C.A."

"Oh, please don't do that. I'm not being cruel to her, I'm being kind. That horrid man I bought her from, he was being beastly, he was taking her to the knacker. My plan was to save her from him. I couldn't bear to see the expression on her poor face."

"Well, but what are you going to do with her, my dear boy?"

"I thought—set her free."

"Set her free? She's not a bird, you know, you can't go setting horses free like that—not in England anyway."

"Yes, I can. Not in Oxford, perhaps, but where I live there is a *vieux parc, solitaire et glacé,* and it is my intention to set her free there, to have happy days away from knackers. Isn't knacker a hateful word, Mrs. Cozens?"

"The grazing at Hampton is let," said Norma. It was the kind of detail the Boreleys could be counted on to tell you.

Cedric, however, took no notice and went on, "She was being driven down the street in a van with her head sticking out at the back, and I could see at once that she was longing for some nice person to get her out of the fix she was in, so I stopped the van and bought her. You could see how relieved she felt."

"How much?"

"Well, I offered the man forty pounds. It was all I had on me, so he let me have her for that."

"Forty pounds!" cried Norma, aghast. "Why, you could get a hunter for less than forty pounds."

"But, my dearest Mrs. Cozens, I don't want a hunter. It's the last thing. I'd be far too frightened. Besides, look at the time you have to get up—I heard them the other morning in the woods, half-past six. Well, you know, I'm afraid it's 'up before seven *dead* before eleven' with *one*. No, I just wanted this special old clipper-clopper. She's not the horse to make claims on a chap. She won't want to be ridden all the time, as a younger horse might, and there she'll be, if I feel like having a few words with her occasionally. But the great question now, which I came to tease practical Fanny with, is how to get her home?"

"And if you go buying up all the horses that are fit for the kennels, however do you imagine hounds are going to be fed?" said Norma, in great exasperation. She was related to several Masters of fox-hounds and her sister had a pack of beagles, so no doubt she was acquainted with all their problems.

"I shan't buy up all the horses," said Cedric, soothingly, "only this one, which I took a liking for. Now, dear Mrs. Cozens, do stop being angry and just tell me how I can get her home, because I know you can help if you want to and I simply can't get over the luck of meeting you here at the very moment when I needed you so badly."

Norma began to weaken, as people so very often did with Cedric. It was extraordinary how fast he could worm his way through a thick crust of prejudice, and, just as in the case of Lady Montdore, the people who hated him the most were generally those who had seen him from afar but never met him. But whereas Lady Montdore had "all this" to help in her conquest of disapproval, Cedric relied upon his charm, his good looks and his deep inborn knowledge of human, and especially female, nature.

"Please," he said, his eyes upon her, blinking a little.

I could see that he had done the trick, Norma was considering.

"Well," she said at last, "there are two ways of doing it. I can lend you a saddle and you can ride her over. I'm not sure she's up to it, but you could see . . ."

"No, Mrs. Cozens, no. I have some literary sense—Fauntleroy on his pony, gallant little figure, the wind in his golden curls, all right, and if my uncle had had the sense to get me over from Canada when I was younger we should have seen that very thing, I've no doubt. But the gloomy old Don on Rosinante is quite another matter, and I can't face it."

"Which gloomy old don?" asked Norma with interest. "But it makes no odds, she'd never get there. Twenty miles, now I come to think of it—and I expect she's as lame as a cat."

She went to the fence and peered over.

"Those hocks . . . ! You know, it honestly would be kinder—oh, very well, very well. If nothing I can say will make you understand that the animal would be far happier dead, you'll have to get the horse box. Shall I ring up Stubby now, on Fanny's telephone and see if he can come round at once?"

"No! You wouldn't do that for me? Oh, dearest Mrs. Cozens I can only say—angel! What a miracle that I met you!"

"Lie down," she said, to the Borders, and went indoors.

"Sexually unsatisfied, poor her," said Cedric, when she had gone.

"Really, Cedric, what nonsense! She's got four children."

"I can't help it. Look at all those wrinkles. She could try patting in muscle oil, of course, and I shall suggest it as soon as I get to know her a little better, but I'm afraid the trouble is more deep-seated. Of course, I feel certain the Professor must be a secret queer—nobody but a queer would ever marry Norma, to begin with."

"Why? She's not at all boyish."

"No, dearest, it isn't that; but there is a certain type of Norma-ish lady which appeals to queers, don't ask me why, but so it is. Now, supposing I arranged for her to come over every Tuesday and share a facial with Sonia, what do you think? The competition would be good for both of them, and it would cheer Sonia up to see a woman so much younger, so much more deeply haggard."

"I wouldn't," I said. "Norma always says she can't stick Lady Montdore."

"Does she know her? Of course, I doubt if anything short of a nice lift would fix Mrs. Cozens, but we could teach her 'brush' and a little charm to help the Waynflete Prof to do his work a bit better, or, failing that, and I fear it's rather a desperate hope, some nice Woodley might come to the rescue. No, darling, not *one*," he added, in response to a meaning look from me. "The cuticles are too desperately anaphrodisiac."

"I thought you never wanted to see her because she reminded you of Nova Scotia?"

"Yes, I thought she would, but she is too English. She fascinates me for that reason; you know how very, very pro-English I am becoming. The cuticles are rather Nova Scotian, but her soul is the soul of Oxfordshire and I shall cultivate her after this like mad."

Some half an hour later, as Cedric went off, sitting by the driver of the horse box, Norma, panting a little from her efforts with the mare, who had stubbornly refused at first to get into it, said, "You know, that boy has some good in him, after all. What a shame he couldn't have gone to a decent public school instead of being brought up in those shocking colonies."

To my amazement, and great secret annoyance, Cedric and Norma now became extremely friendly, and he went to see her, when he was in Oxford, quite as often as he did me.

"Whatever do you talk about?" I said to him crossly.

"Oh, we have cosy little chats about this and that. I love Englishwomen; they are so restful."

"Well, I'm fairly fond of old Norma, but I simply can't imagine what you see in her, Cedric."

"I suppose I see whatever you see," he replied carelessly.

After a bit, he persuaded her to give a dinner party, to which he promised to bring Lady Montdore. Lord Montdore never went out now, and was sinking happily into old age. His wife being provided with a companion for every hour of the day, he was not only allowed but encouraged to have a good long nap in the afternoon, and he generally either had his dinner in bed or shuffled off there immediately after dinner. The advent of Cedric must have proved a blessing to him in more ways than one. People very soon got into the habit of asking Cedric with Lady Montdore instead of her husband, and it must be said that he was much better company. They were going out more now than when Cedric first arrived, the panic caused by the financial crisis was subsiding and people had begun to entertain again. Lady Montdore was too fond of society to keep away from it for long, and Cedric, firmly established at Hampton, weighed down with many large expensive gifts, could surely now be shown to her friends without danger of losing him.

In spite of the fact that she was by way of being unable to stick Lady Montdore, Norma got into a perfect state over this dinner party, dropping in on me at all hours to discuss the menu and the fellow guests, and finally imploring me to come on the morning of the day to make a pudding for her. I said that I would do so on one condition: she must buy a quart of cream. She wriggled like an eel not to have to do this, but I was quite firm. Then she said would the top of the milk do? No, I said, it must be thick rich unadulterated cream. I said I would bring it with me and let her know how much I had paid for it, and she reluctantly agreed. Although she was, I knew, very wealthy, she never spent a penny more than she could help on her house, her table or her clothes (except her riding clothes, for she was always beautifully turned out in the hunting field and I am sure her horses lived on an equine substitute for cream). So I went round, and, having provided myself with the suitable ingredients, I made her a crème Chantilly. As I got back to my own house the telephone bell was pealing away. Cedric.

"I thought I'd better warn you, my darling, that we are chucking poor Norma to-night."

"Cedric, you simply can't, I never heard anything so awful. She has bought cream!"

He gave an unkind laugh and said, "So much the better for those weedy tots I see creeping about her house."

"But why should you chuck, are you ill?"

"Not the least bit ill, thank you, love. The thing is that Merlin wants us to go over there for dinner. He has got fresh foie gras, and a fascinating Marquesa with eyelashes two inches long—he measured—do you see how *one* can't resist it?"

"*One* must resist it," I said frantically. "You simply cannot chuck poor Norma now. You'll never know the trouble she's taken. Besides, do think of us, you miserable boy, we can't chuck, only think of the dismal evening we shall have without you."

"I know, poor you—lugubrious."

"Cedric, all I can say is you are a sewer."

"Yes, darling, *mea culpa*. But it's not so much that I want to chuck as that I absolutely know I shall. I don't even intend to, I fully intend not to, it is that something in my body will make me. When I've rung off from speaking to you, I know that my hand will creep back to the receiver again of its own accord, and I shall hear my voice, but quite against my will, mind you, asking for Norma's number, and then I shall be really horrified to hear it breaking this dreadful news to Norma. So much worse, now I know about the cream, too. But there it is. But what I rang you up to say is, don't forget you are on *one's* side—no disloyalty, Fanny, please, I absolutely count, dear, on you not to egg Norma on to be furious. Because so long as you don't do that you'll find she won't mind a bit, not a bit. So, solidarity between working girls, and I'll promise to come over tomorrow and tell about the eyelashes."

Oddly enough, Cedric was right and Norma was not in the least put out. His excuse, and he had told the truth, merely adding a touch of embroidery by saying that Lady Montdore had been at school with the Marquesa, was considered quite a reasonable one, since dinner with Lord Merlin was recognized at Oxford as being the very pinnacle of human happiness. Norma rang me up to say that her dinner party was postponed, in the voice of a society hostess who postpones dinner parties every day of the week. Then, lapsing into more normal Oxford parlance she said:

"It's a bore about the cream, because they are coming on Wednesday now and it will never keep in this weather. Can you come back and make another pudding on Wednesday morning, Fanny? All right, and I'll pay you for both lots together, if that suits you. Everybody is free and I think the flowers may last over, so see you then, Fanny."

But on Wednesday Cedric was in bed with a high temperature, and on Thursday he was rushed to London by ambulance and operated upon for peritonitis, lying between life and death for several days, and in the end it was quite two months before the dinner party could take place.

At last, however, the date was fixed again, another pudding was made, and, at Norma's suggestion, I invited my Uncle Davey to come and stay for it, to pair off with her beagling sister. Norma looked down on dons quite as much as Lady Montdore did, and, as for undergraduates, although of course she must have known that such things existed, since they provided her husband and mine with a livelihood, she certainly never thought of them as human beings and possible diners out.

IT WOULD NEVER formerly have occurred to me that "touching," a word often on Lady Montdore's lips (it was very much of her day) could come to have any relation to herself, but on the occasion of Norma's dinner, the first time I had seen Lady Montdore with Cedric since his illness, there was really something touching about her attitude towards him. It was touching to see this hitherto redoubtable and ponderous personage, thin now as a rake, in her little-girl dress of dark-blue tulle over pink taffeta, with her little-girl head of pale-blue curls, dark-blue ribbons and a swarm of diamond bees, as she listened through her own conversation to whatever Cedric might be saying, as she squinted out of the corner of her eye to see if he was happy and amused, perhaps even just to be quite sure that he was actually there, in the flesh, touching to see with what reluctance she left the dining room after dinner, touching to watch her as she sat with the rest of us in the drawing room waiting for the men to return, silent, or speaking at random, her eyes fixed upon the door like a spaniel waiting for its master. Love, with her, had blossomed late and strangely, but there could be no doubt that it had blossomed, and that this thorny old plant had very much altered in character to accord with the tender flowers and spring-time verdure which now so unexpectedly adorned it. During the whole of the evening there was only one respect in which she behaved as she would have done in her pre-Cedric days, she piled wood and coal, without so much as a by-your-leave, onto the tiny fire, Norma's concession to the fact that winter had begun, so that by the end of the evening we sat in a mellow warmth such as I had never known in that room before.

The men, as they always do in Oxford, remained an inordinate length of time over their port, so long, in fact, that Lady Montdore, with growing impatience, suggested to Norma that they might be sent for. Norma, however, looked so absolutely appalled at the idea that Lady Montdore did not press it any further, but went on with her self-appointed task as stoker, one spaniel eye on the door.

"The only way to make a good fire," she said, "is to put on enough coal. People have all kinds of theories about it, but it's really very simple. Perhaps we could ask for another scuttle, Mrs. Cozens? Very kind. Cedric mustn't get a chill, whatever happens."

"Dreadful," I said, "him being so ill, wasn't it?"

"Don't speak of it. I thought I should die. Yes, well, as I was saying. It's exactly the same with coffee, you know. People have these percolators and things and get the Bolter to buy them special beans in Kenya. Perfectly pointless. Coffee is good if it is made strong enough and nasty if it is not. What we had just now would have been quite all right if your cook had put in three times the amount, you know. What can they be talking about in the dining room? It's not as if any of them were interested in politics."

At last the door opened. Davey came in first, looking bored and made straight for the fire, Cedric, the Professor and Alfred followed in a bunch, still pursuing a conversation which seemed to be interesting them deeply.

"Just a narrow edging of white . . ." I heard Cedric say, through the open door, as they came down the passage.

Later on I remembered to ask Alfred what could have led up to this remark, so typical of Cedric but so un-typical of the conversation in that house, and he replied that they had been having a most fascinating talk on burial customs in the High Yemen.

"I fear," he said, "that you bring out the worst in Cedric Hampton, Fanny. He is really a most intelligent young man, interested in a large range of subjects, though I have no doubt at all that when he is with you he confines himself, as you do, to remarks in the nature of 'And did you notice the expression on her face when she saw who was there?' because he knows that general subjects do not amuse you, only personalities. With those whose horizon is a little wider he can be very serious, let me tell you."

The fact was that Cedric could bring out edgings of white to suit all tastes.

"Well, Fanny, how do you like it?" he asked me, giving a twitch to Lady Montdore's tulle skirt. "We ordered it by telephone when we were at Craigside—don't you die for television? Mainbocher simply couldn't believe that Sonia had lost so much weight."

Indeed she was very thin.

"I sit in a steam barrel," she said, looking fondly at Cedric, "for an hour or two, and then that nice Mr. Wixman comes down twice a week when we are at Hampton and he beats and beats me and the morning is gone in a flash. Cedric sees the cook for me nowadays. I find I can't take very much interest in food, in my barrel."

"But, my dear Sonia," said Davey, "I hope you consult Dr. Simpson about all this? I am horrified to see you in such a state. Really much too thin, nothing but skin and bones. You know, at our age, it's most dangerous to play about with one's weight, a terrible strain on the heart."

It was generous of Davey to talk about "our age," since Lady Montdore was certainly fourteen years older than he was.

"Dr. Simpson!" she said derisively. "My dear Davey, he's terribly behind the times. Why, he never even told me how good it is to stand on one's head, and Cedric says in Paris and Berlin they've been doing it for ages now. I must say I feel younger every day since I learnt. The blood races through your glands, you know, and they love it."

"How d'you know they love it?" said Davey with considerable irritation. He always scorned any regime for health except the one he happened to be following himself, regarding all others as dangerous superstitions imposed on gullible fools by unscrupulous quacks. "We understand so very little about our glands," he went on. "Why should it be good for them? Did Dame Nature intend us to stand on our heads? Do animals stand on their heads, Sonia?"

"The sloth," said Cedric, "and the bat hang upside down for hours on end—you can't deny that, Davey."

"Yes, but do sloths and bats feel younger every day? I doubt it. Bats may, but I'm sure sloths don't."

"Come on, Cedric," said Lady Montdore, very much put out by Davey's remarks, "we must be going home."

Lady Montdore and Cedric now installed themselves at Montdore House for the winter and were seen no more by me. London society, having none of the prejudices against the abnormal which still exist among Boreleys and Uncle Matthews in country places, simply ate Cedric up, occasional echoes of his great success even reaching Oxford. It seemed that such an arbiter of taste, such an arranger of festivities, had not been known since the days of the beaux, and that he lived in a perfect welter of parties, dragging Lady Montdore along in his wake.

"Isn't she wonderful? You know she's seventy—eighty—ninety . . ." Her age went up by leaps and bounds.

So Cedric had transformed her from a terrifying old idol of about sixty into a delicious young darling of about a hundred. Was anything beyond his powers?

I remember one icy day of late spring I ran into Mrs. Chaddesley Corbett, walking down the Turl with an undergraduate, perhaps her son, I thought, chinless, like her.

"Fanny!" she said. "Oh, of course, darling, you live here, don't you? I'm always hearing about you from Cedric. He dotes on you, that's all."

"Oh," I said, pleased. "And I'm so very fond of him."

"Couldn't like him more, could you? So gay, so cosy, I think he's a perfect poppet. As for Sonia, it's a transformation, isn't it? Polly's marriage seems to have turned out to be a blessing in disguise for her. Do you ever hear from Polly now? What a thing to have done, poor sweet. But I'm mad about Cedric, that's all—everybody in London is—tiny Lord Fauntleroy. They're both dining with me this evening. I'll give them your love, shall I? See you very soon, darling, good-bye."

I saw Mrs. Chaddesley Corbett perhaps once a year. She always called me darling and said she would see me very soon, and this always left me feeling quite unreasonably elated.

I got back to my house and found Jassy and Victoria sitting by the fire. Victoria was looking very green.

"I must do the talking," Jassy said. "Fa's new car makes poor Vict sick and she can't open her mouth for fear of letting the sick out."

"Go and let it out in the loo," I said. Victoria shook her head vehemently.

"She hates being," said Jassy. "Anything rather. We hope you're pleased to see us."

I said that I was, very.

"And we hope you've noted how we never do come nowadays."

"Yes, I have noted. I put it down to the hunting."

"Stupid, you are. How could one hunt, in this weather?"

"This weather only began yesterday, and I've heard of you from Norma, hunting away like anything up to now."

"We don't think you quite realize how bitterly offended we feel over your behaviour to us the last year or two."

"Now, now, children, we've had this out a thousand times," I said firmly.

"Yes, well, it's not very nice of you. After all, when you married we rather naturally expected that your home would open up all the delights of civilized society to us, and that sooner or later we should meet, in your salon, the brilliant wealthy titled men destined to become our husbands. 'I loved her from the first moment I saw her, the leggy little girl with the beautiful sensitive face, who used to sprawl about Mrs. Wincham's drawing room at Oxford.' Well, then, what happens? One of the richest parties in Western Europe becomes an *habitué de la maison* and are we thrown at his head by our cousin, naturally ambitious for our future? Does she move heaven and earth to further this splendid match? Not even asked to meet him. Spoil sport."

"Go on," I said, wearily.

"No, well, we're only bringing it up . . ." Victoria here fled the room, Jassy took no notice, ". . . in order to show our great magnanimity of soul. The fact is, that we know a very interesting piece of news, and in spite of your counter-honnish behaviour we are going to tell it to you. But we want you to realize that it is pretty noble of us, when you take everything into account, his flashing eyes, his floating hair, only seen in the distance. It is such a shame, and I must wait for Vict to come back or it would be too unfaithful, and can we have some tea? She's always starving after."

"Does Mrs. Heathery know you're here?"

"Yes, she held Vict's head."

"You don't mean to say she's been sick already?"

"It's always thrice—once in the car and twice when we get there."

"Well, if Mrs. Heathery knows, tea will appear."

It appeared simultaneously with Victoria.

"Fanny's loo! The bliss! It's got a carpet, Jassy, and it's boiling warm, one could stay there all day. Crumpets! Oh, Fanny!"

"What's this news you know?" I asked, pouring out milk for the children.

"I like tea now, please," said Jassy. "Which shows how long since you saw us. I like tea and I almost like coffee. So the news is, Napoleon has left Elba and is on his way back."

"Say it again."

"Dense. Nobody would think that you were a hostess to the younger cosmopolitan intellectual set, noted for her brilliant repartee."

"Do you mean Polly?" I said, light suddenly dawning.

"Very bright of you, dear. Josh was out exercising this morning and he stopped at the Blood Arms for a quick one, and that's what he heard. So we came dashing over to tell you, Fanny, in sickness and in health. So does one good turn not deserve another, Fanny?"

"Oh, do stop being such a bore," I said, "and go on telling. When?"

"Any day now. The tenants have gone and the house is being got ready. Lady Patricia's sheets and things, you know. She's going to have a baby."

"Who is, Polly?"

"Well, dear, who do you think? Not Lady Patricia. So that's what she's coming back for. So are you admitting that it was handsome of us to come over and tell you?"

"Very handsome," I said.

"So will you invite us to luncheon one day soon?"

"Any day you like. I'll make chocolate profiterolles with real cream."

"And what about closing our eyes with holy dread?"

"Cedric, if that's what you mean, is in London, but you can close them at Jock Boreley," I said.

"Oh, Fanny, you brute. Can we go upstairs and see dear little David?"

Chapter 7

THE WEATHER NOW became intensely cold, and much snow fell. The newspapers came out every day with horror stories of sheep buried in snowdrifts, of songbirds frozen to the branches on which they perched, of fruit trees hopelessly nipped in the bud, and the situation seemed dreadful to those who, like Mrs. Heathery, believe all they see in print without recourse to past experience. I tried to cheer her up by telling her, what, in fact, proved to be the case, that in a very short time the fields would be covered with sheep, the trees with birds and the barrows with fruit just as usual. But, though the future did not disturb me I found the present most disagreeable, that winter should set in again so late in the spring, at a time when it would not be unreasonable to expect delicious weather, almost summer-like, warm enough to sit out of doors for an hour or two. The sky was overcast with a thick yellow blanket from which an endless pattern of black-and-white snowflakes came swirling down, and this went on day after day. One morning I sat by my window gazing idly at the pattern and thinking idle thoughts, wondering if it would ever be warm again, thinking how like a child's snowball Christ Church looked through a curtain of flakes, thinking, too, how cold it was going to be at Norma's that evening without Lady Montdore to stoke the fire, and how dull without Cedric and his narrow edging of white. Thank goodness, I thought, that I had sold my father's diamond brooch and installed central heating with the proceeds. Then I began to remember what the house had been like two years before when the workmen were still in it, and how I had looked out through that very same pane of glass, filthy dirty then, and splashed with whitewash, and seen Polly struggling into the wind with her future husband. I half wanted and half did not want Polly in my life again. I was expecting another baby and felt tired, really, not up to much.

Then, suddenly, the whole tempo of the morning completely altered because here in my drawing room, heavily pregnant, beautiful as ever, in a red coat and hat, was Polly, and, of course, all feelings of not wanting her melted away and were forgotten. In my drawing room, too, was the Lecturer, looking old and worn.

When Polly and I had finished hugging and kissing and laughing and saying, "Lovely to see you," and "Why did you never write?" she said,

"Can I bend you to my will?"

"Oh, yes you can. I've got simply nothing to do. I was just looking at the snow."

"Oh, the heaven of snow," she said, "and clouds, after all those blue skies. Now the thing is, Fanny, can I bend you until late this afternoon, because Boy has got an utter mass of things to do and I can't stand about much, as you see. But you must frankly tell me if I shall be in your way, because I can always go to Elliston's waiting room. The blissful bliss of Elliston after those foreign shops! I nearly cried for happiness when we passed their windows just now—the bags! the cretonnes! The horror of abroad!"

"But that's wonderful," I said, "then you'll both lunch here?"

"Boy has to lunch with someone on business," said Polly, quickly. "You can go off then, darling, if you like, as Fanny says she can keep me. Don't bother to wait any more. Then come back for me here when you've finished?"

Boy, who had been rubbing his hands together in front of the fire, went off, rather glum, wrapping a scarf round his throat.

"And don't hurry a bit," she called after him, opening the door again and shouting down the stairs. "Now, darling Fanny, I want to do one final bend and make you lunch with me at Fullers. Don't speak! You're going to say 'look at the weather,' aren't you? but we'll ring up for a taxi. Fullers! You'll never know how much I used to long for Dover sole and walnut cake and just this sort of a day in Sicily. Do you remember how we used to go there from Alconleigh when you were getting your house ready? I can't believe this is the same house, can you? Or that we are the same people, come to that. Except I see you're the same darling Fanny, just as you were the same when I got back from India. Why is it that I, of all people, keep on having to go abroad? I do think it's too awful, don't you?"

"I only went just that once," I said. "It's very light, isn't it?"

"Yes, horrible glare. Just imagine if one had to live there for ever. You know we started off in Spain. And you'll never believe this, but they are two hours late for every meal—two hours, Fanny—(can we lunch at half past twelve to-day?) so of course by then you've stopped feeling hungry and only feel sick. Then, when the food comes, it is all cooked in rancid oil. I can smell it now, it's on everybody's hair, too, and to make it more appetizing there are pictures all round you of some dear old bull being tortured to death. They think of literally nothing all day but bulls and the Virgin. Spain was the worst of all, I thought. Of course Boy doesn't mind abroad a bit, in fact, he seems to like it, and he can talk all those terribly affected languages (darling, Italian! you'd die!) but I truly don't think I could have borne it much longer. I should have pined away with homesickness. Anyway, here I am."

"What made you come back?" I said, really wondering how they could afford it, poor as Davey said they were. Silkin was not a big house, but it would require three or four servants.

"Well, you remember my Auntie Edna at Hampton Court? The

good old girl died and left me all her money—not much, but we think we can just afford to live at Silkin. Then Boy is writing a book and he had to come back for that, London Library and Paddington."

"Paddington?" I said, thinking of the station.

"Duke Muniment room. Then there's this baby. Fancy, if one had to have a baby abroad, poor little thing, not a cow in the place. All the same, Boy doesn't much want to settle down here for good. I think he's still frightened of Mummy, you know. I am a bit, myself—not frightened exactly, but bored at the idea of scenes. But there's really nothing more she can do to us, is there?"

"I don't think you need worry about her a bit," I said. "Your mother has altered completely in the last two years."

I could not very well say my real thought, which was that Lady Montdore no longer cared a rap for Boy or for Polly, and that she would most likely be quite friendly to them. It all depended upon Cedric's attitude, everything did, nowadays, as far as she was concerned.

Presently, when we were settled at our table at Fullers, among the fumed oak and the daintiness ("Isn't everything clean and lovely? Aren't the waitresses fair? You can't think how dark the waiters always are, abroad.") and had ordered our Dover soles, Polly said that now I must tell her all about Cedric.

"Do you remember," she said, "how you and Linda used to look him up to see if he would *do*."

"Well, he wouldn't have *done*," I said. "That's one thing quite certain."

"So I imagine," said Polly.

"How much do you know about him?"

I suddenly felt rather guilty at knowing so much myself and hoped that Polly would not think I had gone over to the enemy's camp. It is so difficult if you are fond of sport to resist running with the hare and hunting with the hounds.

"Boy made friends, in Sicily, with an Italian duke called Monte

Pincio. He is writing about a former Pincio in his new book, and this wop knew Cedric in Paris, so he told us a lot about him. He says he is very pretty."

"Yes, that's quite true."

"How pretty, Fan? Prettier than me?"

"No. One doesn't have to gaze and gaze at him like one does with you."

"Oh, darling, you are so kind. Not any longer though, I fear."

"Just exactly the same. But he is very much like you. Didn't the Duke say that?"

"Yes. He said we were Viola and Sebastian. I must say I die for him."

"He dies for you, too. We must arrange it."

"Yes, after the baby—not while I'm such a sight. You know how sissies hate pregnant ladies. Poor Monte would do anything to get out of seeing me, lately. Go on telling more about Cedric and Mummy."

"I really think he loves your mother, you know. He is such a slave to her, never leaves her for a moment, always in high spirits. . . . I don't believe anybody could put it on to that extent, it must be love."

"I'm not surprised," said Polly. "I used to love her before she began about the marrying."

"There!" I said.

"There what?"

"Well, you told me once that you'd hated her all your life, and I knew it wasn't true."

"The fact is," said Polly, "when you hate somebody you can't imagine what it's like not hating them. It's just the same as with love. But of course with Mummy, who is such excellent company, so lively, you do love her before you find out how wicked she can be. And I don't suppose she's in all that violent hurry to get Cedric off that she was with me."

"No hurry," I said.

Polly's blank blue look fell upon my face. "You mean she's in love with him herself?"

"In love? I don't know. She loves him like anything. He makes such fun for her, you see, her life has become so amusing. Besides, she must know quite well that marriage isn't his thing exactly, poor Cedric."

"Oh, no," said Polly. "Boy agrees with me that she knows nothing, nothing whatever about all that. He says she once made a fearful gaffe about Sodomites, mixing them up with Dolomites. It was all over London. No, I guess she's in love. She's a great, great faller in love, you know. I used to think at one time that she rather fancied Boy, though he says not. Well, it's all very annoying because I suppose she doesn't miss me one little bit, and I miss her, often. And now tell me, how's my dad?"

"Very old," I said. "Very old, and your mother so very young. You must be prepared for quite as much of a shock when you see her as when you see him."

"No, really? How d'you mean, very young? Dyed hair?"

"Blue. But what one chiefly notices is that she has become so thin and supple, quick little movements, flinging one leg over the other, suddenly sitting on the floor, and so on. Quite like a young person."

"Good gracious," said Polly. "And she used to be so very stiff and solid."

"It's Mr. Wixman, Cedric's and her masseur. He pounds and pulls for an hour every morning, then she has another hour in a hay-box—full-time work, you know, what with the creaming and splashing and putting on a mask and taking it off again and having her nails done and her feet and then all the exercises, as well as having her teeth completely re-arranged and the hairs zipped off her arms and legs—I truly don't think I could be bothered."

"Operations on her face?"

"Oh, yes, but that was ages ago. All the bags and wrinkles gone, eyebrows plucked, and so on. Her face is very tidy now."

"Of course it may seem odd here," said Polly, "but you know there are hundreds and hundreds of women like that abroad. I suppose she stands on her head and lies in the sun? Yes, they all do. She must be a sight. Scene or no scene, I utterly can't wait for her, Fanny. When can we arrange it?"

"Not for the moment. They're in London now, fearfully busy with the Longhi ball they are giving at Montdore House. Cedric came to see me the other day and could talk of nothing else—he says they won't be going to Hampton again until it's over."

"What is a Longhi ball?"

"You know, Venetian. Real water, with real gondolas floating on it, in the ballroom. *O sole mio* on a hundred guitars, all the footmen in masks and capes, no light except from candles in Venetian lanterns until the guests get to the ballroom, when a searchlight will be trained on Cedric and your mother, receiving from a gondola. Fairly different from your ball, Polly. Oh, yes, and I know, Cedric won't allow any Royalties to be asked at all, because he says they ruin everything, in London. He says they are quite different in Paris where they know their place."

"Goodness!" said Polly. "How times have changed! Not even old Super-Ma'am?"

"No, not even your mother's new Infanta. Cedric was adamant."

"Fanny, it's your duty to go to it. You will, won't you?"

"Oh, darling, I can't. I feel so sleepy after dinner when I am pregnant, you know. I really couldn't drag myself. We shall hear about it all right, from Cedric."

"And when does it take place?"

"Under a month from now, the sixteenth, I believe."

"Why that's the very day I'm expecting my baby. How convenient. Then when everything's all over we can meet, can't we? You will fix it, promise."

"Oh, don't worry. We shan't be able to hold Cedric back. He's fearfully interested in you. You're Rebecca to him."

Boy came back to my house just as we were finishing our tea. He looked perished with cold and very tired but Polly would not let him wait while some fresh tea was made. She allowed him to swallow a tepid cup and dragged him off.

"I suppose you've lost the key of the car as usual," she said unkindly on their way downstairs.

"No no, here it is, on my key ring."

"Miracle," said Polly. "Well, then, good-bye, my darling. I'll telephone and we'll do some more benders."

WHEN ALFRED CAME in later on I said to him, "I've seen Polly! Just imagine, she spent the whole day here, and oh, Alfred, she's not a bit in love any more!"

"Do you never think of anything but who is or is not in love with whom?" he said in tones of great exasperation.

Norma, I knew, would be just as uninterested, and I longed very much for Davey or Cedric to pick it all over with.

Chapter 8

So POLLY NOW settled into her aunt's house at Silkin. It had always been Lady Patricia's house more than Boy's, as she was the one who lived there all the time, while Boy flitted about between Hampton and London with occasional visits to the Continent, and it was arranged inside with a very feminine form of tastelessness, that is to say, no taste and no comfort, either. It was a bit better than Norma's house, but not much, the house itself being genuinely old instead of Banbury Road old and standing in the real country instead of an Oxford suburb. It contained one or two good pieces of furniture, and where Norma would have had cretonnes the Dougdales had Boy's needlework. But there were many similarities, especially upstairs, where linoleum covered the floors, and every bathroom, in spite of the childlessness of the Dougdales, was a nursery bathroom, smelling strongly of not very nice soap.

Polly did not attempt to alter anything. She just flopped into Lady Patricia's bed, in Lady Patricia's bedroom whose windows looked out onto Lady Patricia's grave. "Beloved wife of Harvey Dougdale," said the gravestone, which had been erected some weeks after poor Harvey Dougdale had acquired a new beloved wife. "She shall not grow old as we that are left grow old."

I think Polly cared very little about houses, which, for her, consisted of Hampton and the rest, and that if she could no longer live at Hampton she could not take much interest in any other house. Whatever it was in life that Polly did care for, and time had yet to disclose the mystery, it was certainly not her home. She was in no sense what the French call a *"femme d'intérieur,"* and her household arrangements were casual to the verge of chaos. Nor, any longer, alas, was it Boy. Complete disillusion had set in, as far as he was concerned, and she was behaving towards him with exactly the same off-hand coldness that had formerly characterized her attitude towards her mother, the only difference being that whereas she had always been a little frightened of Lady Montdore it was Boy, in this case, who was a little frightened of her.

Boy was busily occupied with his new book. It was to be called *Three Dukes,* and the gentlemen it portrayed were considered by Boy to be perfect examples of nineteenth-century aristocracy in their three countries. The Dukes in question were Paddington, Souppes and Monte Pincio, all three masters, it seemed, of the arts of anecdote, adultery and gourmandise, members of the Jockey Club, gamblers and sportsmen. He had a photograph, the frontispiece for his book, of all three together, taken at a shoot at Landçut, standing in front of an acre of dead animals; with their tummies, their beards, their deerstalker's hats and white gaiters they looked like nothing so much as three King Edwards all in a row. Polly told me that he had finished Pincio while they were in Sicily, the present man having put the necessary documents at his disposal, and was now engaged upon Paddington with the assistance of the Duke's librarian, motoring off to Paddington Park every morning, notebook in hand. The idea was that when that was finished he should go to France in pursuit of Souppes. Nobody ever had the least objection to Boy "doing" their ancestors: he always made them so charming and endowed them with such delightful vices, besides which it gave a guarantee, a hallmark of ancient lineage, since he never would take on anybody whose family did not go back to well before the Conquest, in England, or, who, if foreign, could not produce at least one Byzantine Emperor, Pope or pre-Louis XV Bourbon in their family tree.

The day of the Montdore House ball came and went, but there was no sign of Polly's baby. Aunt Sadie always used to say that people unconsciously cheat over the dates when babies are expected in order to make the time of waiting seem shorter, but if that is so it certainly makes the last week or two seem endless. Polly depended very much on my company and would send a motor car most days to take me over to Silkin for an hour or two. The weather was heavenly at last, and we were able to go for little walks and even to sit in a sheltered corner of the garden, wrapped in rugs.

"Don't you love it," Polly said, "when it's suddenly like this after the winter and all the goats and hens look so happy?"

She did not seem very much interested in the idea of having a baby, though she once said to me, "Doesn't it seem funny to have talcum powder and things and boring old Sister waiting about, and all for somebody who doesn't exist?"

"Oh, I always think that," I said. "And yet the very moment they are there they become such an integral part of your life that you can't imagine what it was like without them."

"I suppose so. I wish they'd hurry up. So what about the ball— have you heard anything? You really ought to have gone, Fanny."

"I couldn't have. The Warden of Wadham and Norma went— not together, I don't mean, but they are the only people I've seen so far. It seems to have been very splendid, Cedric changed his dress five times. He started with tights made of rose petals and a pink wig and ended as Doris Keane in *Romance* and a black wig. He had real diamonds on his mask. Your mother was a Venetian youth, to show off her new legs, and they stood in a gondola giving away wonderful prizes to everybody—Norma got a silver snuffbox—and it went on till seven. Oh, how badly people do describe balls."

"Never mind, there'll be the *Tatler*."

"Yes, they said it was flash, flash all night. Cedric is sure to have the photographs to show us."

Presently Boy strolled up and said, "Well, Fanny, what d'you hear of the ball?"

"Oh, we've just had the ball," said Polly. "Can't begin all over again. What about your work?"

"I could bring it out here, if you like."

"You know I don't count your silly old embroidery as work."

Boy's face took on a hurt expression and he went away.

"Polly, you are awful," I said.

"Yes, but it's for his own good. He pretends he can't concentrate until after the baby now, so he wanders about getting on everybody's nerves when he ought to be getting on with Paddington. He must hurry, you know, if the book is to be out for Christmas. Have you ever met Geoffrey Paddington, Fanny?"

"Well, I have," I said, "because Uncle Matthew once produced him for a house party at Alconleigh. Old."

"Not the least bit old," said Polly, "and simply heavenly. You've no idea how nice he is. He came first to see Boy about the book and now he comes quite often, to chat. Terribly kind of him, don't you think? Mamma is his chief hate, so I never saw him before I married. I remember she was always trying to get him over to Hampton and he never would come. Perhaps he'll be here one day when you are. I'd love you to meet him."

I did meet him after that, several times, finding his shabby little Morris Cowley outside Silkin when I arrived. He was a poor man, since his ancestor, the great Duke, left much glory but little cash, and his father, the old gentleman in spats, had lavished most of what there was on La Païva and ladies of the kind. I thought him rather nice and very dull, and could see that he was falling in love with Polly.

"Don't you think he's terribly nice?" said Polly, "and so kind of him to come when I look like this."

"Your face is the same," I said.

"I really quite long for him to see me looking ordinary—if I ever do. I'm losing hope in this baby being born at all."

It was born, though, that very evening, took one look, according to the Radletts, at its father, and quickly died again.

Polly was rather ill and the Sister would not allow any visitors for about ten days after the baby was born, but as soon as she did I went over. I saw Boy for a moment in the hall. He looked even more gloomy than usual. Poor Boy, I thought, left with a wife who now so clearly disliked him and not even a baby to make up for it.

Polly lay in a bower of blossoms. The Sister was very much in evidence and there should have been a purple-faced wailing monster in a Moses basket to complete the picture. I really felt its absence as though it were that of a person well known to me.

"Oh, poor . . ." I began. But Polly had inherited a great deal of her mother's talent for excluding what was disagreeable, and I saw at once that any show of sympathy would be out of place and annoy her, so, instead, I exclaimed, Radlett fashion, over two camellia trees in full bloom which stood on each side of her bed.

"Geoffrey Paddington sent them," she said. "Do admit that he's a perfect love, Fanny. You know Sister was with his sister when she had her babies."

But then whom had Sister not been with? She and Boy must have had some lovely chats, I thought, the first night or two when Polly was feverish and they had sat up together in his dressing room. She kept on coming into the room while I was there, bringing a tray, taking away an empty jug, bringing some more flowers, any excuse to break in on our talk and deposit some nice little dollop of gossip. She had seen my condition at a glance, she had also realized that I was too small a fish for her net, but she was affability itself and said that she hoped I would come over every day now and sit with Lady Polly.

"Do you ever see Jeremy Chaddesley Corbett at Oxford?" she asked. "He is one of my favourite babies."

Presently she came in empty-handed and rather pink, almost, if such a thing were possible with her, rattled, and announced that Lady Montdore was downstairs. I felt that, whereas she would have bundled any of us into our coffins with perfect calm, the advent of Lady Montdore had affected even her nerves of iron. Polly, too, was thrown off her balance for a moment and said faintly, "Oh! Is Mr.—I mean my—I really mean is Boy there?"

"Yes, he's with her now. He sent word to say, will you see her? If you don't want to, Lady Polly, I can say quite truthfully that you may not have another visitor to-day. You really ought not to, the first day, in any case."

"I'll go," I said, getting up.

"No, no, no, Fanny, you mustn't, darling. I'm not sure I will see her, but I couldn't possibly be left alone with her. Sit down again at once, please."

There were voices in the garden outside.

"Do go to the window," said Polly. "Is it them?"

"Yes, and Cedric is there, too," I said. "And they're all three walking round the garden together."

"No! But I must I must see Cedric! Sister, do be a darling, go down and tell them to come up at once."

"Now, Lady Polly, no. And please don't work yourself up, you must avoid any excitement. It's absolutely out of the question for you to see a stranger to-day. Close relations was what Dr. Simpson said, and one at a time. I suppose your mother must be allowed up for a few minutes if you want her, but nobody else and certainly not a strange young man."

"I'd better see Mummy," Polly said, to me, "or else this silly feud will go on for ever, besides, I really can't wait to see her hair and her legs. Oh, dear, though, the one I long for is Cedric."

"She seems to be in a very friendly mood," I said, still looking at them out of the window. "Laughing and chatting away. Very smart in navy blue with a sailor hat. Boy is being wonderful. I thought he might be knocked groggy by her appearance, but he's pretending not to notice. He's looking at Cedric all the time. They are getting on like mad."

Most astute of him, I thought privately, if he hit it off with Cedric he would, very soon, be back in Lady Montdore's good graces, and then, perhaps, there could be a little modification of Lord Montdore's will.

"I die for the sailor hat. Come on, let's get it over. All right then, Sister, ask her to come up — wait — give me a comb and a glass first, will you? Go on with the running commentary, Fanny."

"Well, Cedric and Boy are chatting away like mad. I think Boy is admiring Cedric's suit, a sort of coarse blue tweed, very pretty, piped with scarlet. Lady Montdore is all smiles, having a good look round. You know the way she does."

"I can just see it," said Polly, combing her hair.

I did not quite like to say that Lady Montdore at this very moment was peering over the churchyard wall at her sister-in-law's grave. Boy and Cedric had left her there and were wandering off together towards the wrought-iron gates which led to the kitchen garden, laughing, talking and gesticulating.

"Go on," said Polly, "keep it up, Fanny."

"There's Sister, she is floating up to your mother, who is simply beaming — they both are — I never saw such smiles. Goodness, how Sister is enjoying it! Here they come. Your mother looks so happy, I feel quite sentimental, you can see how she must have been missing you, really at the bottom of her heart, all this time."

"Nonsense," said Polly, but she looked rather pleased.

"Darling, I do so feel I shall be in the way. Let me escape now through Boy's dressing room."

"Oh, on no account whatever, Fanny. Fanny you'll upset me if you do that — I absolutely insist on you staying here — I can't face her alone, beams or no beams."

Perhaps it had occurred to her, as it now did to me, that Lady Montdore's beam would very likely fade at the sight of Polly in Lady Patricia's room, unchanged in almost every respect, in the very bed where Lady Patricia had breathed her last, and that her repugnance for what Polly had done would be given a new reality. Even I had found it rather unattractive until I had got used to the idea. But over-sensibility had never been one of Lady Montdore's failings, and, besides, the great flame of happiness that Cedric had lit in her heart had long since burnt up all emotions which did not directly relate to him. He was the only person in the world now who had any substance for her.

So the beam did not flicker. She positively radiated good humour as she kissed Polly first and then me. She looked round the room and said, "You've moved the dressing table. It's much better like that, more light. Lovely flowers, dear, these camellias—can I have one for Cedric's buttonhole? Oh, from Paddington, are they? Poor Geoffrey, I fear he's a bit of a megalomaniac. I haven't been over there once since he succeeded. His father, now, was very different, a charming man, great friend of ours. King Edward was very fond of him, too, and of course Loelia Paddington was perfectly lovely—people used to stand on chairs, you know. So the poor little baby died. I expect it was just as well. Children are such an awful expense, nowadays."

Sister, who came back into the room just in time to hear this remark, put her hand to her heart and nearly fainted. That was going to be something to tell her next patients about, never, in all her sister-hood, can she have heard its like from a mother to an only daughter. But Polly, gazing open-mouthed at her mother, taking in every detail of the new appearance, was quite unmoved. It was too typical of Lady Montdore's whole outlook on life for somebody who had been brought up by her to find it odd or upsetting. In any case, I doubt if she minded much about the baby, herself. She seemed to me rather like a cow whose calf has been taken away from it at birth, unconscious of her loss.

"What a pity you couldn't have come to the ball, Fanny," Lady Montdore went on. "Just only for half an hour, to have a look. It was really beautiful. A lot of Cedric's friends came from Paris for it, in most striking dresses and, I am bound to say, though I have never liked the French, they were very civil indeed and so appreciative of anything one did for them. They all said there hadn't been such a party since the days of Robert de Montesquieu, and I can believe it. It cost £4000, you know, the water for the gondolas was so heavy, for one thing. Well, it shows these foreigners that England isn't done for yet; excellent propaganda. I wore all my diamonds and I have given Cedric a revolving diamond star (goes by clockwork) and he wore it on his shoulder—most effective, I must say. We thoroughly enjoyed every minute and I wish you could read the letters I've had about it, really touching, people have had so little pleasure the last year or two and it makes them all the more grateful, of course. Next time we come over I'll bring the photographs. They give a wonderful idea of what it was like."

"What was your dress, Mummy?"

"Longhi," said Lady Montdore evasively. "Veronica Chaddesley Corbett was very good, as a prostitute (they were called something different in those days) and Davey was there, Fanny, have you heard from him? He was the Black Death. Everybody made a real effort, you know. It's a terrible pity you girls couldn't have come."

There was a pause. She looked round the room and said with a sigh, "Poor Patricia—well, never mind that's all over now. Boy was telling us about his book, such an excellent idea—*Three Dukes*— and Cedric is very much interested because young Souppes, the son of the Prince des Ressources whom we used to see at Trouville, is a friend of his and Chèvres-Fontaine, which Cedric used to take every summer, belongs to his first cousin. Isn't it a curious coincidence? So of course Cedric can tell Boy a great many things he never knew about them all, and they think later on they might go to Paris together to do some research. In fact, we might all go, wouldn't that be amusing?"

"Not me," said Polly, "no more abroad for me, ever."

At this point Boy came into the room and I discreetly left it, in spite of a furious look from the bed. I went into the garden to find

Cedric. He was sitting on the churchyard wall, the pale sunshine on his golden hair, which I perceived to be tightly curled, an aftermath of the ball, no doubt, and plucking away with intense concentration at the petals of a daisy.

"He loves me, he loves me not, he loves me, he loves me not, don't interrupt, my angel, he loves me, he loves me not, oh, heaven, heaven, heaven! He loves me! I may as well tell you, my darling, that the second big thing in my life has begun."

A most sinister ray of light suddenly fell upon the future.

"Oh, Cedric," I said. "Do be careful."

I NEED NOT have felt any alarm, however. Cedric managed the whole thing quite beautifully. As soon as Polly had completely recovered her health and looks, he put Lady Montdore and Boy into the big Daimler and rolled them away to France. The field was thus left to a Morris Cowley which, sure enough, could be seen outside Silkin day after day. Before very long, Polly got into it and was driven over to Paddington Park, where she remained.

Then the Daimler rolled back to Hampton.

"So here we are, my darling, having lovely cake and eating it, too, which is *one's* great aim in life."

"The Boreleys think it simply terrible," I said.

ALSO BY NANCY MITFORD

THE BLESSING

When Grace Allingham, a naïve young Englishwoman, goes to live in France with her dashingly aristocratic husband Charles-Edouard, she finds herself overwhelmed by the bewilderingly foreign cuisine and the shockingly decadent manners and mores of the French. But it is the discovery of her husband's French notion of marriage—which includes a permanent mistress and a string of casual affairs—that sends Grace packing back to London with their "blessing," young Sigismond, in tow. While others urge the couple to reconcile, little Sigi—convinced that it will improve his chances of being spoiled—applies all his juvenile cunning to keeping his parents apart. Drawing on her own years in Paris and her long affair with a Frenchman, Mitford elevates cultural and romantic misunderstandings to the heights of comedy.

Fiction/978-0-307-74083-0

DON'T TELL ALFRED

Fanny Wincham—last seen as a young woman in *The Pursuit of Love* and *Love in a Cold Climate*—has lived contentedly for years as housewife to an absent-minded Oxford don, Alfred. But her life changes overnight when her beloved Alfred is appointed English Ambassador to Paris. Soon she finds herself mixing with royalty and Rothschilds while battling her hysterical predecessor, Lady Leone, who refuses to leave the premises. When Fanny's tenderhearted secretary begins filling the embassy with rescued animals and her teenage sons run away from Eton and show up with a rock star in tow, things get entirely out of hand.

Fiction/978-0-307-74084-7

ALSO AVAILABLE:
The Pursuit of Love, 978-0-307-74081-6
Wigs On the Green, 978-0-307-74085-4

VINTAGE BOOKS
Available at your local bookstore, or visit
www.randomhouse.com

Nancy Mitford

LOVE IN A COLD CLIMATE

Nancy Mitford, daughter of Lord and Lady Redesdale and the eldest of the six legendary Mitford sisters, was born in 1904 and educated at home on the family estate in Oxfordshire. She made her debut in London and soon became one of the bright young things of the 1920s, a close friend of Henry Green, Evelyn Waugh, John Betjeman, and their circle. A beauty and a wit, she began writing for magazines and writing novels while she was still in her twenties. In all, she wrote eight novels as well as biographies of Madame de Pompadour, Voltaire, Louis XIV, and Frederick the Great. She died in 1973. More information can be found at www.nancymitford.com.

NOVELS BY NANCY MITFORD
AVAILABLE FROM VINTAGE BOOKS

Wigs on the Green (1935)
The Pursuit of Love (1945)
Love in a Cold Climate (1949)
The Blessing (1951)
Don't Tell Alfred (1960)